Saturday Comes

Saturday Comes
by Carine Fabius

Kouraj Press
6025 Santa Monica Boulevard
#202
Los Angeles, CA 90038
323-460-7333
info@kouraj.com
www.kourajpress.com

Cover Design: Pascal Giacomini, Jeannie Winston Nogai

Cover Artwork: Edouard Duval-Carrié

Fabius, Carine

Saturday Comes

Printed in the United States of America

ISBN: 0-9785-0033-4
ISBN-13: 9780978500337

Saturday Comes

A Novel of Love and Vodou

Carine Fabius

2011

Also by Carine Fabius

Jagua, A Journey into Body Art from the Amazon
Sex, Cheese and French Fries:
Women are Perfect, Men are from France
Ceremonies for Real Life
Mehndi: The Art of Henna Body Painting

ACKNOWLEDGEMENTS

Writing a book is a long, hard journey requiring, among countless things, the help and support of those whose encouragement, generosity, expertise, tough criticism and positive feedback help to remind an author that there *is* an end in sight. I am grateful to those of you who read the manuscript and provided critical insights. I won't even attempt to name you all because this book has been so many years in the making that I will surely forget someone crucial! I owe endless gratitude to Maddie Perrone of Literary Artists Representatives, my first agent, who fell in love with this story and believed in me as a writer. I am also grateful to Deborah Ritchken of Castiglia Literary Agency, who pushed hard to help this story see the light of day, and to my friend Karen Kaplan for introducing me to Deborah and championing this book from day one. Many thanks to Donald J. Cosentino for helping me get closer to the ultimate trickster, *Baron Samedi*; and to Henrietta Cosentino for her guidance to a better understanding of *Vodou* ceremonies. Frank Weaver remains the best editor known to mankind. Thanks to Edouard Duval-Carrié for his gorgeous artwork, which graces the cover of the book. As always, huge thanks to my husband, Pascal Giacomini, for his enduring support.

The Baron

If Christians paid more attention in school they would remember about Saturday night. They would know that the Miraculous One goes by other names too, like Lord of Saturday, Father of the Dead, Spirit of Death; or, the one my Haitian children use: *Baron Samedi.* What's that you say, baby? *Yesss...Samedi* is French for Saturday, the day He died. But the Christ's valiant journey to the underworld to gather lost souls never gets much play; it's his return on Easter Sunday to rise in glory from the dead that steals the show every time. Not surprising, really, since everyone makes such a fuss about life. Call me biased, but I'm into death.

I love it down here in the land of the dead, where it's icy and dark, with no need to protect my sensitive eyes from all that light—although these shades do look sharp with my black suit and hat. And you've got to admit that my purple scarf hits just the right note! I let myself be lured up there, but I don't like to stay too long. Sliding into a human body is no easy thing. My throat gets funny too. I hear them saying I'm nasal and that I speak so slowly... But, there are matters to deal with above ground—like encouraging humans to carry on feeding their obsession with sex.

No death without life, I like to say. 'Round and 'round it goes, from the grave to the stage and back again! You want my job, you better be an expert on *getting down*, baby, and, *yesss*, dying. Haitians love that delicious and *dangerous* combination. Mmm...That's why I like hanging with them and will attend their ceremonies, but only IF properly plied with the right rum and cigars. And it is true that I love, love, love to dance. Watch this smooth move. Uh huh. You get my groove.

Love me, hate me, fear me—doesn't matter. Just get used to me 'cause I'll be dropping in from time to time to cast a shadow or two. I can't help it. I have a stake in this story, as in all stories, which have to end in my cold but welcoming arms. Haitian people say that if a person does not merit death, I will reject it. I am not sure if I agree or disagree—about it being a question of merit. Why don't you read on and judge for yourself?

Prologue

I am going to kill him!

In a feral flash of brilliance, Maya St. Fleur knew what to do. As glacial resolution spread through her body, the dark, long-limbed child wondered at the sense of peace and thrill that filled her heart. She understood that her prayers to the *Baron* had been answered. As he bowed before her now, his tall black hat removed in at-your-service parody, she watched his vacant face melt into shaded topcoat, and vanish into the gloom around her. And she accepted the unthinkable. Yes, it was perfect—and so right that she should kill the very one who had introduced her to love.

A defiant tear willed itself down her cheek as angry waves slapped against the rotting, hollowed-out, 14-foot tree trunk that doubled as a boat. She frowned, wiping at the tear. *I have to stay strong. I have to stay alive.* But she knew that the probability of reaching Miami was slim at best. It was folly even to try.

The hopeful crew of twenty-five that had waved goodbye to relatives and friends had dwindled down to two: Maya and the determined young man named Antoine, who had collected their tattered filthy dollars for the price of passage.

Perhaps two weeks (or was it months?) had passed since the group's departure. But the anxious resolve, swollen aspiration, and devil-may-care disposition had been theirs, not Maya's. No willing participant was she, sentimentally blackmailed and prodded like a pirate on a plank to leave her family and friends, home and hopes. How was it that she, who would have chosen Haiti's desperation over Miami, was the only one still alive? One by one, day after wretched day, night after terrifying night, they'd gone. Three nights into the voyage, two aged women, an overweight girl, and a middle-aged man had been swept away by choppy waves. Blue-cold wails haunted the air around them as the moonless sky aided the sea in its conquest. And the others: that blur of black faces and bodies so wrenchingly skinny and scared. What did it matter? They were gone, and Maya dared not reflect on the gruesome, sometimes scandalous remembrances—of tightly packed bodies made slippery by vomit, of soggy bodily wastes crushed between toes, of the increasing fights among them for the food their own excrement had become, and then much worse as their hunger turned vicious. And the stench, the unbearable, never-ending stench...

As the sun started to rise in the sky, she looked over at the once-cocky captain of their boat. He didn't seem to be breathing. *It would be so simple, so beautiful just to die here now, floating like this*; *at least there's more room now, so much better than before*...But she would not allow that. She would continue to breathe, and a miracle would get her to this cursed land they called Florida. She mustered up what strength she could to hum a song to *Agwe*, Ruler of the Sea. *Please, please.* She had work to do. She dropped her burnt and blistered arm over the side into saltwater below. Knowing it wouldn't help, she lifted a few drops to her mouth, dripping acid down her throat. Why not? Desperation had inspired worse things.

A strong wind picked up.

Thankful for a respite from the heat, Maya turned over and prayed for sleep—*a dreamless sleep, please God.* But she would not be spared.

"Ou konen Jedi se jou pa ou."

"You know Thursday's your day," she heard him say. Maya peered around a half-opened door to a concrete room, dank and windowless, and froze before a familiar spectacle: M'sié Chenet, the man of the house where she and her mother worked, stood as close as he could behind her manman, his right hand squeezing her breast in a painful pinch. His left hand clutched a coiled red rope. His dark green shorts pooled around his ankles as he pushed rhythmically into Manman Jizzeline's dark brown behind. As Maya watched, her mother turned, noticing her. Two ragged-edged black holes burned in place of her eyes. She smiled but her teeth were gone, replaced by sharp, pointed fangs that dripped dirty, brown blood. Maya opened her mouth to scream in terror, but something stopped her.

"It's okay," her mother said without words. "There's nothing we can do to change it. I die, he lives on. That's the way it's always been. Don't try to change it, you'll only get hurt. Now go!"

"No!" she shouted, running toward them, fists flailing, a hollow scream bouncing against clammy gray walls; and she saw the red rope come to life, becoming a thick purple-edged snake that flung itself around her scrawny body. As she watched herself disappear down the serpent's orifice, she wondered at her vanishing resolve. "I am like a stone. I can't move or fight. And this heat,

this smelly, horrid heat. I'm going to hell...But I didn't kill him yet! So hot...so hot...so hot..."

When Maya opened her eyes, it was hot indeed, and the horrid smell a vapor from her own body. A strange, gritty sensation filled her mouth and surrounded her tongue. She sat up groggily and gazed upon turquoise water, sensing a change. *The boat was missing!* She looked down, imagined she saw sand, and thought, *Shore!*

And then a voice said something she could not comprehend. Dazed, her eyes clouded, Maya slowly raised her head. The boy looked a couple of years her junior, and she stared up at him: at his black hair, steel-gray eyes, and mouth that did not smile. He uttered more sounds, insisting...

A surge of nausea defeated the exhausted child. A void filled her chest, and like a lifeless ragdoll, she crumpled onto the coveted solidity of Miami Beach.

Part One

I

One Year Earlier

Tragedy had befallen the Chenet family the year that Jizzeline St. Fleur and her daughter Maya arrived to interview for the position. Thanks to *télé-djol,* the island's rumor mill, they knew that the Chenets' thirteen-year-old son, Sylvain, had survived the car crash, but that the younger daughter, Christine, had perished. Word also got around that the family who lived up on Thomassin 23 near the firehouse in Laboule needed a new housekeeper. Although aware of *Monsieur* and *Madame* Chenet's dubious reputation, the reality of empty change purses and emptier stomachs had driven Jizzeline to apply just the same. So it was with a mix of apprehension and hope that stringy Maya and her densely built, sturdy-footed mother climbed to the house on top of the hill—the one that shone bright white in the fierce spring sun, the one with the emerald green awnings and sculpted wood front door that must weigh boulders. A beautiful house. A *mulatto* house.

A black manservant with watery brown eyes and raggedy clothes answered their knock and ushered them in through the back door, common entry for all former slaves in modern Haiti. The stained-glass windows on the side of the house reflected light pink, blue, and yellow popcorn patterns on the black mosaic that covered the entire first floor, making impossible attempts at warmth. They were led to an ultra-stylish, black and white and stainless steel kitchen, and told to wait. After twenty long minutes on their feet, mother and daughter managed to look up while keeping their eyes respectfully on the floor when

Madame Chenet arrived in a sweeping motion meant to convey activity and importance.

Though she tried to disguise it with a flurry of light words, heavy makeup, rock-hard bouffant black hair, and swishing skirt, the lady of the house had a tough time hiding her right hand's missing middle finger. Jizzeline and Maya knew not to notice the gap and concentrated on the in-between look they'd come to master when communicating with members of the island's bourgeoisie.

"Do you know how to cook?" *Madame* Chenet asked right off in Kreyol painted with a slight French accent. Her light pink skin shimmered with a slight sweat, and her pale brown eyes looked outside the window at something that seemed out of place.

"*Oui*," Jizzeline said.

"I need someone who knows how to cook vegetables in a variety of ways. My son, Sylvain, has decided that he no longer eats meat. Thirteen years old and he refuses to eat meat. *Ça complique.* So what kind of dishes can you prepare?"

"I make very good vegetable stew; I can make good soufflés and soups; I make *gratinées* and—

"Is that right?" *Madame* Chenet said.

"*Oui, Madan* Chenet. I even know how to make vegetable pies, like quiche," Jizzeline added shyly in lilting Kreyol that came straight out of the hills of Haiti via Africa.

"Just how would you know anything about quiche? Quiche is a French dish, although Americans seem to like it too."

"Years ago, I worked in the restaurant down by the pier where the boats used to come in, and I learned how to cook things that tourists like to eat, but with Haitian spices. They loved my food," she added. *I know my stuff* was left unsaid.

"Is that right?" *Madame* Chenet said again. "Well, my husband likes his food Haitian. Meat every night for *Monsieur*

Chenet, is that understood? Can you cook a good *griot*? He loves his *griot*."

"*Madan* Chenet, I make the best *griot* in Haiti. The pigs, they run when they see me coming 'cause they know I make them taste so good."

Madame Chenet hazarded a toothy, somewhat charming smile.

"And I prefer fish," she added, as if to test Jizzeline's resilience. "I would rather eat fish any day of the week. I love shellfish. Are you good with shellfish?"

"It will melt in your mouth, *Madan* Chenet," Jizzeline said now, as if this was all child's play.

"We'll see," said the lady of the house. "I expect you to clean the house every morning, do the laundry twice a week, cook breakfast, lunch, and dinner six days a week. You can live in the room out back. Dieuseul will show it to you. Dieuseul!" she called. The black manservant reappeared, shoulders hunched in perpetual grief.

"Dieuseul," *Madame* Chenet said, "show—oh, what's your name?" she said, turning to look at her new maid. "And what about your child here? What's her name?"

"My name is Jizzeline and this is Maya. She is very good at gardening. She can make anything grow. If you want fruits, they come out of the ground *so* fast if she's the one who plants the seeds. If it's vegetables you want, no problem, *Madan* Chenet; even flowers, she knows how to make them climb to the sky."

"Oh yes? Well maybe she can help Sylvain with his projects. He loves that sort of thing. Does she go to school?"

"No *Madan* Chenet. There's no money for that."

"Well, as long as she doesn't get in the way. If she makes herself useful, she may stay. But you should get her into a school. How old are you, child?"

"Twelve," Maya said, eyes still cast downward.

"That's a shame. Just a shame, a young girl like you with no education. You should learn how to read and write so you can teach your mother how to read and write."

"If I make your garden grow, maybe you can pay for my school," Maya ventured.

"We'll see," *Madame* Chenet said, smiling inwardly at the kid's spunk. "I pay $50 a month. All right with you?" she said to Jizzeline.

"I used to make $60 at my last job, *Madan* Chenet."

"Well, we'll start you at $50, and if you work out, we'll see."

"We'll see, we'll see. Everything is we'll see," Jizzeline muttered as she surveyed the minuscule room that would be her new home six days out of the week. On Wednesdays, she and her daughter would get to go back home and spend the night with Raoul, Maya's father and Jizzeline's husband. "I guess we'll see," she sighed.

Monsieur Chenet liked Jizzeline's *griot* just fine. He liked it, and everything else she cooked so much that he took to patting her on the fanny whenever she walked by, just so she'd know how much he appreciated her cooking. To Jizzeline's dismay, he didn't mind showing his appreciation in front of his wife. On these occasions, *Madame* Chenet would smile, embarrassed, and look away, as if she hadn't noticed. Jizzeline went about her business as if she hadn't felt his hand on her. But as time went by, the pat turned into a rub when *Madame* Chenet wasn't around, then into an intrusion as he began to stroke her derriere's cheeks right through her dress while she stood at the oven, stirring something he knew would be *so delicious!*

A rather handsome man in his fifties, Henri Chenet's skin was many shades darker than his wife's, a milk chocolate brown burned even darker by the sun. He controlled the pleasure boating industry in Haiti because he owned the island's only dealership. Taking potential clients out on yachts melted into entertaining friends on his latest prized possession, a 50 ft. Silverton. Henri Chenet cared about three things in life: his looks, his boats, and his son, Sylvain. His looks and his boats he loved with a passion. His son he loved with fear. Protecting Sylvain, making him happy, and being loved by Sylvain was of paramount importance. He had never felt the same emotion toward Christine, his younger daughter, now gone. While the accident rerouted his wife into a world of half-finished sentences, haphazard glances toward far-off places, and sobering returns to a world where her baby no longer existed, *Monsieur* Chenet did not mourn his daughter long. He celebrated the existence of his son, instead. Lately he'd taken to coming home early on Thursday afternoons to spend time with him—to watch a video together, take interest in his homework, or kick a soccer ball around the yard. He also visited Jizzeline and Maya on Thursdays.

One sunny blue Thursday, while his housekeeper frantically rubbed at his touch with a hog-bristled brush, a light-footed Henri Chenet emerged from Jizzeline's gray room, and stopped short. *No wonder Maya wasn't around to play audience for me. She's out here with Sylvain again!* In the recesses of this overlord's mind, an alarm went off, rooting him in place, breath held short as he watched them unobserved. The youngsters basked in the earth around them and in the air, brushstroked with the hopeful flavor of mint. Maya's sloping, glittery eyes looked up at Sylvain as he spoke, her licorice body leaning toward him as she listened. The light brown boy with soft, curly black hair was serious in his manner, like that of a teacher toward a student as he hunched into the ground next to her. She stopped him to ask a question and, momentarily thrown off balance, he smiled at her, shaking his head no.

Was that a smile of affection? He'd have to explain things to Sylvain. Just that morning he'd been talking with his wife about their help.

"Didn't I tell you Dieuseul couldn't handle the task?" he'd complained, as Dieuseul stood close by. "I knew he wouldn't remember who to give that package to! There's nothing to be done for ignorance."

"Of course," she'd agreed. "It's no use teaching them anything; it's a waste of time. Asking Jizzeline to cook anything out of the ordinary is a ridiculous exercise."

Henri Chenet approached the two children gingerly, trying to remain unseen in order to hear their conversation. But as he stepped closer to them, Sylvain looked up. Seeing his father, he waved him over.

"I was just telling Maya that I think I'll be an environmentalist when I grow up."

"Really? That's interesting. You think Maya understands anything about the environment?"

"She understands plants and trees," the boy responded, looking at Maya for confirmation.

"Why don't you go inside and see about helping your mother prepare dinner," *Monsieur* Chenet said to Maya, who quickly pranced away, the braids in her short hair sticking straight out of her head like puffy black cotton balls. But as she rounded the bend leading to the house, she stopped to hide behind a thick wall of purple bougainvillea, curious to hear their conversation.

"Come inside and tell me all about this," *Monsieur* Chenet said, turning to his son. Is it something you're learning in school that has you interested in the environment?"

"Why didn't I know that practically all our trees are gone? Why isn't someone doing anything about this? Haiti will die if all our forests are chopped down," the young boy said.

"The reason we've lost so many of our trees is because the peasants keep chopping them down for cooking, and for the price that our exotic woods bring," *Monsieur* Chenet explained.

"So why doesn't somebody teach them that it's wrong? They would understand! This is their country too!"

"That's just it. They don't understand because it's a concept that's too complicated for them to grasp. All they know is that they need to eat and to earn money, so they keep chopping."

"There must be other ways for them to make money. If I can learn, so can they. They're no different from us."

"Well you're wrong there, son. They are an underdeveloped people. Their brains don't function like ours. They don't think like us. You were too young to remember what happened when we hired someone to teach Dieuseul to read. After a few weeks, he just refused to show up for his lessons; said he could be making money instead, doing odd jobs for people in the neighborhood."

"But just because Dieuseul did that, doesn't mean they all...In any case, Maya's not like that. She's smart. "

"Maybe she is. But tell me something. I was watching you two talk back there for a while, and I thought I saw a look on your face that was...affectionate, maybe?"

"I don't know. We were just talking, and she says funny things sometimes. I like her," Sylvain said.

"But I just want to make sure you don't misunderstand your feelings for her. You have to be careful. She's from a different class. You wouldn't want to encourage her in any way, or have her thinking that you and she could have a relationship that's anything other than one between a house girl and her boss' son."

"Papa, I don't know what you're talking about. I don't care about girls, anyway. Maya is just fun to talk to."

Sylvain turned his head to hide his blushing cheeks as he walked toward the house with his father, whose arm lay possessively around his son's shoulder.

"Wait till you see what I brought home for you," Maya heard *M'sié* Chenet say as they walked past the point where she could hear them.

He sure does love his son, Maya thought to herself. *And he sure hates us.*

Later that night, as Jizzeline's soft snores competed with the sound of crickets outside, Maya lay awake, reliving her few moments with Sylvain. It had been so wonderful until *M'sié* Chenet interrupted. She thought he looked like a lizard, all slippery and sneaky and...*Don't want to think about him.* Instead, she imagined Sylvain's strong cocoa-colored arms, the way he creased his brow in thought, the devastating effect his smile had on her, and the way he sometimes touched her as he spoke.

As she smiled herself to sleep, the stars in the sky giggled and danced with the flush of Maya's infatuation.

Sylvain smiled, too, as he thought of his mother's garden, which had flourished under Maya's touch. He had watched her one time as she watered and talked to the plants when she thought she was alone. Afterward, he had asked her questions, which she answered openly in her singsong voice. A timid, embarrassed smile often tinged her responses, which made him want to ask her more questions.

Maya thought his soft black curls were the most beautiful things she had ever seen.

Sylvain enjoyed spending time with her in the garden.

She thought he was kind.

He thought she was pretty sharp.

That night, as he lay in bed, remembering something she'd said about the nature of roses, he thought about her smile and realized for the first time that she had really prominent dimples. He didn't know how he'd missed them before.

The next morning, at breakfast, Sylvain turned to his mother, "*Manman*, Maya's clothes are all so old and torn, why don't we give her some of Christine's clothes? Maya's so skinny, she'd probably fit into *some* of them anyway."

Two sets of eyes turned to stare at Sylvain, and all motion stopped except for the clinking of spoon against bowl as Sylvain attacked his American corn flakes, an expensive treat from his father.

In the year since his sister's death, Sylvain had never mentioned Christine's name. *Madame* Chenet's eyes opened wide in horror, dark clouds gathering about her head and breaking loose as she burst into tears.

"I would think of her too much if Maya walked around here in her clothes! It would be too awful!" she said.

Monsieur Chenet's eyes also popped open, unleashing miniature crocodiles that snapped at imagined enemies in the air. His fist came crashing down on the table.

"I'd rather burn those clothes than give them to her!"

Sylvain stood up, confused at the uproar his suggestion had caused. He walked over to his mother, put his arm around her and said, "I'm sorry, *Manman*. It was a silly thing to say."

To his father he said nothing and walked out of the room.

Wednesdays were special for Jizzeline and Maya. That was the day they gathered their few meager belongings and headed into town, away from the big house with the black mosaic floor, away from the staggering views of Port-au-Prince and into the heart of the city itself, past tree-fertile La Plaine, then further north, up the road leading to the border that separates Haiti from the Dominican Republic, and into the town of Croix-des-Bouquets. Outwardly a small, quiet town, the interior teemed with the activity of forgers and artists cutting and banging away at oil drums destined to hang in Port-au-Prince's prestigious galleries at prices the artists could only dream of. Out on the main road, overcrowded, open-air public mini trucks called *tap taps* barreled through town with exhaust pipes barking, horns honking, and loud inspirational messages painted on their sides, back and front. That Wednesday, as mother and daughter extricated themselves from the sweaty bundle of people who shared their ride into town, friends of the pre-teen and forty-year-old waited for the royal blue *tap-tap* whose sides proclaimed in painted white script, *Min mwen St. Christof*—Here I am, St. Christopher!

Pulling at the ribbon in Maya's hair, and waving it in the air, a skinny kid with large white teeth and black saucers for eyes kicked up dust as he made off with the day's prize. Once again, Jacquy had stolen her ribbon before being tagged with Maya's stick of chalk. He taunted her mercilessly.

"Ha! Ha! Ha! You know I always win! No matter how you plan it, I always get you first!"

"It's not fair!" Maya screamed, her laughter slowing her down. "Your spot at the foot of the *tap tap* is too easy!!"

"So all you have to do is get to the river first and you can win!" he shouted back.

She couldn't run as fast as him either, but for hours afterward, they played tag and hunted for hidden treasures and dangerous snakes. Practicing their usual game of "who will end up in the water first?" they circled each other, casually inching closer to the water's edge. Once in, flailing in mock drowning, they pleaded at the top of their lungs: "*Agwé*! *Agwé!* Please save us from having to live underwater forever!" And magically, the ability to swim was there, enabling them to glide like the silver fish that slid underneath their feet. Their fantasies wrapped the two friends in a wondrous silken cocoon until it was *time*. Jacquy decided when it was time, and Maya knew the signal by the look in his eye.

As the familiar ritual dictated, they raced out of the water in anticipation of the day's most important event. Maya stripped down to her underwear and located a sunny spot, while Jacquy walked over to the foot of the giant avocado tree, lifting up a well-placed stone. There lay hidden two items, which he beheld as if they were gems: a grammar book and a notebook half-filled with large, awkward words—his and Maya's words.

Jacquy was one of the lucky ones. Blonde, pretty, and well-meaning, Laura Nielsen was a young American missionary who had taken a liking to him at first sight. She couldn't help it. Sitting on a lonely side road in her stalled car one night, trying hard to forget about the *lougawou*, she'd reacted to Jacquy's smiling face as if to an angel dropped down from heaven. He'd returned with his father, a mechanic with the magic touch. The next day, laughing at herself and Haiti's mythical werewolves of the night before, she'd gone looking for her savior to repay his kindness. *Nothing like a dark night in Haiti to get the imagination rolling!* In bad Kreyol, she asked him what he wanted most in the world.

"To read and write," he answered, as if he'd rehearsed it a hundred times.

So they'd struck a deal. She paid for him to attend school in the mornings; in exchange he ran errands and tended to her small house in the afternoons. To constant ridicule from other missionaries in the area, she also gave Jacquy extra pocket cash, even though it wasn't part of their agreement.

"He's taking advantage of your soft spot," the one named Horace warned.

"The new ones always get sucked in like this," the older, more experienced one had sneered.

To hell with them. She tought he was smart and fun, and he made her laugh, which was more than she could say for either one of those idiots. Jacquy's teacher said he was the brightest kid in her class. Maybe she was being naïve, but she liked helping him out. Jacquy offered to teach his best friend everything he learned. Maya lapped it up like a starved cat at a milk bowl. She was beyond the simplicities of writing her name and such. She was composing complete sentences now.

Back at the *tap tap* stop, Jizzeline's friend, Josette, and her boisterous laugh had been there too, as she was every Wednesday, anxious to hear the latest news, although it never much differed from her own stories. In the end, she'd left the Chenet family's employ in a huff, hand held high on her hip, swearing never to return. Their cackles flip-flopped over the brown earth and through stoic trees as they swished and swayed all the way to Jizzeline's place, a tiny concrete-floored hut without electricity where time passed all too quickly as they caught up. Some time after lunch, as moist sunshine pounded pitilessly on bony animals and humans languishing in the heat of the large *lacou*, big-bosomed Vesta, the red-lipped town lush, sauntered in for her weekly drop-in.

"Hello ladies, I need a cigarette, a snack, and the 'goods.'" Vesta's greedy interest offended Jizzeline, but the feelings of degradation often dissipated in the telling—if just for a while—as so many women she knew had been in a similar situation at one time or another.

Vesta spat as she listened, shaking her head back and forth, lips pursed.

"You got it bad, honey, but just imagine being that wife of his. Imagine what she must have to go through every day! You know, they say that one day she pointed that middle finger of hers one time too many at him, and he dragged her into the kitchen, pulled out a chopping knife, and—"

"Vesta, you crazy. That is probably the twentieth story I heard on how that poor lady lost her finger," Josette said.

"Well, now you know the truth."

"Mmm hm."

One after another, the friends, the cousins, the aunts, the grandparents came through Jizzeline's small shack with stories, the latest joke, and news of the most recent burial, wedding, christening, or scandal, as if years had passed since their last reunion. Later that evening, as the heat dissipated and sounds of the day whispered to a close, Raoul arrived, changing the evening's tone and mood. Voices lowered and giggles faded until one by one, everyone's eyes turned to Raoul for a signal that the ceremony would soon begin.

Earning a living as a sculptor in the area's cutout metal tradition was the least of Raoul's abilities. He also presided as the most renowned *ougan* in Croix-des-Bouquets. Though small of stature, Raoul was an imposing man who commanded attention—through a glance, a flick of his wrist, or the shake of his head. He moved deliberately, it seemed, so that people might notice the way sunlight or moonlight reflected off his pearly black skin. His frown devastated the faint of heart, and his anger reduced the mightiest of men to quivering jelly at his approach. He was known to obey the *lwas*—spirits of the Haitian *Vodou* religion—first and last, thus drawing a steady flow of people, who came from near and far to seek his counsel. Thanks to Jizzeline's presence, the Vodou priest's Wednesday ceremonies were always well attended; his intensity edged down a notch, and people liked that.

Returning from their time at the river, Maya and Jacquy entered the courtyard where her family and their friends sat in hushed stillness just as Raoul made his announcement: "Tonight, we invite the *Baron* to visit."

Excited and apprehensive murmurs swarmed the sweaty air as various people scurried away to fetch their *Baron Samedi* regalia. Maya and Jacquy turned to each other with excitement. *Finally, the Baron.* Even though he was the wise and important Spirit of Death, his forbidding black-clad demeanor often dissolved into amusing and naughty entertainment. They couldn't wait!

The ceremony began with Raoul saluting the four corners of the temple with rum. Next came the *drapeau Vodou* ritual to consecrate the space: worn across the shoulders of several attendants, the *drapeaus*—sequined and beaded banners patterned with symbols of *Vodou* deities—became a whirling splash of color that dazzled the eye as the attendants ran and danced around the *poto mitan*, the center pole and doorway for spirits to enter and exit. By the start of Raoul's call-and-response prayer sequence to the Catholic spirits known as *Action de Grace*, Maya and Jacquy itched with impatience. The drums helped pick up the pace as the invocation of African spirits known as *règlement* commenced, followed by the salutation of the drums themselves with rum and song. As the rhythm of the drums increased, movement within the circle of participants began to spread like an alcohol-induced fever, while Raoul, seemingly oblivious to the mounting tension, proceeded to formally salute the *poto mitan*, and then various visiting *mambos* and *ougans* with whom he exchanged ritual hugs and handshakes.

Although the two young people anxiously awaited the invocation of *Baron Samedi*, Raoul still was not ready. Yet to come was formal recognition of all the major spirits. *Papa Legba* was first, since he alone could open the doorway for spirits to come. Only after a long list of greetings did Raoul finally turn to the Baron, inviting him to honor this crowd and ceremony with his presence. Soon, the drum pitch reached a frenzy, as nearly everyone—dressed in black with powdered whiteface—danced, many already in the throes of possession by *gede*, children of the Baron. Transported too, by now, Raoul danced and drank, drawing the Baron's black goat offering into the ring in an attempt to entice the reluctant spirit. It wouldn't be much longer.

Just minutes later, Raoul's eyes rolled into the back of his head, and his body shifted from dancing in wild abandon to uncontrolled flailing. They knew the Baron had arrived. A priestess in training, dressed in traditional white *hounsi* dress, stepped forward to bring him his favorite black coat and drink of *clerin*—raw liquor spiked with pepper and herbs. Pushing the bottle to his lips, the Spirit of Death drank long until quenched. Later, completely attired in his signature black suit, top hat, and sunglasses, pelvis forward, phallic wooden cane in hand, the Baron casually hopped toward the altar to the beat of the drums. Reaching for the pipe and matches handed him by someone in the crowd, he stopped to light his tobacco in a slow, deliberate way. Satisfied at last, he looked around the circle of people, his cold, dead eyes bringing all activity to a grinding, shivering halt. Then, without warning, he threw his hands up in the air, cane pointing at the sky, and he began to dance. Springing back to life, the drummers worked up a feverish tempo as the Baron flew into a series of fast and complicated steps mixed with vulgar thrusts of both cane and pelvis, throwing the crowd into screams of laughter and fiendish consent. Dancing feet recommenced in earnest as the crowd let loose into the magical *Vodou* night.

Affected too, the leaves in the trees called out shocking stories to one another while wretched scraggy wild dogs howled their hunger into the night. The moon sang a song of exultation at having overpowered the sun once more, and the extinguished king of light whispered burning promises of return from his hiding place in the sky.

Mesmerized, Maya stood partially draped by Jizzeline's wide skirt, flames from various log fires flicking dancing shadows across her smooth, dark skin. Now oblivious to Jacquy's presence at her side, Maya breathed in air heavy with the smell of raw, potent liquor, letting it envelop her, as everyone around her laughed out loud and danced in delirious rhythm with the Spirit of Death in their midst.

The Baron was laughing uproariously now, mocking death with wild enthusiasm, swirling his body around and around, his cane held out before him, caught in a gripping circular motion that seemed destined never to stop.

And then he stopped.

And his cane pointed directly at Maya.

All drumming and activity halted. Standing beside her, Jacquy froze in sympathy with his friend, whose eyes opened wide in horror and embarassment. Crushing heat now rushed through Maya's frail body, adding to the wooziness in her head, but she didn't dare budge. The Baron unfolded to full, regal stature. Later everyone would swear that Raoul grew double in height. Dropping the cane to the ground, he walked stiffly toward Jizzeline and Maya, his shoes scraping on dirt now the only sound. He stood facing them for interminable seconds, his dead, frightful eyes boring a hole through Jizzeline. Finally an eerie, nasal, halting voice seeped from his lips.

"There is...trouble coming," he said, "*terrible* trouble. It's your trouble but not your trouble. Keep looking past yourself to your own...extension."

After taking a deep breath, Jizzeline whispered in a thin voice, "I don't understand *Papa Baron.*"

"You better seek to...understand."

Turning his back to her, he added, "Money's not everything! Your child will suffer, suffer, suffer."

"But if I don't work, my daughter won't eat!" Jizzeline cried out, "Everything I do is for her!"

"Be careful," the nasal voice sputtered as he turned back, piercing Jizzeline with his black eyes, "the ocean is...waiting; confusion is...king. You better look out!"

"I don't know what you mean!" Jizzeline said in frightened exasperation.

"But you can comfort yourself with this," the infuriatingly slow voice said as if she had not spoken. "*Agwé*...Yes, *Agwé* will keep a special eye out for little Maya."

And with that Raoul's body collapsed to the ground. *Baron Samedi* was gone.

Hysterical now, Jizzeline turned to Maya, "Does any of this make sense to you?! Is there something I should know? Tell me! Tell me!!"

Maya couldn't think. If only she knew something that might ease her mother's frenzy! Later, as she reflected on the night's events, she noticed moonlight sliding in through the window toward the mattress where she lay on the floor. Heeding her grandmother's warning about the moon, she quickly turned her face away to avoid monstrous disfigurement. Distracted momentarily by the moon, then by the soft whimpering sounds of her parents reuniting in the room next door, Maya's wandering mind returned to the Baron and his strange words. No matter how hard she tried to squeeze together the puzzle pieces of his visit, she still could not understand. Aside from *M'sié* Chenet's disgusting and still incomprehensible Thursday afternoon sessions with her mother and her, life was good. She was learning to read and write; her flowers and vegetables grew at a furious pace; and Sylvain lit a spot in her heart that made her warm all over.

Six months later, the Baron's words were just an uneasy memory for Jizzeline. Maya remembered now and then, but the message behind his words slid through her mind like silver water over hard white rocks. Her thoughts strayed more often now to that special time in the afternoons, between three and four, when Sylvain arrived home from school. Invariably he would stroll down to the garden where she tended to the plants in her care, and they would talk. He told her that he learned much from their chats. His interest in the *Vodou* religion her family practiced had spawned fascinating discussions between them, though he mostly asked questions and listened while she responded, shy and polite at first, then with confidence as she recognized her own ability to impart knowledge.

She told him about *Papa Loko*, the leaf doctor in the *Vodou* pantheon of spirits, and about *Cousin Zaka*, the spirit known as the farmer. She believed that service to these spirits helped her gain insight into the life of plants, and she pointed to her success in his mother's lush garden as proof. In turn, he talked with her about his deepening interest in the role of plants and trees on the earth, and in Haiti in particular. They spoke in Kreyol to each other, but she often wished she could speak proper French. When she mentioned it to him one day, he said, "I could teach you. It's so close to Kreyol, I bet you'll pick it up in no time. You understand it already, all you have to do is speak it. We'll start right now."

"And just what are you planning to start right now?" came the voice of Sylvain's father as he came around the driveway, surprising them both.

She hated the sound of his voice. It reminded her of the grunting sounds he made as he pawed and pinched her mother's breasts on Thursday afternoons, insisting Maya not only watch, but also applaud on command. And lately, he'd been trying to put that big thing in her, too. It hurt the last time he tried.

"I was just telling Maya that I could help her learn to speak French."

"Don't you have schoolwork to do?"

"Yes, but I can—"

"I think you should be worrying about your own education, mister. Go ahead now. I want to have a talk with you about this later."

"Okay. See you, Maya."

"*Oui, M'sié* Sylvain," she answered, lowering her eyes.

She didn't lift them up again until she heard *M'sié* Chenet's steps retreat. She noticed that he didn't go back to the main house but headed instead toward her mother's room. Quietly, she followed and crouched down by the shed's open back window in order to hear what he had to say.

Monsieur Chenet was boiling inside when he entered Jizzeline's room, but he managed an air of nonchalance. She was in her slip and bra and let out a small cry of surprise at the sight of him in her space on a day that was not Thursday.

"I want to talk with you about something, Jizzeline. Why don't you put something on."

"*Oui, M'sié* Chenet," she said, grabbing the dress she'd just removed, and slipping it back on over her stocky hips.

"I notice that Sylvain and Maya are spending a lot of time together lately, and I don't like it. They're always laughing together; now he wants to teach her French. That boy has some strange ideas. Next he'll be wanting who knows what else. I don't like it."

"I'll tell her not to talk to him anymore, *M'sié*. That's no problem."

"No, no. Here's what I want to do. It seems she wants an education, so I'll make it possible for you to send her to the United States."

"*Oh, M'sié*!"

"I'll pay for you to put her on one of those boats to Miami, and I'll give you an extra $500 a year for the next few years to make sure she has everything she needs."

Jizzeline felt the crawl of a deadly spider rising up her spine. *$500 a year! That could change our lives.* But the chill in her back and neck reminded her of something else.

"But I don't want to send Maya away, *M'sié*, and those boats are dangerous. Most people never make it over there."

"There's a guy I know who's good. Safe boat, knows his stuff. He brings things from Miami for me all the time. He'll take her."

$500 a year!

"But Maya is my only child! You have the money. Why don't you pay for plane fare? Those boats hardly ever make it in one piece. She might die," Jizzeline protested, her voice rising above the shock and attraction of *$500 a year!*

Monsieur Chenet was running out of patience. "Jizzeline, you either send that kid away on that boat or you're out of a job, okay? And I'll be forced to call the police and tell them that you stole from us here."

"But I didn't!"

"Now, you'll take that money; I don't care what you do with it. Build a new shack, buy a car, whatever you want. But you're putting that kid on one of those boats day after tomorrow, and most importantly, you won't mention it to *Madame* Chenet. I talked to Sylvain about it yesterday, and he agrees that this is a good idea. He told me that the only reason he is nice to her is because he feels sorry for her.

"Does he know that the chances are stacked against her? That she will probably drown before she ever gets there?"

"Yes, he knows. He's young but he knows the value of an education and he thinks it's worth the risk."

"I'd rather just leave, then. I'll go pack up our things."

"Don't be an idiot, Jizzeline..." Henri Chenet started to say, then stopped. "I didn't say that you leaving was an option. Didn't you hear me? I like having you around. You either stay and send Maya to Miami or I'm calling the police."

He saw Jizzeline's eyes go hazy, but she didn't say anything.

"Take what God offers when He gives it. $500 is a lot of money. You will never have this chance again," he prodded. And when she did not respond, he said, "Now I'll go see Antoine down at the docks. I'll let you know what time the boat leaves when I get back."

He closed the door quietly as he left.

"No, *Manman*!"

Panic took hold of Maya by the throat as Raoul and Jizzeline tried to convince her of the good in it for them all.

"You'll be the first in our family to have a real education," her father said, smiling a smile he hoped would reassure her.

"Yes, *chéri*," Jizzeline added, "and you can stay with my sister when you get there. I have her address; all you have to do is get in a taxi and go. She will be so happy to see you."

"She lives in a neighborhood called 'Little Haiti' in Miami, so you will not feel so far from home," Raoul said as he hugged her, tears wetting his eyes.

"I hate him! It's all his fault! I don't want to go! Please don't make me go," Maya said through steel-hard vocal chords.

Her mother had explained that this was all because of the growing friendship between her and Sylvain, as she already knew. That *m'sié* Chenet had threatened to report Jizzeline as a thief to the authorities if she refused to send Maya away; he'd also offered her money—lots of money. *And Sylvain didn't care!*

"Now, now. Be brave," Jizzeline whispered. "I'm afraid of going to jail, Maya. No one ever comes back..."

She changed tack in midstream.

"This is a wonderful opportunity for you, *cheri mwin*. And things will change for us here, too. We can barely eat on the money we make. Think of this as a sacrifice for your family. Besides, everyone dreams of going to Miami. You'll love it. You probably won't ever want to come back!"

Maya stared at her mother as if through sticky cobwebs from an era long gone. Suddenly, a strong breezed fluttered the tattered curtains of her parents' small bedroom, and Maya thought she heard the sound of familiar laughter. She looked up at the window, and as her parents followed her gaze, lightning flashed in the sky and the Baron's cane fell to the ground.

That night, as Maya lay awake, dreading the tomorrow that would take her away from all she knew—her family, her home, Jacquy—she vowed revenge against *M'sié* Chenet and his traitor son. Somehow, one day she would make them pay.

2

Close your eyes and taste my revenge, M'sié Chenet. Know what it is to lose everything, rich man. Feel the sadness, how does death...

"Hey, wake up! Are you dead or what?"

Startled out of her semi-conscious reverie, Maya shook her head, frowning at the task that lay ahead.

"Did you come in on that boat?" the boy with the gray eyes asked, pointing to a spot behind her.

She turned to see where he pointed and saw the rotted wood hull that had carried her and Antoine for a miserable eternity. It lay on the beach, smashed, much the way she felt herself. Antoine was nowhere in sight. She sat up and stared at the wood heap, transfixed, wondering how it was that she still lived.

"So?" the voice intruded.

She didn't look at him. She looked down at herself instead. The light blue dress she wore since leaving Haiti was torn in several places, soiled like a mechanic's rag and caked with dry vomit, blood, and shit. Her shoes were gone. She stood up, fighting to maintain her balance. The boy just watched. On oatmeal legs, she walked toward the boat; he followed. When she reached the shattered remains of the vessel that would never return to Haiti, it seemed the pounding in her heart might crush her. The bag with her few dollars and scant belongings was gone. With eyes slanted nearly shut against the glare of the sun, she stared in horror at the debris.

My aunt's address! All my things! All along, she'd clung to her little cloth bag as if her sanity depended on it; its absence now symbolized everything she'd lost. She crumpled to the ground, her breath coming in short, staccato heaves that ached in her constricted chest.

"If you come to my house, I'll show you my drawings," the boy said. "I live right over there," he added, pointing to a two-story shingle house that was painted pale pink with white wood shutters opened to the ocean breeze.

She didn't know what he was saying, but his voice shook her out of the dark hole that beckoned. She lifted the cannonball that had replaced her head and stared at where he pointed. With a small gesture inviting her to follow, he started off in the direction of the house. *I just can't.* And then she knew she could. *Work to do. Water. He'll give me some.* She willed strength into her body and rose, wavering on her feet.

"Good," he said as he walked, occasionally looking back to make sure she trailed him. Maya willed her eyes to focus on his winter-white legs until they stopped at the pink house. The door was unlocked and he walked in, beckoning for her to come. A sunny kitchen with flowered yellow curtains and dozens of photographs stuck to the refrigerator led to a deco green-carpeted dining room where a glass chandelier presided over a solid mahogany table and matching chairs. He headed for the staircase that led to a second floor. She knew she couldn't follow. Turning to look at her, he understood.

"Okay, I'll help you." Turning around and placing her arms around his neck, he lifted her onto his back. "Hey, you're pretty light! But, whoa, do you smell bad!"

As he climbed up the stairs, she stole a glance at the comfortable living room down below. Floppy forest-green couch and love seat, television, entertainment center, plants, pretty flower-shade lamps on mahogany end tables. *They must be as rich as the Chenets.*

Judging from the heat of the sun, she surmised that the time of day had to be around noon. This boy's parents were not home. He carried her into his bedroom, an extremely neat room with a single bed under a window that looked out over the ocean. Next to the bed was a white Formica desk with reams of blank white paper stacked on one corner and at least twenty black pencils splayed out on the other. Rear center, a miniature brown tree that sprouted a shaded light bulb served as a desk lamp. When he put her down, her legs gave way and she fell to the floor.

"Here," he said, propping her up against one leg of the bed. She let her eyes stray to the walls. They were covered in a systematic way with drawings, all of them black and white, all of them the same size. Each drawing, spaced a half inch apart, was pinned to the wall with black pushpins. Maya tried to take them in one at a time. A large tongue swallowing a tiny person; the head of a mouse in the clutches of a murderous cat; an enormous bus running over the body of a woman; a house on fire with a small boy crying at a top floor window; a form standing on a cliff, about to jump.

She turned to look at him; he was waiting for her reaction. It seemed to matter to him. Finally, brow furrowed and summoning her best voice, she said to him, *"Poukisa ou desinin tout bagay dwòl sa yo?"* Why do you draw all these strange things?

"What language are you speaking?" he demanded as they both heard the sound of the back door opening and closing. A woman's voice called from below.

"Colin! Are you up there?"

Maya froze.

"Yes, Mom!" He turned to Maya, his finger on his lips, indicating for her to be quiet.

"What are you doing? I thought we were meeting on the beach?"

"I feel like working on my drawings. Can we go a little later?"

"Only if you draw something more inspiring than your usual, okay?"

"Hey, Mom!" he called out, ignoring her request, "If I find something on the beach, can I keep it?"

"Depends on what it is. What did you find?"

"I'll tell you about it later."

"All right. I'm going out for a swim. See you in a little bit?"

"Maybe."

"You need some sun, Colin. Don't stay in all day!"

They heard steps on the kitchen tile and the door close with a soft click.

"What were you saying?" he asked, turning to her. She was still paralyzed with the thought that that woman might have climbed the stairs and found her sitting there. She said nothing. "Well?" he insisted, "What did that mean?" Still nothing. He gestured toward his drawings and, nodding his head yes, he asked, "Do you like them?"

She understood what he meant and shook her head no. *Water.*

"Why?"

"M'pa konn pale anglè," she rasped, holding her throat. The pain was too much.

"What is that language you're speaking?" Colin said again, puzzled by the strange, melodic sound of the words she spoke. "Aren't you one of those boat people from Haiti? Shouldn't you speak French?" Pondering her frustrating blank face, the boy remembered that he knew one line of French, so he tried again:

"I," he began, pointing to his chest, "*parlez vous* English. *English,*" he repeated. "And you? *Parlez-vous Français?*"

She thought she understood *parlez-vous Français* and deduced the rest. She also realized that she had just learned her first English word: English. She repeated it under her breath two or three times before whispering, *"M'pale Kreyol, oui."* I speak Kreyol.

"You are not from Haiti, then?"

Blank stare. Colin sighed heavily and walked past her to his desk where he picked up a pencil and wrote on a blank sheet of paper: HAITI. He brought the paper over to her, pointing at the word he'd written. *She knew that word!* She raised her head and smiled large at him, nodding furiously, forgetting for an instant the pain that hammered between her ears.

"Oui! Mwen vini de Haiti!" And then the room started to spin, and she could no longer control her body. Consciousness slipped quietly away as she fell to the floor.

When Maya awoke, she was in a tight, dark space. She vaguely remembered drinking water the boy had offered, then falling back into the void that claimed her once more. Alarmed at first, she felt around her. Shoes. Something above her tickled her neck. Cloth. Clothes. She was in a closet! She remembered the boy dragging her in here when sounds from below had sent him into an eye-popping flurry of activity. Weakly, she pushed against the door, which creaked open easily at her touch. She could hear voices downstairs and sounds, along with the tell-tale odors that meant it was dinner time. Her stomach groaned in agony. She wondered if the American boy meant to hide her from his parents forever.

"There was something on the radio today about that broken boat down on the beach," Paul Gardner was saying to his wife, Yvette, as she passed him the plate of roasted chicken. The aroma wafted upstairs and tugged at Maya's tongue. "You know how usually there are dozens of people on those boats? Well this time, all they found was the boat. Nothing else. Not a trace of any people."

"How awful!" said Yvette Gardner, a pretty woman with wavy brown hair and a ferocious pair of breasts. "They must all have died at sea this time. And that broken-down boat practically right at our front door! That's never happened before."

"What do they usually do with those people when they find them?" Colin asked in the most casual voice he could muster.

"They are turned over to the authorities, who either send them back to Haiti or keep them in detention centers until they figure out what to do with them," Colin's father said between bites of baked potato.

"What do you mean by detention centers? Is that like jail?"

"In a way it is."

"Those poor people," Yvette Gardner said, shaking her head.

"Why do they come here if they know what will happen to them?" Colin asked.

"I guess they imagine it won't happen to them," Paul Gardner said, fingering his graying mustache. "I suppose they just come hoping they'll make it. They're very poor, you know. To them, anything is worth escaping the poverty and terror they have back home."

"What terror?" Colin asked.

"Oh, it's been terrible!" his mother said. "The military overthrew that priest, and since then, there has been killing and rape left and right. Just awful..."

Colin considered his words carefully. "If one of those people on the boats came to us looking for help, what would we do? Turn them over to the police?"

"Why do you ask?" his mother said, suddenly suspicious.

"I was just wondering what you would do if one of them came knocking at our door."

Paul Gardner chuckled into his salad and looked at his wife. "Those damned annoying hypothetical questions."

"Well thank God we don't have to deal with that," she said. "I just don't know what I'd do, really. What a question, Colin! Really, you and your theoretical dilemmas!"

"Can I finish eating upstairs?" he asked, trying to change the subject. "I was in the middle of a really neat drawing."

"You should eat at the dinner table, Colin, not in your room."

Colin ignored his father and pleaded with his mother, "Please, Mom. I'll even eat these radishes and I swear I won't drop a crumb. And I'll wash my dishes later."

Yvette Gardner turned to her husband, "It's okay, honey; there's something I want to talk to you about anyway."

"What?" Colin wanted to know.

"Hey! Do you want to finish your dinner upstairs or not?" his mother said, laughing.

"I'm going," he said, seizing the moment. He was out of his chair and up the stairs before either one of them could remind him not to drop food on the carpet.

Entering his bedroom, Colin found Maya sitting on the floor, propped up against the wooden bedpost. She was staring vacantly at the drawings on the wall. He handed her his plate.

"You should have stayed in the closet, you know. What if my mother had come in instead of me?"

She wasn't listening. All she could focus on was the taste of food in her mouth, as her famished body greedily absorbed the nutrients it craved. He watched her eat in silence, gravely weighing the acceptable options before him. There didn't seem to be too many, and by the time she finished his meal, he knew what to do.

"You can't stay here," he said decisively, gesturing with great emphasis on YOU and CAN'T and HERE.

The simultaneous look of comprehension and panic in her eyes was what he expected.

"Don't worry," he said. I'll fix it. I think."

She wished she could understand this strange boy with the aluminum-gray eyes, who never smiled, who offered help one minute then scared her with threats the next. She knew she was helpless to do anything other than what he wished. So when he handed her a glass of water and gestured for her to wait, she accepted her fate and the glass he proffered, drinking deeply of the clear, quenching liquid that glided past her throat and hinted at hope that life could start anew.

Maya didn't know when she'd fallen asleep again, but she awoke with a start to find Colin's face close to hers at the foot of the bed, his finger pushed up against his lips.

"Shhh," he whistled through his finger as he stood, motioning for her to follow. Feeling a little stronger now, though still disoriented and unwell, she crept behind him down the stairs through the quiet house and out the back door. She noticed the kitchen clock on the way out. It was 8:15.

The night breeze kicked up gently as the waves revisited the shore in their timeless ritual. A palm tree just to the side of the house shielded them from the blue-white shine of the moon that glowed in the vast dark sky.

"Come on," Colin whispered, "fast now!" He grabbed her around the waist and took off down the beach, lifting her off the ground when he felt her slipping. Forgetting the weakness in her bones, Maya tried to keep up, knowing he led her now to her destiny. They passed ten, fifteen, twenty houses as his sneakered feet kicked up sand behind them. After what seemed like an eternity of breaths heaved in and out of her chest, she was relieved to see Colin finally slow down and come to a stop. He let her go, then, ignoring her, he looked up for long minutes at the shuttered windows of a dark red house that looked old and abandoned even in the dark. Maya didn't notice the dilapidated state of the place, transfixed as she was by the sight that greeted her at the blood-red house's front door. Laid out on an earthenware platter were a couple of green bananas, cleaned white chicken thigh bones, and a heaping handful of white rice: offerings to *Papa Legba*, Master of Passageways!

Fighting the chill that slithered up her spine, Maya whispered to Colin, *"Li bon, oui!" It's good!*

Eyes large, he watched for a few seconds as Maya advanced toward the house in a hypnotic state. Swallowing hard, he brushed past her and pounded on the door. As they waited, the boy and the girl looked into each other's eyes, sharing a connection neither one understood.

"What's your name?" he asked her. "My name is Colin." He pointed at his chest, "Me, Colin. Colin Gardner. Colin Gardner, me."

Earlier, she had heard his mother call his name.

"Maya," she answered, pointing at herself.

Neither one smiled; they were waiting.

Suddenly, they could hear a whirring tone advancing toward them from inside.

"Here she comes," Colin hissed, sweat running down his back.

Then the door opened, and what they saw first was the chair, its stainless steel wheels banging up against the inner doorjamb. The gigantic black woman overflowing from the chair resembled a cross between a mirthful carnival queen and a wrathful khan. Her head was wrapped with a red satin bandanna, which was knotted at the base of her neck. Multiple strings of glass beads, African resin beads, Indian wood beads, charms, trinkets, and gold strands swathed around her neck and chest competed with the intricate pattern of the silver-threaded cloak layered onto her shoulders and draping down into her lap. Underneath was a red satin dress that cut deep down into plunging cleavage and fell down around her bare feet.

"What do you want?" she demanded in a loud, heavily accented voice made more resonant by the scowl on her face.

Colin spoke quickly, falling over his words.

"Maya's boat...from Haiti...arrived on the beach today. She needs help. I have to get back home before my parents miss me...they're just watching TV in their room...*What am I saying?*...so, I thought maybe she could stay with you a few days until she figures out what to do."

The gargantuan creature in the shiny red dress barked out a hoarse, eccentric laugh. "Oh, is that so? Is that what you think? Ha ha ha ha!"

He cut her off, his gray eyes shining daggers. "I don't know you, but I don't think you're bad like they say you are. I have to go now. Goodbye, Maya."

Then he was gone, his heels kicking up sand, her laughter ringing in his ears.

Colossal creature and spindly waif stared aghast at Colin's retreating form. Maya was the first to recover. Shyly she ventured, pointing to the offerings on the ground: *"Se pou Papa Legba ou mete sa yo isit la?"* Did you set these here for *Papa Legba?*

The queenly form turned back to Maya and looked her over from head to foot. Lifting a pudgy fist to her side, *Madame* Mirta laughed out loud once more.

"Ou tou konn sa, cheri!" Honey, you know it! *"Vini non, ann gade sa'n pral fe avè ou."* Come on in so we can figure out what to do with you.

The living room had been transformed into an *ounfò,* a living, breathing *Vodou* temple. In the middle of the room a *poto mitan*—the sacred center pole through which spirits arrive—stood planted like a bare tree. Chairs and ceremonial drums lined one wall. Sequin-emblazoned *Vodou* flags, dazzling to the eye, decorated the walls. The wood floor, painted black, showed leftover markings of recent *vévés* drawn in white chalk. A large crucifix for *Baron Samedi* looked out over the fireplace mantel, its presence strong and looming. On the other side of the room, worn brown shag carpeting, a beat-up plaid sofa, a coffee table, and a television indicated to Maya that this was where *Madame* Mirta kicked back when she wasn't attending to business.

To the right of the living room was the kitchen. Steam floated from a cup and saucer set on a small, round table in a separate alcove. Four hard plastic garden chairs surrounded the table covered with a vinyl cloth featuring poinsettias in feverish bloom. A standard white roll-up shade prevented the curious from looking into the window above the sink. *And believe me, plenty of busybodies around here!* A pot of delicious-smelling stew simmered atop an oven burner, lighting up Maya's appetite all over again. *Map fe bouyon sa pou demen depi kounye a. Konsa lap pi bon!* Unfortunately it was being prepared for the following day. *Madame* Mirta offered her tea instead.

"Se yon te ti bom qui sot jus an Haiti!" Mint tea all the way from Haiti.

Maya accepted gratefully, and her cup joined *Madame* Mirta's on the table across the room. While the tea leaves steeped, Maya got the tour of the house. She followed her host out of the kitchen, down a short hallway, and into her bedroom. When *Madame* Mirta pushed open the door, a gigantic bed covered with a red, ocean-sized, satin spread leaped out at Maya and she took a step backward. Her hostess laughed as she entered the room, speaking to Maya over her shoulder.

"Madan Mirta bezwin pwoteksyon! Rouge se koulè Bosou!" She needed Lord *Bosou*'s protection, and red was his favorite color!

Maya nodded her comprehension as she gazed around the room, the walls of which glowed like a dying fire. Perfumes and lotions, hair pomades, and multiple family photos tumbled over each other on a dresser with open drawers bulging with scarves, flashy costume jewelry, and undergarments. An open closet door revealed more red satin dresses, shawls, slippers, and shoes.

Clutching a glass decanter retrieved from her night table, *Madame* Mirta now rolled toward Maya, indicating with a tilt of the head that it was time to leave this ruby-hued chamber. Once out of the bedroom, she pointed her wheels to the door just to the left, then stopped, her hand on the knob. Turning to look into Maya's eyes with a mischievous gleam in hers, the queen threw open the door with a flourish. Maya's breath stopped short.

Overwhelming the small room stood two epic altars made up of shelves, each packed with objects honoring individual spirits, indicating a living, breathing sanctuary of *Vodou* works in progress. Liquor bottles, candles, and multiple household items elbowed each other for space. Client photos leaned up against dishes filled with stones or mysterious potions. Skulls, cigarettes, and sunglasses sidled up against beaded rattles called *asons*. Bound medicine packets, known as *paket kongos*, silently spread their power alongside clear glass bottles carrying dolls' heads and crucifixes. Hand-made dolls used as messengers to the *lwas*, books, mirrors, and money all congregated together in joyful chaos.

After staring at the shrines for some time, the mesmerized child forced herself to look away. All around the room, charms called *wangas* hung from the ceiling. They were crafted out of boxes and vials wrapped in string, rope, hair—whatever *Madame* Mirta, Miami Beach's own *mambo*, saw fit to get the job done. Decanters filled with countless herbs and powders displayed on wall shelving proclaimed the *Vodou* priestess' knowledge of the healing arts. A furry, rust-orange carpet covered the floor. The room was stuffy and crammed from floor to ceiling with the accoutrements of *Vodou* magic and ritual.

"This is where I do my work," *Madame* Mirta said after awhile. She placed the glass decanter taken from the bedroom onto one of the shelves. "Come with me, let's go have our tea."

Seated at the kitchen table among riotous vinyl poinsettias, Maya listened carefully to the words of her savior—the second in one day.

"...I make a special ceremony to *Marassa* for a child like you. Nobody ever see so much food in one ceremony. The *Marassa,* they were very happy. I am not greedy, so I did not ask for two; no, just one because I just need a little help. I got a bad hip, and since the operation, it get worse. But I can't lie, I no only ask because I am in a wheelchair. I ask also because I never had no children, and I always wanted a little girl. I made the ceremony one month ago, and tonight, you knock at my door. I knew; I feel it in my bones that the *Marassa* twins be good to me and send me a child. You perfect. You so pretty, and little, not fat like me, and you get strong. I know you probably come in on that boat they find on the beach, right? You got family here?"

"Yes," Maya whispered, "one aunt, but I don't know how to find her. Everything I had is in the sea now."

"Did you have an address for her? Do you know what part of town she live in? Is it Little Haiti?" These questions *Madame* Mirta asked with dread in her heart.

"Yes, Little Haiti."

"Then we try to find her for you. If we find her, you not the one. If we don't, I make extra special ceremony to thank *Marassa* for this lovely gift. What's your name, child?"

"Maya."

"I don't suppose you know how to read and write French?"

"A little."

"Hmpphhh. You go to school in Haiti?"

"No, but my friend Jacquy did, and he taught me. At least he *was* teaching me until..."

"Until what?"

"Nothing."

"Hmpphhh. Nothing, huh? Where's your mother? Where's your father?"

"In Haiti."

"Why they send you and they not come themself?"

The look in Maya's eyes hardened and darkened, sending a slight shiver through *Madame* Mirta.

"Because they wanted to send *me*," she said in the dry, matter-of-fact voice of a tired adult.

Madame Mirta changed the subject. "How you manage to survive the trip? Most people don't make it."

"I don't know."

"Do you feel all right?"

"I don't feel so good. My throat is dry. My skin hurts. My eyes burn. My stomach hurts." Two heavy teardrops made their way down to her chin as she spoke.

"Well, drink that tea, then. It will make you feel better. And then we get you to bed."

"What do you want me to do for you?"

"I want us to take care of each other, like mother and daughter."

"I have a mother."

"Do you want to stay here with me? You can help me prepare for my ceremonies. Help me in and out of the bathtub; help me get dressed; help me get around. And if everything work out all right, if we don't find your aunt, then I'll take care of you. I am legal here, you know! I can get you your papers! You can go to school! Learn English! Get special lessons in French! That sound all right with you?"

"That sounds very good."

The older woman stifled a chuckle. She had never seen such a young grown-up. *After that trip, I suppose anyone would forget how to smile.*

"Were you always this serious, baby?"

"No. But I am now."

"Okay, Miss Serious, finish your tea, and we go fix a bed for you in the other room."

The other room was behind a door, which Maya had assumed to be a closet. Just on the other side of the altar room, it contained little more than a small cot and a night table; a low wood-and-straw chair stood by itself in a corner. Maya was instructed to remove her soiled clothes, slip into a queen-sized nightgown, and climb into bed. After pulling back the sheets, *Madame* Mirta whirred her wheelchair out of the room. She paused at the door to look back at the child.

"You can call me *Manman* Mirta," she said.

In response, Maya stood by the bed, staring at her with vacant eyes. The large woman closed the door with a firm click.

Maya was running down a dark, deserted beach, but it wasn't a beach; it was a forest, because there were so many trees. Breathing heavily, she stopped to listen. Was that a sound over there? Was he hiding behind that big avocado tree? She could almost smell him. She thought she saw his light brown skin peering out from behind the dark brown bark. Was that an elbow? She plunged head on, fists clenched. But what she found were the remains of one of her boat mates, human bites marks still apparent on the now festering limbs. "NO! You can't make me!" she screamed at the others who tried in vain to convince her it was merely survival. She had to get away...but WHAT WAS THAT? Footsteps retreating to her left made her turn, eyes full of fear mixed with anticipation. She ran full speed toward the sound, her breath catching, throat dry. I wish I had some water, she thought, it would taste so good right now. I've been in this sandy forest for so long now; I'd give anything for water...then I could keep looking...

When Maya woke up, her throat was parched, her thirst a hurting thing. The rising sun slid unnoticed past the small, uncovered window. Sitting up, she looked around, dazed, confused for a moment. Then she remembered. Still so weak, she stepped out of bed and dragged herself to the kitchen, where she poured herself a tall glass of water and drank, refilling the glass three times. Satisfied, Maya looked around the room until she spied the things she needed. A yellow-ruled note pad and two pens lay next to the telephone. Choosing a pen and tearing off a sheet of paper, she tiptoed back to her room. Once inside, determination in her step, Maya walked to the bed and kneeled down. But she did not intend to pray. Her trembling hand laid pale yellow paper against dimpled sheet. In contrast, her pen seemed to attack as she wrote several words in large, awkward letters. Then, flicking off exasperating tears, she studied her work.

"*Msié* Chenet will pay. I will find him. I will kill him."

Later that day, *Madame* Mirta looked in several times on Maya, only to find her hidden beneath the tangle of sheets, head down, soft snores the only audible sound in the room. She was excited that her ceremony had worked. She knew this child would be staying. Although her house was old, compared to the other well-kept homes on the beach, and she knew the neighbors found it an eyesore, *Madame* Mirta had other ideas about how to spend her money. She had been saving up for years in anticipation of the day she would have a child to take care of. This child would have everything. The best! And if things went well and their relationship blossomed like the flower she hoped for, Maya would inherit everything—the tidy sum she had in the bank, the house, and hopefully, her business. The joy in her heart made her want to leap up out of her wheelchair. *God is good*, she thought. And immediately after, *But she may not want to make her living like I do. If she doesn't, that okay, too,* she decided, *she will be able to choose anything she want to do, and I will help her.* Pushing away the possible disappointment of having to leave this earth with no one to assume her important work, she wheeled herself into the kitchen, where she set about preparing a festive welcome feast for her new daughter.

It would take a while for the feast to be consumed.

From a semi-conscious haze, Maya battled then surrendered to the pain that hammered her eyes, throat, chest, and every bone in her body. At times, she woke to the sound of hushed voices—of *Madame* Mirta and some other woman discussing her condition and how best to heal it. Other times, she would be made to sit up for an astonishing assortment of vile-tasting potions. She submitted to the coarse hands of her benefactress as she applied soothing creams to the hideous sun blisters she'd developed all over her face and body; sandpaper lips that could not smile welcomed smelly balms that tasted like glue but comforted all the same. Often during those days, *Madame* Mirta found her half-asleep, the tears on her face like orphan creatures in search of a home. And in the middle of the night, *Madame* Mirta sometimes jolted awake to the sound of Maya's voice screaming the name, "Sylvain!"

On the fifth day, the sound of persistent ringing at the door woke Maya, and feeling stronger for the first time, she staggered out of her room and into the hallway, wondering where her new friend might be. Then she saw her, staring out the open front door, shoulders slightly hunched.

"What's the matter?" Maya asked softly.

The large woman turned around, replacing her look of resignation with a hasty smile. "Oh, you're up! That good. How you feel?"

"Better. What's the matter?"

"Oh, nothing. Just those kids, coming around to bother me. They think I do black magic. They scared of me, but they like to push their luck, hoping to see me do some evil spell so they have something to talk about. They just kids," she added with a sigh.

"Why don't you make them stop?" Maya said.

"I can't make them stop doing what they want to do," she said, closing the door. She turned her chair around and headed up the hallway toward Maya. She wore a bright red dress with big white flowers and summery green leaves. It fell down to her shins; her feet were bare. She wore no jewelry today, and her face, devoid of makeup, looked pudgy, round and fresh, but lines of sadness napped around her eyes.

"What do you mean you can't make them?" Maya insisted. "You know magic."

Madame Mirta rolled along to the kitchen without answering. A flavorful and tempting aroma wafted past Maya's nose, and she followed the scent as the large white cotton nightgown she had been commanded to wear billowed and trailed on the floor behind her. At the oven, *Madame* Mirta stirred without interruption as her young charge sat down, head hanging between her hands.

"You hungry?" *Madame* Mirta asked, finally turning around to look at her.

"Yes. Why don't you answer my question?"

Madame Mirta set the table for two, filling two bowls with her steaming vegetable and beef stew. Setting them down, she arranged herself across from Maya before picking up her spoon, blowing with elaborate attention to cool its contents. Apparently satisfied with both herself and her dish, she looked up at Maya, who was slurping spoonfuls, oblivious of temperature. *Madame* Mirta let a few moments pass before asking: "What you know about magic?"

"I know you can make spirits work for you if you serve them," Maya answered.

"And you think you can make the spirits do things to other people for you?"

"Yes."

"Then you don't know nothing, *cheri mwen.* If you are going to help me with my business, first thing you need to know is, whether you call it *Vodou* or magic, I only do good. I don't take no chance that what I do come back on me. The only way magic work is if you do it on yourself. You make ceremonies and pray to the spirits to make change *for you,* not *to* anyone else!"

Maya looked up at her, head cocked, disbelieving. They stared at each other for a moment in silence. And then the doorbell shrilled again, making them jump.

"I will go open the door for you," Maya offered, standing and heading for the hallway.

Madame Mirta followed, curious. The non-stop ringing jarred the house with the sound of intrusion. Hidden from view, she watched Maya's walk go from small frail child to willful fighter; head up and back, shoulders set. She stood for a few seconds in front of the dark wood door, then forcefully threw it open.

"What do you want?" she asked of the two boys who stood, giggling nervously, obviously on a dare. She had spoken to them in Kreyol.

"Where's the witch?" one of them asked. "I have some water in this can. If she's not a witch then nothing will happen to her if I sprinkle some drops on her, right? Where is she? Who are you?"

Maya said nothing and stared at them with contempt.

"What's the matter with you? Don't you know how to talk? Can't speak any English?"

She shifted her eyes from the two boys and looked up at the sky, at the blue jays flying overhead. Not five seconds later, a chilly breeze replaced stagnant humid summer air, and the boys looked around with apprehension. As they glanced around them, wondering at this unexpected change in weather, one of the birds swooped down, grazing one boy on the head with its claws, causing them both to turn and run, screaming at the top of their lungs. Maya closed the door, turned around, and headed back to the kitchen. Stupefied, *Madame* Mirta watched the child settle back into her seat at the table, casually slurping her stew.

"You always been able do that?" the older woman asked finally.

"What?"

"You don't seem surprised at what you just did."

"I didn't do anything."

"Anyone can do magic, child. Anyone can work with nature; it's just that most people have to work really hard at it. They have to concentrate for a long time and really want something *bad!* You got natural magic in you, baby, but using it in anger can be very dangerous. That what I trying to tell you before. You got to decide what you want for yourself—maybe you want those kids to stop bothering us—then you ask the spirits to take care of it and let them decide how to do it; the spirits know best, child."

Maya just kept eating.

"You hear what I saying to you, child?"

Maya took another spoonful of stew and chewed the meat slowly, savoring the taste in her mouth before answering. "I didn't do anything. I just wanted them to go away. Maybe the spirits did it."

"When the spirits do something, they do it right. Whatever they decide to do, it is fair and it don't hurt nobody."

"Hmph," Maya said into her spoon. She hadn't heard this philosophy before and it dawned on her that she'd never stopped to question her family on the inner workings of the religion they practiced.

Madame Mirta's voice insisted. "Child, what happen to you make you so mad? Who you so mad at? Who is Sylvain?"

Maya looked up, fear in her eyes.

"How do you know that name?"

"These past four days, while you so sick, I must have hear his name fifty time. Sometime you say it like he your favorite person; sometime you say it real sad; and sometime there so much hate, I get scared."

Maya refused to answer. She looked at *Madame* Mirta for a moment, fighting back tears that had their way in the end as they tumbled down her cheeks.

"Oh Lord," the priestess sighed, looking up at the ceiling. "You never know what you get when you pray for something. I see I have a lot of work to do with you, *ti cheri*. I hope you can accept what I have to teach you."

The Baron

The months moved on at their usual glacial pace. But as they always do, the years flew by at breakneck speed. That's time for you, baby. It's *never* on your side. No, no, no.

3

Ten Years Later

Maya stepped out of the coffee shop with a light step, her quiet, brooding demeanor replaced by a dimpled smile that made people turn and stare at the striking young woman with cigarette-thin, waist-long dreadlocks and black silk for skin.

"Are you a model?" a young man entering the cafe asked as she held the door open for him. "You look very familiar to me."

She would have ignored him normally, but today was different.

"No, I'm a dancer!" she smiled broadly, ducking out before he could further engage her

Today she was excited. She had just finished an hour-long interview with Penelope Long, a *Dance* Magazine writer who planned to feature her as an up-and-coming dancer in the eye-catching shaded box that appeared in every issue. She never thought anything like this would happen to her so soon. After the sixth performance of her starring role in the company's latest show, the concave, mousy-haired woman with the thinnest imaginable lips had tapped her on the shoulder as she exited the theater and asked if she would like to be featured in the magazine.

"Me? Why?" Maya had asked, surprised.

"Because I think you just may have created an entirely new dance concept. The choreography is yours, right?"

"Supervised by Mr. DeVilla, but yes."

"Am I wrong or do I recognize elements of *Capoeira* in the way you move?"

"You have it right."

"Where can we talk?"

Maya had suggested The Korner Kafe, where she stopped in almost daily for a quick bite to eat after rehearsals. For a little over an hour, she explained to Penelope Long the origins and motivation behind her Brazilian-inspired style, which was gaining recognition in local dance circles. Maya couldn't quite get a read on this Fanny woman—she was edgy, not very friendly—but she felt the interview had gone well. She wanted to run and phone *Manman* Mirta, but her cautious nature decided against it. *Just wait until the issue comes out and simply show it to her.* She would be so proud! Maya chose instead to knock on Colin's door to see if he might be up for a celebratory dinner. Upon entering the yellow stucco, three-story apartment building where the two friends lived—he on the ground floor, she on the second—she detoured first to her mailbox. *Great!* There was a letter from Jacquy. *This must be my lucky day.* Tucking it into her large black leather carry-all, she walked around the staircase and down the ever-so-deco-green painted hallway—just like eighty percent of the buildings on Miami Beach—where ambient strains of unpleasant metallic music resounded. It meant Colin was home, getting stoned on pot and gazing at the drawings on his living-room walls. They had not changed much in subject matter since the day he rescued her on the beach.

She quickened her step, hoping to avoid running into Simon, the smarmy building manager who wanted Colin *bad.* She also wanted to get upstairs to her own space, where she could luxuriate in the news from Jacquy. Just as she rang Colin's doorbell, Simon's door opened (as she knew it would), and the painfully unattractive, large-headed, pockmarked building manager peeked around it.

"Hi, Maya!" he smiled, his brown teeth making their usual stomach-churning impression.

"Hi, Simon."

He dispensed with the small talk. Anyone who knew Maya did that.

"Would you tell Colin to knock on my door at some point? I have a question about his rent check."

"No problem."

She turned back to face the door just as Colin opened it.

"Quick let me in and close the door, fast."

"Gotcha."

Colin grabbed Maya by the shoulder and shoved her into the apartment, shutting the door with a flourish.

"Simon?"

"Your lover-in-waiting my dear."

Colin stood a long, slim 6'2" in straight-legged, tight black jeans and a plain white shirt that buttoned down the front—his usual. And he sported small, round, black-framed glasses. His dark, tightly cropped hair with not a highlight in sight was combed forward to hide the receding hairline that had begun to make itself noticed at the early age of twenty-three. His pale-as-death skin flashed its only hint of color—red-rimmed eyes contoured in kohl.

Maya stepped gingerly through several scrunched-up balls of white paper strewn throughout her friend's black-carpeted apartment, walking around a large black-lacquered coffee table covered with comic books, and over to his black corduroy couch. She plopped herself down, anxious to tell him her news. In her dark, sleeveless leotard and sweatpants, she nearly blended right into the couch. Looking at her sparked an idea in Colin for a story about a people-swallowing couch, but something in Maya's demeanor cut his thought short.

"So, what gives? I detect a smile or a twinkle or some such thing. Are you really Maya, or her despicably happy-go-lucky twin sister?" He spoke in an affected manner that suggested homosexuality but left most people unsure.

"Oh stop, Colin. You'd just love for me to be as morbid as you." Her island-accented English hinted at long-ago French lessons from the Haitian teacher *Madame* Mirta had insisted upon.

"Honey, you won that contest ages ago."

"You know what? I just figured it out about you! You're like one of those gay guys who swears every hetero man is gay but won't admit it; except with you, your secret belief is that everyone is as obsessed with death and creepy things as you are!"

"Busted. Hey, at least I'm not one of those gay guys."

"No, the jury's still out on what you are."

"Look who's talking. When did you last get laid? Name one guy you ever had a crush on, one guy you would even consider potential boyfriend material?"

Maya's face darkened momentarily, then lightened up just as quickly.

"Well, in all the years I've known you, I have never seen you lust after woman or man. Care to enlighten those of us who would love to know?"

"You love to answer questions with questions when things get personal, don't you?"

"Really, Colin, just this once can you answer the question: Are you asexual or or just gay but closeted?"

"Really, Maya," he parried, "are you a lesbian or do you just like getting yourself off?"

"Okay, okay. Want to hear the news I came here to tell you?"

"3-2-1 go."

"I just had my interview with Penelope Long, and I think it went really well! She asked very intelligent questions, and I tried not to say *um* and *uh* and *like* and stuff like that so I would sound thoughtful and brainy and devastatingly creative and brilliant."

"And you pulled it off?"

"Fucker," she laughed.

"Just kidding. That's just monstrous, Maya! When does the issue come out?"

"Next month. She was past her deadline and rushing to get back to the magazine to get it in. Apparently, they had to trash the guy they were planning to feature at the last minute—I didn't ask why—so I got lucky. Anyway, I wanted to see what you're doing later for dinner. I'm in the mood to celebrate."

"Maybe the celebration should wait till the piece comes out."

"Ever the optimist."

"Hey, if you had to choose between being swallowed whole by an alligator or a giant rat, what would you choose?" Colin asked, changing the subject.

"Oh great, here we go. And what happens if I decide not to choose?"

"You never hear from Jacquy again."

"Oh boy. Always for the jugular. All right, I take the alligator."

"Why?"

"Not fair. I have no reasons and you can't make me have one. This is just a comic book."

"You know, I have something to celebrate, too," he said. "I've been nominated, along with thirty other comic book artists and storywriters, for an award. If they choose me, I get a $10,000 grant."

"No!"

"Yes!"

"Don't you want to wait till they decide before celebrating?" Maya asked with a sly grin.

"Fucker," he muttered with what passed for a laugh. Colin hardly ever laughed. He thought it was unbecoming to a creepy-story writer such as himself.

"So, how about dinner? I'll go Dutch if you will," Maya sing-sang.

"How can I refuse such a tantalizing offer?"

"What time?"

"A couple of hours. Want to walk down Jefferson till we see something that looks horrifying?"

"Sounds good." Maya got up, and as she did so, Jacquy's letter dropped out of her bag.

"Hey, this must be your lucky day! Mail from the Jack-o."

"That's just what I thought to myself when I saw the letter," she said opening the door to leave. "And by the way, Simon has a question about your rent check. Wants you to knock on his door about it. Did you forget to sign it on purpose? Looking for a reason to step into the lair of our gorgeous landlord?"

"My rent check? Oh, screw him. Nothing can lure me into *that* angel's den." To Colin, all deadbeats were defined as angels and darlings.

Maya chuckled, clutching her bag and hurrying up the stairs to her apartment. She opened the door to a small studio filled with potted plants, herbs, and flowers, with a bed by the window that looked out on the street. The bedspread was a bright, satiny red with sequins sewn in as stars—a gift from *Manman* Mirta. In the middle of the room was an old wood palette she'd found in the trash. It stood on a couple of milk crates covered with a white lace tablecloth, also a gift from the queen. She'd scored with a floor that was hardwood instead of the usual crappy carpeting. Four large, well-placed cushions served as chairs, and several short tree stumps from a lumberyard up in North Miami Beach served as end tables and repositories for candles, vases, and more plants. The kitchen was a tiny alcove that opened onto the main room; again she'd been lucky—all the appliances and cabinets were white, and the counters were gray. Across the room, to the right of the kitchen, was a door leading to the bathroom, which didn't fare so well in the luck department. The wall and floor tiles were black and a sickly khaki-green. The vanity cabinet was also black, made of cheap plasterboard; the white sink, bathtub, and toilet were stained that typical Miami Beach rust-brown. Simon had promised to replace them within three months, but she'd given up waiting. Two years had passed since she'd moved out of *Manman* Mirta's home, much to the lady's chagrin.

"You don't want stay with me no more?"

"You know that's not true."

"Then why you want go? You so young still."

"It makes sense for me to be closer to the studio since the only time I'm not there is when I'm sleeping. My career is in dance, Manman. I know this doesn't fit in with your plans but...you knew this was coming."

Madame Mirta sighed. "Yes, child, I know that."

"But don't look so sad! I'm not moving out of the country. I still want to help with the big Saturday ceremonies whenever I can."

"Really? You still want do that?"

"Of course. This way we'll see each other at least once a week."

After thinking about it for a moment, Madame Mirta grumbled a little, but then added, "Once a week don't give me enough time to keep an eye on you."

"Why do you think you need to?"

"Don't play Miss Innocent with me."

"Are you back on that again?"

"You know you have power in you mind."

"That's what you keep telling me. God, how I wish I could make things happen as easily as you think. And if I was so powerful, don't you think I would use this power the right way? I think I learned something *from living with you all this time."*

"I hope so. And I hope you remember some of those thing when the time come."

The only remaining space in the small apartment was to the left of the front door, and that was where Maya's altar stood, hidden behind a pretty, painted white Indonesian wood screen. No one had ever been permitted a look behind that screen, though many had tried and stopped short upon seeing *The Look* on Maya's face. It was her private space, she told the few friends she invited in, and she expected them to honor that. The tone accompanying The Look worked beautifully, keeping the nosiest at bay, even Colin. She had always been able to do that—stop the flow of conversation, freeze people in their tracks, and rearrange intentions with one glance. They knew instinctively not to cross her—to stop in midstream, go back and start again.

She moved the screen over now and stepped closer in, reaching for a small bowl in which a dead rose floated in water. She walked to the kitchen, threw out the faded flower, and rinsed the bowl, returning it to the second of the three shelves that made up her personal sanctuary. She sat down on the floor in front of the homemade temple, looking it over, checking on a candle here, changing incense there, rearranging certain items; all the while, she breathed deeply, taking in the energy that poured forth from this living shrine that served as sanctuary to the lonely, angry child that still lived inside the young woman Maya had become. Her altar, in sharp contrast to *Madame* Mirta's, was almost stark. It was lacking in the stacked, closely crowded objects that featured so prominently in the working altar of a busy *Vodou* priestess.

The items on the second and lower shelf changed, depending on the circumstances of her life at any given time. If she felt under the weather, the middle shelf might display a photo or crudely drawn symbol for *Simbi*, lord of healing, along with a glass of water to represent where *Simbi* is said to reside.

Ground powder from medicinal plants placed on charcoal might be burned for restoration of health. In times of confusion, she might invoke the spirit of *Papa Legba* with numerous crosses of all shapes and mediums. It was said that the cross's vertical line linked heaven above with those who have passed below. The intersecting horizontal line between the living and the dead served as symbol of *Legba*'s power to facilitate communication between the physical and metaphysical worlds from which the spirits speak wisdom to their kin on earth. But the top shelf never changed, and it never would until justice was wrought. Covered in black cloth and overlaid with a purple velvet, triangular-shaped shawl that hung down over the center, the rack stood devoted entirely to *Baron Samedi*, Lord of the Dead. Known to dwell in cemeteries in order to assist spirits in the transition from life to death, the Baron always dressed like an undertaker. His familiar black top hat sat imperiously at the center of the shelf, surrounded by various items associated with the beloved but ghoulish spirit. The Baron's black sunglasses; a wooden, phallus-shaped walking stick; and a bowl of flour—worn like powder on the face to represent the whiteness of the human skull—rested next to a cigar, a photo of a cemetery cross, and lastly, a framed 8" × 10" pencil sketch that was a dead ringer for Henri Chenet.

Maya sat for a while, gazing at the photo of her nemesis, smiling for a moment at the brief image that flashed through her memory of the street artist she had chosen to draw the image of the man she needed always to remember.

She'd spotted him while strolling through a crowded and noisy street fair in Coconut Grove one weekend. Working as if a motor powered his fingers, he drew a spot-on likeness of the young woman who sat opposite him. She'd waited her turn and sat in the chair, fixing him with a long, hard gaze. The young art student in search of enough beer money to make it through the weekend in a drunken haze had tried to shake the stringy brown hair from his rugged, pleasant face but found that he couldn't move. Neither, it seemed, could he speak, so he waited, caught in the grip of an inexplicable moment. Finally, the black-skinned girl opened her mouth to speak. He could barely hear what she said, but he knew he must break through the fog that suddenly enveloped his brain to listen and to understand what she wanted.

"I am going to describe a man to you, and I want you to sketch his face for me," she said in a quiet voice.

As if he had imagined the fog just a moment before, his head cleared and the rascal in him returned.

"You mean just like a police sketch?"

"Yes," she nodded.

"What the hell," he ceded good-naturedly, "could be fun."

Maya described in minute detail every aspect of Henri Chenet's face, character, and demeanor, down to the sound of his voice. When she was done, he looked up from his pad and into her brooding eyes.

After his last pencil stroke, he turned the pad to show her. "Somehow, I suspect you're gonna tell me my drawing is this guy's spitting image," he said.

At the sight of the man who so filled her with hatred, Maya felt heat rise up through her body, and a film of sweat covered her skin. She suddenly felt weak and wobbly.

"Hey! Are you gonna faint or somethin'?" the young man said, alarmed. This chick was flipping him out. He wanted her out of his chair. "You want some water?"

Fighting hard for composure, Maya willed herself to stand up, and, holding on to the back of the chair for support, she rasped: "How much?"

"Nothing. You can have it for free." He was feeling an urge to move her along, get her as far away from him as soon as possible. She stood still as a statue. "Really, it's okay," he insisted.

"Thank you," she whispered. " Is there something you would like instead of money?" She was beginning to feel better. That nauseous,

feverish feeling was fading, and she was becoming aware of people around them staring, waiting for her to wrap up her business.

"Sure," he chuckled, "make my bookie disappear." He looked over his shoulder at a fat, balding guy in shirtsleeves and a bad wig heading his way. He was dodging cars and screaming profanities as he went.

Maya looked across the street, and laughed inside at the sudden image of the lumbering rhinoceros that entered her mind. She reached out to take the sketch from the young man's hand, and held his gaze. All motion stopped for an instant. He watched her as she looked once more at the man heading their way, then nodded slightly, walking away without a backward glance. Before he knew it, the man to whom he owed more dollars than he cared to count was on him, bad breath pouring like liquid crap from his mouth and into the artist's face. The customers were scattering.

"So, what's it gonna be, shithole? You think you're gonna pay me back the cash you owe me drawing pitchers?" THWACK, went the sound of fleshy backhand on skinny face.

"Frank, don't worry, I'll have it by the end of the week!" the young man screamed in a frightened, high-pitched voice.

Before Frank could respond, another voice filled the air, growling like a beast.

"Hey, Frankie, harassing minors again? What did I tell you about breaking your parole?"

A pug-nosed, middle-aged guy in sideburns and bell-bottomed blue jeans had materialized as if from thin air.

"Whaddaya mean, Len? What minors?" Frank blubbered, his eyes frantically seeking escape.

"Oh yeah? How old are you kid? Make my day, tell me you're under eighteen."

"I'm seventeen," the young man lied, swallowing nervously, thanking a God he didn't believe in for the rescue.

"Did you know this guy was a pervert? Broke his parole twice before; reported just the other day for peeping through the schoolyard fence down on 21st. Been looking for him." As he announced this blessed *news, the man named Len grabbed handcuffs from his back belt loop, nailing Frank. "Funny thing is, I was looking for a shop on Main Street; needed to pick up a cake for my wife. But I came down here instead. No fuckin' idea why. Musta been to pick up Frank the perv, here, whaddaya think?"*

"I guess so,..."the artist started to say, but Len wasn't listening. He was already walking away with "Frank the perv" in tow. Alone now, the artist spun around, half-expecting to see the girl loitering nearby, smiling wickedly or some weird shit like that; but she was nowhere to be seen.

Looking up at Henri Chenet's picture, Maya summoned the concentration needed for her daily ritual of the past ten years: focus, focus, focus on forming the image in her mind of *Monsieur* Chenet weeping miserably, begging forgiveness. She did this now, seeing the scene play itself out like a movie, feeling the man's hopelessness and pain, reveling in the joy it brought her.

Fifteen minutes later Maya was sitting cross-legged, stone-still in concentration, when the phone rang, jarring her out of the ritual that always left her perturbed but energized with the relentless power of her intention. She reached the phone just as the answering machine picked up, and lifted the receiver. It was Eliana Higuerra, a petite, high-energy dancer who had persisted long enough to break through Maya's wall. Their friendship was new but growing. Raised in a strict Catholic Cuban household, Elly often found ways to bring up *Vodou*, drawing Maya into conversations that sometimes brought them to the brink of parting ways, but they liked each other too much.

"I'm dying to know how the interview went!" Elly asked in her perky, lightly accented voice.

"Hi, Elly," Maya smiled, rousing herself from her interrupted reverie.

"So?"

"I'm hopeful that it went well," Maya said.

"Is that all I'm going to get, Maya? Come on, tell me what she was like; she can be such a bitch in her column sometimes. Was she at least nice to you?"

"Sort of," Maya said, feeling more in her skin now. "I'm not a hundred percent sure, because she's all sharp angles and corners, you know what I mean? But I have a feeling it will turn out all right."

"Well, your feelings are usually right, *mija*. But what kind of questions did she ask you?"

"Hey, why don't you join Colin and me for dinner tonight? This way I can fill you both in at once."

"With Colin? He's so weird, Maya; but then again, so are you, right?"

"That's what my friends keep telling me."

"Come on, even you have to admit you're not the average...anyway, where are you going? Maybe I *will* meet you."

"Not sure. We were going to walk down Jefferson until something just *horrible* leaps up and grabs us."

"You're quoting that weirdo, right?"

"Yes," Maya chuckled, "he's such a riot."

"A king-size riot—as in Rodney King." She giggled at her own joke. "What time are you guys leaving?"

"In an hour and a half or so. Meet us downstairs?"

"Okay, see you soon. I'm starved already."

Hanging up the phone, Maya headed to the bathroom for a shower, delaying the moment she would sit with Jacquy's letter, inhaling the scent and essence of Haiti, along with news of the Chenet family's activities. A half hour later, she was refreshed, bare-footed, and draped in a white cotton bathrobe. A cup of mint tea in hand—courtesy of *Manman* Mirta's garden—she sat on her bed, leaning against the wall, relishing the moment. The sun was setting, and the sky getting ready to turn dark blue. If she strained, she could hear the faint sound of waves breaking on shore. Two candles and a small bed lamp served as the only light in the room. She closed her eyes, smiling, then tore open the envelope and read the letter, which was written in semi-broken French:

My Dear Sister Maya,

Good News! By the time you get this letter, I probably already be in Miami! I finally receive word from Benjamin Porter (the man my cousin work for) that he have finally get the authority to bring me in to work for him. With the help of Laura Neilson—remember that missionary? Yes, she still here—somehow he get the immigration people to believe that his factory work no good without me! I hope they never make an inspection because I expect I must to be working as Mr. Porter's house-boy until I can get a job using my welding hands. In any case, I am very happy because things in our country are more terrible than I can ever memorize. It only beginning of the 90s but it looking like it won't be no better than the 80s. Just yesterday, the whole Ignacel family was killed with machete blows. We think it is because one of the boys are suspect of involve in an anti-government group. We hoping the elections still go on. I am sorry not to vote, but I preferred get out if I can.

Your manman and papa are fine and ask me to send you their love. They are very sad that you refuse to communicate with them, but you already know this. Think you ever change your mind someday?

You never tell me why you always so interesting in that family your manman work for, but as you know, I always try do whatever you ask and tell you anything what I hear about them. I miss you really and being friends, and I am happy to see you again when I get to Miami. Is it not strange to be see each other again after all these years of writing letters? I ask myself how you look now? You probably won't even recognize me!

In any case, the last news from the Chenet family is that the son, Sylvain, is studying to be lawyer of the environment at the University of Miami. I not even sure if I tell you the right thing because I don't understand what that is, but that is what your manman say.

Shocked, Maya let the letter drop to her lap as her hand reached up to cover her mouth. Her heart beat like a jackhammer against her breast, causing an uncomfortable sensation. She breathed in deeply, trying to calm herself down. *Sylvain in Miami!* After a moment, she picked up the letter again.

He there since six months now, and both parents are sick for missing him. Your manman say the Chenets have been in horrible mood since he left and treat her like a useless dog. She hope Sylvain stop his lawyer plan and come back soon because she say she no can stand to work there anymore. She especially has horrible things to say about the man of the house...I guess it is the same thing all the time.

Anyway, since it is only a 90-minute flight, I will try bring you some goodies from home (the stuff I know you love, like griot—your manman say she make some special; and guava jelly and those crackers you always like better than bread). I hope they don't catch me and make me throw them out at the airport.

So don't be surprise if I am at your door some time soon. I don't have your telephone number—why that so, anyway? Are you still afraid I will give it to your parents? You should know better by now.

Your good friend from home,
Jacquy

Maya re-read the letter over and over until she knew the words by heart. *Sylvain in Miami!* resonated again and again in her mind, blotting out all other thoughts save for the other message in Jacquy's letter: *Jacquy in Miami!* It was all too much to handle. She didn't know whether to jump up and down and scream with joy or cry with relief. She couldn't think. After so many days, months, years, and dreams of wondering how she would meet Sylvain again, Maya wondered if she might be dreaming now, too. She folded the letter, put it back in its envelope, and walked over to the phone on shaky legs. In a no-nonsense tone her friends knew not to question, she canceled their dinner plans, then headed to the spot that beckoned behind the screen. Laying the letter down on the floor before the altar, Maya began preparations for communication with the Baron.

Stripping off her clothes, she pulled a white sheet from the top drawer of the wooden dresser across from the bed. Choosing to remain bare-breasted, she wrapped it like a sarong around her waist. She picked out a CD of Haitian *Vodou* drum rhythms, setting the volume to a barely audible level. As low rumbling quietly filled the room, she walked to her closet and pulled out the rounded, six-foot-tall wooden staff that she had mounted on a flat base and painted black, covering it from top to bottom with white chalk *veves*. After lighting several candles on the altar and around the apartment, she turned off the lights. Lifting a small brass bell from her altar, she walked around her *poto mitan* in a circle, ringing it lightly as she concentrated on the Baron. The tinkling sound of the bell made her feel warm and happy inside, and she continued in this way for some time before putting it down on the floor and walking over to the stereo to raise the volume up high. Turning back to the altar, she lifted a black and white-beaded *ason*, shaking it loudly up and down as she started to dance around the pole, not caring if her neighbors might wonder at the strange sound. A few minutes later, she turned toward the kitchen counter, where a clear, unlabeled bottle of *clerin* stood waiting in service. Drinking directly from the bottle of Haitian moonshine, she filled her mouth to capacity and, walking back to the *poto mitan*, she looked up and sprayed the spicy liquid into the air to salute the space, the spirits, and the drums. Her face now wet and shining, her long locks beaded with glistening drops, she began a series of prayers to invoke the one she sought.

When Maya came to forty-five minutes later, her body was in a heap on the floor and she felt parched and thirsty. But she knew exactly what to do.

The Baron

Our visit was short but she heard me. I don't waste time mincing words, darlin'. Some people say they can't understand me when I speak. That's only 'cause they don't want to know the truth. And I sure as hell won't spend one extra second on humans who insist on ignoring their destiny. Hear what I'm sayin'?

4

She waited for him just as she had the last three weeks at different times of the day and night outside the main University of Miami gates. Patience dictated that in time, he would appear, and that she would know him instantly despite the years. Today, the wait seemed longer than usual, since a torrent of what seemed like powerful liquid diagonals of steel pounded the ground in a fury that announced the official arrival of the rainy season in America's sun-anointed city. It was a deluge that darkened the skies to a woolen gray, that discomforted the skin and dampened time, turning the world moldy and mean.

She stood like a statue, facing the wrong way among the throngs of students heading home. Rushing, bumping umbrellas collided while curses at the rain competed with shouts of hallelujah from the heat's reprieve. Maya stared hard at the faces, searching, neck straining, while somewhere, another part of her obsessed over the feature story that Penelope Long had penned. The thought of it made her burn, and she wondered if she might be getting sick from being in the rain for so long.

Her heartbeat pounding like an African's drum, Maya had run to the newsstand that morning to pick up the newly published issue of *Dance*. She had frantically flipped through the magazine's pages until—*finally!*—she found what she was looking for. Reading quickly, she felt her trepidation turn to pleasure, then just as rapidly to annoyance, then anger, and at length, to nausea. In tiny black print against a gray background, the writer had reported:

MAYA SAINT-FLEUR: A VERITABLE STAR IN THE MAKING?

Carlos DeVilla's fifteen-year-old dance company, DeVilla Modern, certainly broke new ground last month with its daring ten-show presentation of new choreography and concept entitled "From Sunset to Full Moon." Although this writer hardly ever gets this captivated, I returned three times to see the show because of a star-making performance by one of the company's principal dancers, Maya Saint-Fleur. The twenty-three-year-old Haitian dancer's symmetry and fluidity cracked with the suddenness of a new form of movement, which I correctly identified as a restatement of Brazilian Capoeira, a form of martial arts.

Later, backstage, the dancer admitted to having herself conjured up the potent blend of traditional modern dance with the wildness of this attack-and-response school of self-defense. Eager to find out more, I asked her to meet me for coffee. At The Korner Kafe, with a haughtiness befitting a first class-diva, Ms. Saint-Fleur proceeded to give me a history lesson on Capoeira, lecturing me at length on the merits of this somewhat primitive "art form," and never really answering my questions, remaining stubbornly mysterious as to just how she came up with the rather unusual idea of combining the two forms of movement. Could it have been someone else's idea to begin with? After all, according to her, she's a Haitian of low-echelon roots. This writer came away wondering just that, while also conceding the possibility that this naturally gifted young dancer just may be a true-to-form "star" (with some of its unfortunate side effects) in the making. In any case, both Maya Saint-Fleur and her neoteric but undeniably exciting dance concept—oddly, she hasn't given thought to its potential name—are definitely worth keeping an eye on.

Later for this, she'd decided, thrusting the magazine in her carry-all and plunging Penelope Long down into the boiling well within her. She needed to go looking for Sylvain.

Yet, *Dance* Magazine and Penelope Long had somehow snuck around the back way, re-entering her psyche and pissing her off all over again.

It's past six and growing darker by the minute, she thought, disgusted. *Maybe I'll just call it a day.* But suddenly, she thought she recognized a face. Sylvain's face. Could it be? She strained her eyes, trying to lock onto the approaching figure that seemed to be coming directly toward her. Yes! She was sure of it. *It's HIM*. Her mind zigzagged in one hundred directions at once, trails of unfinished thoughts intertwining in her brain. She stood transfixed like Lot's wife, as heavy as a mound of salt. The rain pounded her red umbrella as she watched him walk right toward where she stood, then turn around to face the still oncoming but thinning crowd. He didn't seem to notice her, though their umbrellas nearly touched. Several moments later, she exhaled, realizing that he, too, waited for someone to come.

A quarter of an hour passed as she stood immobile, while beside her he fidgeted and shifted from one leg to another, obviously annoyed at the person's tardiness. The crowd slimmed to occasional solitary rushing figures huddled under jackets as they fled the rain. Then she heard his voice, surprised that she remembered its warm tone.

"Someone stand you up, too?"

She turned slightly, answering in a too-loud voice.

"Seems that way."

"The rain managed to get in through the neck of my shirt," he said in a recognizable Haitian accent. He shook his head, shivering. "I'll give her one last chance to show up, but I definitely deserve a cup of coffee. It's a straight view from the coffee shop's window," he added, pointing across the street. "What do you think? Looks like you've been here a lot longer than I have."

She was sure he could hear the erratic tick-tocking of her heart.

"That sounds like the best idea I've heard all day," she smiled, showing dimples.

He cocked his head to look at her, experiencing something like *déja vu*, but he said nothing as they crossed the street, striving to avoid the enormous puddles that blocked their way.

The coffee shop was one of those modern hamburger joints that tried to emulate the look and feel of an old-fashioned ice cream parlor, replete with quaint counter and chrome fixtures. The lighting glowed a warm gold with pink hues, blessing everyone with that just-kissed look. They chose a table near the wide glass window where, through large, carefully scripted letters that blasted the usual specials, they could both keep an eye out for errant dates.

After having ordered two hot coffees, black with sugar, he chitchatted as she studiously kept watch on the street. Maya was having difficulty looking at him, but she could see that he had grown into a beautiful, honey-tinted man. There was a disarming ease about him that felt all too familiar; a friendly smile showed even, white teeth and deep brown eyes that readily expressed concern.

"Were you waiting for a ride, too?" he asked.

"No," she answered, daring to look him in the eyes, "not a ride, just a friend."

The waitress arrived with their coffees and set them down in the middle of the table. He slid a cup toward her.

"Well, I'll think twice before loaning my car again to *this* friend. This is the first time I've seen rain like this since I've been here!"

"And how long has that been?" she asked, knowing the answer.

"You know," he said, suddenly changing the subject, "your accent sounds Haitian. Are you Haitian?"

"Yes," she said, unable to stop the smile, then the question. "You don't recognize me, do you, Sylvain? I thought I recognized you while we were standing out there, but I wasn't sure. Now I know it's you."

"You know my name!" he laughed, surprised.

"Sylvain Chenet," she spoke quietly, looking down into her cup, then lifting her eyes up at him.

"Okay, you know me, so I must know you," he said, perplexed, the resonance of his cherry tobacco voice pinching her chest. "I'm so sorry not to recognize you. But wait, let me see; give me a clue. Where did we meet?"

"In Haiti. We were very young. I—my mother—we worked for your family." She was feeling overwhelmed, remembering. *Conversations in the garden. M'sie Chenet following her mother into her room, making her watch. Unable to fall asleep while thinking of Sylvain...*

A shadow passed over his face, then cleared, and he shouted: "Maya? Maya! Oh my God, it's you! Could it be?" He was beside himself with—was it relief? Guilt? But, what for? Mixed, aberrant thoughts and emotions raced through his head, confusing him. He was excited and suddenly exhausted at the same time, and damned if he could make sense of it.

"Wait," he said, his eyes round like miniature glowing moons, his hand reaching across the table to touch hers. "How could this be? What happened to you? Where did you go? One day you were gone, and no one would tell me why. It was so weird." His accent was so pronounced when he said "weird" that she nearly laughed out loud. She held it in, afraid it would sound like a bark.

"You didn't know why I disappeared? No one told you?" she said, daring him to lie.

"No," he said. "How did you get here? Have you been living here a long time? Must be because your accent is so slight; it's just that a Haitian can spot another Haitian accent no matter how faint, you know what I mean?"

She chuckled but didn't say anything; didn't know what to say.

"I'm really carrying on, aren't I? Whew!" he blew out a long breath. "What a trip! This is too crazy! And here we are speaking in English, just like strangers—which I guess we are, in a way, huh?"

"No, we're not strangers. I thought about you over the years," she said. "I remember enjoying our talks out in the garden. You were always so pleasant, different from the others. You always treated people—me—with respect. That was nice."

Sylvain's face turned serious. "I'm sorry about that."

"What? *Les Bourgeois Haitiens?* The way they treat people in my class?"

"Yes. I'm from that world, and so too I am guilty of being—. Wait, Maya, do you speak fluent French now?"

"*Oui*," she answered, perfectly comfortable with the totally unexpected development that had become her reality. She could speak French, Kreyol—although it got rustier every year—and perfect English. Eighty-five per cent of Haitians like her were illiterate, dirt poor, with little or no chance of ever changing the rules. "Are you surprised that I could learn to speak French?"

"No. I'm just surprised, period. At everything, this whole evening, this chance meeting, *you*! You look so, so beautiful! And, so different. My God, I have a million questions. Tell me everything."

She laughed in spite of herself, again showing dimples that made him smile. He kept shaking his head and looking at her in wonder.

"Maya, Maya," he murmered, momentarily lost in his thoughts. "What are you doing now? I mean, what do you do, like, for a living?"

"I'm a dancer, and I work at The Mysterious Light bookstore, too. They sell metaphysical books and such."

"Really? Where do you live?"

"Miami Beach."

"I'm in the Bal Harbour area."

"I'm not surprised," she smiled.

"Should I be embarrassed about living there? Bourgeois and obnoxious, right? Oh well, that's how it is. It's a great little place, really. Ground floor, charming courtyard. There's a jasmine bush that smells so sweet, I always sleep with the window open. It's not so bad."

"I'm sure it's not," she laughed now, openly and good-naturedly making fun of his politically correct rich boy insecurities.

While she had lost all pretense of looking for her "friend," he had not, and at that moment he finally spied his car.

"There she is!" he cried with relief, jumping out of his seat, poised to bolt out the front door; but midway he turned back and pleaded, "Please, wait, I'll be right back, okay?"

She nodded and watched as he ran out into the rain, flagging down the woman behind the wheel of his car. He stooped down to talk with her, pointing to the coffee shop, then to a parking spot. Realizing that he was inviting this person to join them, Maya froze, then in a quick burst of motion, she scribbled a note with her number, left it on the table, and ducked out the back door. When Sylvain returned, he found her message: "It was time for me to go. Give me a call if you like." He looked around, hoping to catch her, but she was gone. Shaking his head, pleasantly perplexed, Henri Chenet's son headed home, completely disinterested in his companion's conversation, and later, utterly unable to sleep the night.

Barely able to drive herself home, Maya hoped the vehicle would remember the way as she tried in vain to navigate the tugging currents in her heart, mind, soul, and body. Incapable of keeping her eyes closed once in bed, Maya willingly and repeatedly relived her historic date with destiny until dawn.

"What I want to know is how it is that that woman is still above ground, walking, talking, *breathing* even?!" Elly was ventilating, waving her arms up and down as she shouted, echoes reverberating throughout the studio.

Two days had passed since the article's appearance on the newsstand, but no one had heard a word from Maya until now. Her usual quiet presence was even more palpable this morning as she entered the studio. Maya answered her friend in an amused tone that belied her annoyance at the innuendo.

"And what is that supposed to mean?"

Elly smiled, busted.

"Shoo, you know I know you know about Voodoo, Maya."

"I do know about it, so am I supposed to make a doll that looks like Penelope Long and stick pins in it until she bleeds to death?"

"That would be beautiful, *chiquita.* If you don't want to do it, you just show me and I will! God forbid she would just write that you're a natural born star. No, she had to insinuate that you were lying! She just had to counter every positive thing she said with some snide negative. What a bitch! We were worried about you, weren't we, Mr. DeVilla? Where you been, honey?"

Carlos DeVilla looked up from his warm-up at Maya's entrance and Elly's outburst. Others were streaming into the large, open space with its well-used wood floor, ballet bars across the back and side walls, floor-to-ceiling mirrors, and generous helpings of natural sunlight. He walked across the room now to give Maya a hug.

"I knew she was fine," he said. You're a loner. This is your first review, and I knew you would want to be by yourself with it."

Maya looked up at the looming hulk of a man whose still-svelte and smooth silhouette aptly fit the description of elegance. The forty-four-year-old dance master was special. He liked talky, meditative films, and dancing up close with wide-hipped older women; and he swooned over the scent of vanilla. He could spot talent whether he'd seen the subject lift a toe or tush, or not. He insisted that the subtle scent of vanilla emanated from such people, and his nostrils had filled with that sweet fragrance the very first time he laid eyes on seventeen-year-old Maya.

The young girl's life had changed forever the day she happened onto a PBS documentary on famed African singer Miriam Makeba. Eyes glued to the singer's backup dancers as they twisted isolated bottoms from shimmying shoulders that moved independently from undulating stomachs, Maya became possessed with the urge to dance. She was up on her feet, trying to imitate the figures on screen when *Madame* Mirta rolled into the living room, catching her unaware. Caught in the act, Maya stopped, an embarrassed smile frozen on her face as she turned to look at the woman who had become her mother.

"It feel good to dance, no?"

Maya nodded, turning back to the television.

"You could take classes in African dance if you want to."

Maya tore her eyes away, pirouetting to face *Madame* Mirta. "Really?"

"Sure. There a woman not too far from here who give classes. We go talk to her later this afternoon, if you want."

That very day they signed her up. She was fourteen. Over the years, as teachers encouraged her to explore her natural talent, Maya's love affair with dance soared to unexpected heights. African classes led to Haitian folkloric classes to creative dance, and even belly dance, finally coming to rest on modern dance. While other girls her age went to the movies and to parties, Maya attended performances, seeing as many shows as her adopted mother could afford. When not in school or at home studying, the solemn young student could be found in class, rehearsing for an upcoming production or performing on stage. For her seventeenth birthday, *Madame* Mirta granted her daughter what she wanted more than anything in the world: to participate in the summer intensive at the American Dance Festival in Raleigh, North Carolina. Some would call it a fateful decision; *Madame* Mirta called it intuition confirmed by the *lwa*.

With several classes taught by Carlos DeVilla's professional dancers, the festival had catapulted Maya's fascination with dance from minor obsession to major career path. Alerted by one of his protégées of a young noteworthy dancer, the great Carlos DeVilla himself had observed an afternoon class with a special eye on the gazelle-like creature with smooth, charcoal skin. As he watched, a smile crept up from within his breast to touch the corners of his mouth. There was something about this dancer's energy that was new, *raw*, and somehow lacking in the perhaps overly refined dancers of *Carlos DeVilla Modern*. He had asked the teacher to arrange a meeting with the girl.

When she walked into his hotel's lobby and stopped to look around for the "blue couch next to the tallest ficus tree in the room," Carlos DeVilla had to rub his eyes and look again, because he would have sworn a tall black cat had entered the building. Perfectly feline in her movements and demeanor, Maya halted for a moment to observe her surroundings. Watching her, Carlos expected that she might lick the back of her hand and stroke the ropes of hair that cascaded down her back. The black cat turned back into a girl upon locating her prey. Recovering quickly, he waved to her, fascinated now by this human being with the look of a panther in her swift, yet elegant, slow-motion walk. He stood to meet her, struck at first by her intensity as she approached, then by the waves of vanilla that wafted into the room.

"Wait," he whispered when she reached him. "Wait."

With eyes closed, sniffing the air like a curious hound, he allowed the familiar vanilla feeling to overwhelm him. Reacting as if to a perfectly reasonable situation, Maya waited. When he opened his eyes, she smiled.

"Where do you live?" he said.

"Miami."

"The city where Carlos DeVilla Modern is based," he said, nodding to himself and smiling. "Have you heard of our company?

"I have seen it perform."

"And?"

"I think you're a genius."

"You say this like you mean it."

"I never speak words I don't mean."

"I believe you."

After a pause, he invited her to take a seat. And as they did so, he invited further. "I would like you to join my company."

He heard her sharp intake of breath as her hand flew up to her heart.

"I am honored," she said, looking through his eyes to another place.

"When you get back to Miami, I want you to go to that little video store on Meridian and 18th. They carry all sorts of hard-to-find films and documentaries."

"I know the one."

"Ask for *Capoeirista.* It's an obscure drama based on the life of the genius who pioneered the art of *Capoeira!*" This last he'd uttered with great care, as if honored to speak the word. "Don't ask me why I think you should see it. I go by my instincts, and my instincts tell me I am not wrong!"

"What is *Capoeira*?"

"It is like your martial arts, here, but different."

"All right," she agreed.

"When the festival is over, and you are back in Miami, call me and we will arrange a meeting to go over all the details—what it means to be a dancer in my company, what I expect from you, and what you can anticipate."

As she stood to leave, Maya noticed the maestro wave to a stunning woman, who appeared to be at least ten years his senior. Out on the street, as Maya stooped down to unlock her rented car, she saw her new teacher and his sultry companion hold hands as they walked out of the building like royalty.

Capoeira grabbed hold of Maya with an iron grip and refused to let go. After watching the video recommended by Carlos, she had become obsessed with learning more. Like a detective, she'd sought out the small but growing Brazilian community in Miami, and found a studio where men and women, young and old, came together twice a week to learn and practice the art so familiar to them back home. She'd signed up right away and, over the years, learned to fight like the best of them.

The savage rhythm of battle laced with indefinable grace came to be recognized as Maya's personal style. Although Carlos' method came from traditional though edgy modern concepts, he allowed her to stray and to experiment. He often stayed late into the night with her to observe, counsel, educate, and direct her toward the path he somehow knew she would choose from the start. A brief five years since she first stepped into his studio, the novice had blossomed into assistant choreographer of one of the most important sections and solo performances of the company's new show.

Looking up at Carlos now, Maya assured him, "Oh, don't worry about me. I'm fine. In any case, Ms. Long had wonderful things to say about you and the company and the show in general, didn't she? She can't be all that bad."

"We still hate her," Elly insisted, a *forgive me?* look in her eyes.

On her way to the back of the room to deposit her gear, Maya winked at her friend, who smiled gratefully at the reprieve.

"Want to have dinner tonight?" Elly asked her.

"Mind if we try that threesome with Colin one more time? He's been calling me, too."

"Only if you don't cancel this time."

The company rehearsed for two hours, sweating, perfecting, repeating the tricky parts and begging for relief from Carlos Devilla's demanding quest for flawlessness. What everyone noticed but didn't mention, however, was how little the teacher demanded from his star pupil.

After class, Maya rushed to change out of her tights and leotard and into a pair of loose jeans and worn T-shirt. Wishing the well-meaning students would leave it alone, she accepted their gestures of loyalty with what she thought was good spirit, while most walked away wishing they'd kept their *esprit de corps* offerings to themselves. As a group of three walked out, Maya heard one of them whisper, "I mean, that Fanny bitch should eat dirt and all that, but you gotta admit, some of what she said wasn't so far off. I mean, Maya's just not all that friendly."

Just how I like it.

She waited until the studio was nearly empty before making a beeline for her teacher.

"I don't need special treatment because of that woman, you know."

Maya expected a soldierly attitude from her teacher. This unexpected softening had embarrassed her during rehearsal, and she wanted to growl at him now; but she tempered her voice, trying to cover the frustration she felt while waiting for everyone to leave so she could talk to him in private.

"And why shouldn't I give you special treatment if I feel like it?" he snapped, surprising her.

"Because it's just a review. Aren't I supposed to not let it bother me? Thicken my skin so it all glides off me, knowing my talent is what really matters?"

"Don't you think your skin is thick enough? You've been working at toughening it for so long you don't even know it's already turned to leather. Maybe one of these days you'll tell me why."

Maya turned away from him, her eyes hard.

"Nothing to write home about," she said dryly.

"By the way, just what *were* you doing these last two days?"

"Just like you said, being alone."

"And does Penelope Long have a giant headache today?"

"I don't see why she should."

"No? I'm glad to hear it."

They both remembered a day five years earlier.

"Are your toe shoes on the right feet?"

The young dancer taunted Maya in a cruel, childish way about missteps she'd made throughout the day as they partnered. After class, as the girl walked out of the studio, Carlos noticed Maya's eyes turn to stone as she watched the dancer's retreating figure. Suddenly, the girl gripped her stomach in pain, leaning on the wall for support. He ran over to help, but a few seconds later, just as suddenly, the pains disappeared. He looked across the room to the spot where Maya stood, and felt a chill. Her eyes still had that dead look, but now they bore into the wall as if the girl were still there. The next day, the girl's mother called to say that her daughter had been ill all night with strange stomach pains, and was resting today. Carlos called Maya into his office.

"I know you're responsible for Lydia's mysterious stomach problems."

"I don't know what you're talking about. What's wrong with her?"

"You don't need to pretend with me, Maya. I can tell. I'm Brazilian, remember? I had a friend like you back home. I know what you're capable of, but it's wrong to use your power that way; but you already know that, don't you?"

"I didn't do anything to her, Carlos. I can't say I was feeling love for that little witch, but I didn't have anything to do with her stomach problems. I kind of felt bad for her."

He acted as if she had not spoken.

"You must try very, very hard to keep your abilities under control. Never use them when you are angry. From anger you cure no one, least of all yourself."

She remembered Manman Mirta's words to her so long ago and sighed. "You remind me of my mother. Neither one of you hears a word I say."

"Your mother in Haiti?"

"No, my mother on Miami Beach. She was always telling me stuff like this, even though I kept telling her that I wasn't responsible for—"

"What makes you so mad, child? I have watched you. There's a deep-seated anger in you. Why?"

"Now you really sound like her."

"Well?"

"Never mind. It's just how I am. I was made this way."

"No, I don't think so."

They looked at each other now, holding each other's gaze several beats. Then she grinned, and he relaxed.

"Remember Maya," he called out softly, as she walked out of the room, a solitary silhouette. "From hunger, you feed no one."

"I'm not hungry," she said, laughing.

"Are you sure?"

"I'm having dinner with Elly and Colin tonight, but I'm definitely not hungry anymore!"

The older man shook his head, a worried look on his face.

5

The arresting threesome was seated at a low table in one of South Beach's trendy restaurants. This one was a low-lit Asian place with handy hidden spaces beneath the tables that gave diners the appearance of sitting cross-legged, Japanese style, while their legs and knees enjoyed western style stretched-out comfort. Outside, heavy rain pelted parked cars with a steady beat. Occasionally, lightning criss-crossed the sky, and thunder pealed in response.

After they'd ordered sake and sushi, Elly said, "So, I know I've asked this question before but I never seem to get a straight answer. Just how did you two meet, anyway?"

Maya and Colin looked at each other as if they'd just been asked to name the capital of every state in the country.

"Uh, you two look like you're trying to decide which version you'd like to tell today," Elly said, impatient.

Maya broke the silence, chuckling.

"I guess it's because he's so white and I'm so black that we get asked that question all the time. So we made a game of coming up with one outrageous story after another. We're always trying to top the last one. It's fun."

"It's not because you're black and he's white; it's because you're both so weird. Anyway, what was the last story you told?"

"That Maya came over here on one of those boats you hear about in the news all the time, and that I found her on the beach," Colin deadpanned.

"Yeah, and I was half dead and he brought me to his house and hid me from his parents."

"And later that night, I took her down the block to the only black woman who lived on the beach, and asked her if she would take Maya in."

"Yeah, and then she said, 'Oh my God, my prayers have been answered! I always wanted a little girl of my own, and now here you are, a present from the Lord himself.'"

"That's a good one. Did they buy it?"

"Oh, if they don't buy it, it means we both failed," said Maya. "And the punishment is that I have to seriously consider not one, not two, but three of Colin's horrible theoretical situations and give him truthful answers."

"And I have to listen to more new stuff on *Capoeira*. Just when you think you've heard them all, BAM! She hits you with another one. For hours. In fact, why do you think that darling Penelope Long wrote all that drivel about Twinkle Toes here? Because Maya probably went into her 'latest theory on *Capoeira*' mode. It'll drive anyone insane."

"Thanks for coming up with such a good excuse for Miss Longlegs, Colin."

"Okay," Elly broke into what was becoming the Colin and Maya Show, "so how did you really meet?"

"Oh, we grew up on the same street. Isn't that ever so boring, though?" Colin asked her.

"That's it? Come on, there's gotta be more to it than that! How did you become friends?"

Maya smiled wistfully at the memory.

A year had passed before she'd seen him again. When he'd left her at Madame Mirta's door that night, summer was getting ready to hand over the reins to fall. He was away at school during the day; and on weekends, Maya stayed busy, helping Madame Mirta prepare for her ceremonies. Weekends were the time neighborhood tongues wagged most because so many black people filed in and out of that dilapidated old house down the beach. But Madame Mirta never paid attention. She just went about her business, and Maya helped. She assisted with the preration of the offerings to the spirits, which meant loads of food—rice and beans, chicken Creole, boiled plantains and fried plantains, potato casseroles and eggplant casseroles baked in the oven late in the day because earlier on, the sweet cakes and desserts took up all the room. Then she checked all the liquor bottles to make sure there was enough for that night's visiting god or goddess. Sometimes, Maya played a cassette of Haitian drumbeats just to get the throng of visitors in the mood. Sometimes, she got too caught up and started the festivities early, with this or that spirit possessing her body, sending it into twisting, sweaty paroxysms of religious ecstasy. She loved those times.

During that year, Manman Mirta had hired a tutor to teach her "daughter" the English language. Between her lessons, the tapes her teacher left, and watching TV, Maya's language skills grew quickly, as they often do with the very young in a new country. After a brief six months, the Queen was able to enroll Maya in public school. Then, Madame Mirta insisted on the French tutor.

"Why do I need to learn French? I am in America now."

"Because one of us should know how to speak it, child."

So she made a practice of applying herself to her lessons, and then taking a long walk on the beach to review verb tenses and new vocabulary words in her head. And that was when she'd seen Colin on the beach, late one afternoon, sitting in the sand, staring at the ocean, drawing tablet in his lap. A sketch of an evil and oversized shark devouring a swimmer was in the works.

She still thought he was strange.

"Hey, want to see my new drawings?" he'd said to her first thing.

Just like that day so many months before, she followed him silently back from the beach and up the stairs to his room, where new horror scenarios filled the walls.

"Your drawings are scary," she said to him.

"Oh, you speak English now? Great! You think they're scary? That's great!"

He was excited, but she couldn't quite understand why.

"Thank you for helping me," she said, turning her attention away from the walls. "Why did you do it?"

"Didn't you need help?"

"Yes."

"So that's a dumb question."

She looked down at her feet.

"Hey, you want to see more drawings?"

"I have to go now. My French teacher is coming in ten minutes."

"French teacher? You have a French teacher?"

"Yes."

"And he teaches you French in your house?"

"Yes. My mother wants me to learn it."

"So, she adopted you, huh?"

"Yes."

"If my mom says I can, could I come and learn French with you?"

She shrugged her shoulders, wondering why he would want to learn French. The back screen door slammed shut downstairs, startling them. "Here she is!" Colin whispered, "Let's go ask her!"

He ran out of the room and down the stairs, two steps at a time. She followed slowly.

"Hey mom," she heard him say, "Can I take French lessons with my friend from down the beach if her mother says I can?"

"Who's your fr—?" Maya heard Yvette Gardner say. She stopped talking as she noticed the little girl coming down the stairs. "Who's this, Colin?"

"That's my friend, Maya."

"Hello, Maya," she said, friendly.

"Hello."

"Where do you live?"

"On the beach."

She saw a worried look cross Mrs. Gardner's brow as she began to suspect which house on the beach was the residence of this little girl.

Colin broke in. "Her French teacher is coming in a few minutes. Can I take lessons with her?"

"Well, I don't know, Colin. We'll have to talk to your father about it; and we will have to talk to Maya's mom about it, too. Do you think your mom would agree, Maya?"

Maya shrugged her shoulders.

Later that night, when the subject came up at the dinner table, Paul Gardner thought it all sounded a bit mad. But a week later, after several tantrums from their young son and a worrisome case of what seemed like depression, the parents decided to go knocking on the "witch's" door. Worried more about the fact that they'd never made any effort to be neighborly to this woman, who for years had been the subject of so many rumors, the Gardners decided to take a walk after dinner to introduce themselves and to present their case. A warm wind stirred, blowing sand into the air as they made their way—the well-built man, his cinnamon-sweet wife in her careful white Bermuda shorts, and their intense young son with ghostly skin. As they approached the house that nearly swayed with age and that clearly was in desperate need of a new coat of paint, Colin broke from his parents and hurried up the bricked walk to ring the bell. A moment later, Maya opened the door. Her face looked down at the ground while her eyes looked up at the family, the dark silhouette of her delicate body framed by a long hallway, at the end of which sat Madame Mirta in all her red-satinned glory. Tonight she'd read the cards for three different clients. They'd just left, satisfied, each in their own way, that the spirits would take care of the issue at hand. Madame Mirta wondered if the family had seen them leave.

"Honey, this is Colin's friend, Maya," Mrs. Gardner turned to her husband, breaking the silence. "Hello dear, may we speak with your mother?"

They heard the whirr of the wheelchair, and Maya turned, staring at the royal appearance along with the rest of them.

"Come in! Come in!" the queen beckoned. "What's wrong, Maya? Where your manners? Why don't you invite these nice people in?"

Two hours, mint tea, sweet pastries, a card reading appointment for Mrs. Gardner, and many stories later, it was all set. Colin would take French lessons with Maya; the Gardners would pay half the fee, and the unlikely pair of children would begin the kind of friendship that lasts a lifetime.

Maya trailed back into the present as Colin was summing things up.

"...so basically, Maya thought my drawings were just horrible, and that endeared her to me immediately. We've been friends ever since. But trust me, the minute she says anything good about my work, it's curtains."

Elly laughed, giving up on getting any real sense of the bond that drew these two creatures together. But her laughter ended when Maya's quiet voice shattered the moment.

"So tell me honestly, am I that haughty and arrogant? I think of myself as withdrawn maybe, even a loner, I guess, but is that woman right? Am I really—what's the word—off-putting?"

Elly spoke up first. "She was right about one thing, and one thing only! You are a star, honey. You know your shit, and you give it up on stage! And what's more, you know the roots of your shit. You're informed! You ask me, she was just intimidated. I say she should get another job, maybe shining dancers' shoes or picking candy wrappers off the theater floor after the audience leaves!"

"Or brushing alligators' teeth at the zoo," Colin offered before downing a swig of sake. "And, just the fact that she would dare fuck with you like that proves she has the sensitivity and intuition of a doorknob."

"And why is that, Colin?" Maya wanted to know.

"Most people are intimidated by you, dear, in case you didn't know. Ever wonder why men aren't flocking to your door, inviting you to have coffee or walks in the park. Or sex? It's the way you look at them. Sends them scampering back under the couch to play in the dust along with the other mice."

"Boy, I thought I was direct," Elly muttered, spearing her sushi.

"Well guess what I'm doing tomorrow night, smartass?"

"Wait, don't tell me. Throwing a bon voyage party for Penelope Long? I hear she's going straight to heaven if you have anything to do with it."

"No. Want to try another guess? Never mind, you'll never guess, I'll tell you." She took a deep breath then blurted, "I'm going on a date."

Colin gasped dramatically. Elly choked on her swallow of miso soup, and a couple walking through the front door of the restaurant let in a rush of wind that blew out the candle on their table. A waiter appeared to relight it. After he'd gone, an impatient Elly demanded, "So! *Who is he?*"

"He's an old family friend. I haven't seen him in years," Maya said.

"Do I know him?" Colin asked.

"No. I'm talking about an *old* family friend, from Haiti."

"From Haiti? So you mean you haven't seen him since you were twelve years old? How did you run into him? How did you recognize him?"

"I ran into him at the coffee shop across the street from the University of Miami. There was something familiar about him, and it went on from there."

Colin was skeptical.

"Wait. You saw someone who looked vaguely familiar, and you just went up and struck up a conversation? Come on, Maya, tell us the real story. And what were you doing at the U of M coffee shop?"

Elly interrupted, perplexed. "And what is so strange about Maya striking up a conversation with someone?"

"Because Maya does not do that sort of thing," Colin explained, as if to a child.

"Colin! Would you stop exaggerating!" Maya broke in, turning to Elly, "Pay no attention to him. He thinks he knows everything, but obviously, he doesn't." Pivoting to face him once more, she added, "Yes, Colin, I did strike up a conversation with a total stranger, because—well, there was something too awfully familiar about him. And besides, he was so damned good looking!"

"Catch me, I'm about to faint," Colin said, managing to look a little paler.

"Yeow!" Elly screeched. "Right on, *mija*!"

Maya smiled and refused to say anymore, no matter how much Elly pleaded. Colin feigned disinterest.

Later, under cover of rain ponchos, the three friends walked briskly back to Colin and Maya's apartment building, where Elly's Datsun was parked. Oblivious to the steadily falling rain, Elly chattered on. Although he tried to hide it, Colin failed in his quest to alter the pained expression on his face. Maya, who noticed, but found it impossible to comment, fell back into her usual silence. She couldn't wait to be alone. Tomorrow was her date with Sylvain, and she needed to think.

The Baron

Maya wants to think about her mulatto boy again. The way he looks, how he makes her feel, and what she needs to do to stop thinking about all that. That baby girl should ask me. *Yesss...*The Baron would tell her there is still time to change her mind.

Although she wanted to plan the next evening, Maya fell asleep when her head touched the pillow, and soon she was twisting and turning like a woman possessed by demons.

She was in a sandy forest, where light-skinned brown monsters hid behind every tree. The smell of dead, putrid animals flowed out from among the trees, encircling her so she couldn't move. When she was overcome completely by the stench, one after another the monsters emerged from the shadows—all replicas of Henri Chenet. As one of the monsters strode toward her, a coiled blue snake in his hand, she knew that he meant it for her—to force it into her body. And he laughed at the thought of it. As he chortled, Maya was gripped by the image of herself on a leaky boat surrounded by her dead boatmates in the middle of a cold, black ocean. His laugh rose to a screaming pitch as she stared at him. I'm going to get you, she thought in her dream; I know how to do it. And then the image of Sylvain appeared, filling her field of vision. He was beaming his friendly, open smile. No, she thought. I can't use him. But another thought pushed its way through, overpowering her hesitation. Yes, I can, yes, I can, yes, I can, yes, I CAN!

Awake now, sitting straight up in a pool of sweat, Maya nodded to herself. *Yes, I can.*

Not quite ready to have Sylvain in her apartment, Maya explained to her date that the doorbell downstairs didn't work and that she would wait for him in the lobby. She took special pains with her appearance—her favorite fitted jeans that showed off her butt just so, and the brown boots that passed the more-chic-than-clunky test. She refrained from changing tops more than once—thank God, her light blue, sweater cropped just above the belly button blended with her mood tonight. Just for the hell of it, she added a variety of blue beads to her dreadlocks, gathering them all up into a ponytail high up above her head. Cascading as they did around her face, the hard-to-hide intensity she exuded softened just a bit.

Once again, the city's tourist-perfect weather was highjacked by drizzling rain. Loud, angry thunder trumpeted in the sky. Waiting for Sylvain in the lobby, she reflected on the dream she'd had the night before. She dared herself to relive it, letting it fill her with the fury she needed to do what she must.

So immersed was she in her thoughts that she failed to see the figure who walked to the door. He watched her quietly for a moment until she detected his presence. Startled out of her rumination and a bit flustered, Maya's heart jumped and she froze.

"I'm sorry I frightened you!" Sylvain shouted through the glass door.

"You *did* scare me," Maya said, both anxious and relieved at once, anger dissipating. Her big-dimpled smile greeted Sylvain as she opened the door.

Not knowing quite exactly what to do—whether to shake hands or kiss on the cheek—they stood awkwardly together for a moment, until Sylvain took hold of her arm to draw her under his umbrella.

"You were so lost in thought back there," he said, looking at her, a question mark on his face. She couldn't speak; his proximity left her at a loss for words. "My car is just over here, across the street," he pointed, dropping the subject. "It's starting to rain a little harder; let's make a run for it." He led her to the passenger side of a navy-blue four-door Isuzu Trooper and unlocked the door, holding the umbrella over her as she stepped in. She watched him run around to the driver's side, studying the way he moved, carefree and light as a zephyr.

Seatbelted and settled into his seat, Sylvain suggested Italian food. "I could eat it every day, and I know this great little place just around the corner from where I live. We could go there or anywhere, really. Any ideas?"

"I love Italian," she said, "but are you sure you want to go back to Bal Harbour and then all the way back here to South Beach?"

"I don't mind, if you don't. We've got a lot of catching up to do!"

"Let's go, then."

Sylvain maneuvered out of his tight parking spot, then drove a block or two in silence, thoughts swaying up, down, and around like a child on monkey bars. *The maid's daughter! My mother would have a heart attack, and my fathe—well, he'd just think I was out of my mind having dinner at a restaurant with* "yonn nan moun sa yo." *One of those people.* Yet missing was the clumsiness he had expected might creep in between them.

She saw him shake his head just a little.

"What are you thinking about?" she asked, curious.

"To be honest with you, I was just thinking about how comfortable this all feels. I thought it might be a little awkward or strange or something, but I am so happy to see you. It feels great."

"Yeah, I guess your friends in Haiti would wonder if you were on drugs or something if they saw me in this car."

"I guess they would. Crazy isn't it?"

"Not that crazy, really. I mean, that's how you were raised. Us, and them. That mentality must have seeped into you to some extent, I would think."

"Of course it has—probably to a *great* extent. My whole life I've been taught that I am superior to the people who work for us and walk our streets. Not richer and more educated, but *superior.* But I have never felt at ease with it, and I fight my own prejudices constantly. It's not easy figuring out how to be in that group and not be a part of it, but I figure it's a worthwhile goal."

"So, is tonight an experiment in fighting your prejudices?" she asked.

They had come to a traffic light, and he turned to look her in the eyes.

"No. Tonight is a chance for me to spend time with someone with whom I once felt a connection, and who then disappeared from my life. It's an interesting opportunity, don't you think?"

Maya said nothing but just stared into the street before her, head tilted to the side, as if studying the question.

"I mean, think about it," he went on. "Given the chance, you and I could have become partners. Given your knowledge of plants, your way with them, and my interest in trying to preserve Haiti's environment, we could have done great things together, no?"

"Sure, Sylvain," she laughed. "Right."

"No, I'm serious! Take away the attitudes, the rules about who gets to interact with whom; and let two intelligent people with similar views be themselves together. Don't people like that often go on to accomplish great things?"

"So you want to give me a job as your legal secretary when you become a hot-shot lawyer?" she teased.

He laughed out loud. "Yeah, and then you could sit on my lap while I dictate letters."

"Well then, I better sign up for a typing class quick."

They both laughed, shocked at how easily he'd flirted and at how she'd responded in kind. She changed the subject in a hurry.

"No, I don't think typing is in the stars for me."

"Ah, yes, that's right, you're a dancer. What kind of dance?"

"If you like, you can come see our next performance this weekend. Our company—it's called DeVilla Modern—we're performing the next three weekends at the Jackie Gleason Theater on the beach. I don't know if that's your kind of thing, but I could probably get seats for you and a friend, if you like."

"I do enjoy dance, although I have to admit I haven't been to many performances in my life. Do you have a big part?"

"Kind of. I choreographed a solo piece for the company, and people apparently like it. The show is getting good reviews overall."

"That's great! I would love to come. Is it modern dance or ballet, or—"

"It's a modern dance company, but what I do is a little different. It's my own mix of modern dance and Brazilian *Capoeira*."

"*Capoeira*? What is that?"

"It's a dance-based form of martial arts."

"Really? Sounds fascinating."

"It's very beautiful. Not just the movement, but the spirit behind it. The movement is kind of a body-play of attack and counter-attack in a constant flow, and the music is just as important because of its special rhythm. When they really get caught up in it, practitioners travel to another dimension, almost losing track of their physical bodies."

"Sounds a little like what happens in *Vodou* ceremonies."

"Right! Same slaves, different countries. The Africans came with their own traditions and managed to keep some, including how to fight. *Capoeira* is one of those cultural expressions that stuck around."

"Does *Capoeira* look like what happens in Vodou ceremonies?"

"No, not at all. It's real fighting with a lot of fancy footwork. It supposedly comes from the Angolan region, where they have something called a *zebra* dance. By the time it reached Brazil, the zebra dance was transformed into a tradition of fighting with the feet. So, it's a combination of very elegant footwork with some heavy physical skills. With modern interpretation, it becomes something else altogether."

"I can't wait to see this!" Sylvain enthused. "And you thought this up all by yourself?"

"Now you sound like that witch who just interviewed me," Maya said, smiling at the memory of Carlos' fear that she'd struck Penelope Long with a giant headache.

"Who interviewed you?"

"A woman from *Dance* Magazine."

"Hey, I'm impressed."

"Don't be. She was impressed by the dance but not so much by me. She said I came off like a high-handed bitch when I explained the history of *Capoeira* to her."

"To hell with her, then."

"Yeah, that's what I say," Maya said with that same smile.

They arrived at the restaurant, a tiny box of a place with red-checked curtains in the windows, very few tables, and dim lighting. A green neon sign flared *Paolo's* over the doorway. Sylvain walked around to Maya's side with the umbrella and extended his hand to her. Under the steady onslaught of rain, a nearby gardenia bush in full bloom whispered its fragrant but diluted scent into the night air.

Once seated and their menu selections made, Maya and Sylvain were served two glasses of what a pot-bellied and bearded Paolo promised was hearty red Chianti from the old country. After toasting their reunion, the two young people picked up the thread of their easy-flowing conversation once more.

"So what about you?" Maya said. "Saving Haiti's environment—that wasn't just a childhood thing?"

"No, it's still with me. But I didn't end up becoming a plant doctor or an activist as I thought I might at various times while I was growing up. I decided the best route would be to try instead to change the laws governing the way we treat our environment on the island. But wait a minute, did I tell you that the last time we saw each other?"

"No, I don't think so," she answered uneasily, knowing what was coming.

"Back in the car, though, you said something about me becoming a hot shot lawyer, didn't you? How could you have known?"

"Hmmm," she answered, thinking fast as Jacquy's letter floated through her mind's eye, "must have been a lucky guess. Or maybe you did mention it over coffee."

"Strange, I don't remember that. You must be psychic," he decided.

"I sometimes think so," she said. "I often know what people are thinking or what they are going to say; many times, I could swear I make things happen just by wishing hard for them, but I'm never sure."

"Like?"

"Like...I think I always hoped I would see you again," she said, evading his eyes by looking into her glass. Picking it up, she took a liesurely sip of her wine, commenting on its heartiness.

"Did you really?" he asked, ignoring her wine review. "Interesting. Because over the years, I would periodically flash on your face and wonder what happened to you. So what did happen? Why the sudden disappearance? Why did your mother keep evading the issue? Why didn't you say goodbye?" Now it was his turn to pick up his glass and drink. Feeling his fingers tense around its stem, he wondered why her answer should be so important to him. *She's just Jizzeline's kid! What do you care?*

Maya was taken aback. *He really seems clueless about why I left. What a great, fucking liar! And why does he suddenly seem so tense? As if the reason I didn't say goodbye matters so much?* The thought made her heart flutter like lilacs blown asunder by the wind, and she hated herself for it.

"I didn't disappear," she said. "I left because my parents wanted me to have a better life. To be educated, to be regarded as a human being with feelings and a brain. And because they wanted to give me the opportunity to become more than Jizzeline's barefoot kid in the torn dress. I don't know why my mother didn't answer your questions. She probably made up some story for your parents, since I was part of the package deal when they hired her. If they knew that she was merely sending me off to make something of myself, they might have thought that wasn't a good enough reason to lose their *makeshift gardener.*" Her eyes hardened as she said the last two words, and she saw that her tale affected and embarrassed him. Softening her voice, she added, "And I didn't say goodbye because I didn't think you'd care..."

"Really? I—" he started to say, seemingly crushed.

Confused by his reaction, and before she could stop herself, she added, "And also because *I didn't have the opportunity.*"

Maya let that sink in a moment before continuing. She had rehearsed this next part a hundred times. "It all happened very quickly. My aunt who lived here had applied for my green card. On his side, my father had worked for two years on the immigration people. Then all of a sudden, one day it all came together. I don't know all the details, but my parents found out that a friend of theirs was leaving for Miami, and since they didn't want me to travel by myself, they decided it was then or never, and poof, I found myself on a plane. Goodbye Haiti, goodbye family, goodbye everything. It was pretty scary."

"I was afraid you were going to tell me that you came here on one of those terrible boats," Sylvain said.

She sucked her breath in, shocked, and looked deeply into his eyes. *What the hell?*

"Well, it could have happened that way, no?"

"Yes, it could have," she said, "but no, I flew—and man, were my arms tired afterward," Maya laughed as she waved her arms like a bird, thrilled that she could come up with a joke.

Sylvain burst out laughing.

He really is handsome, she thought, watching him laugh. He was wearing an ivory crew-neck cotton sweater with khaki-colored pants that looked at ease on his body. *His hands are clean and strong and friendly,* she observed, then instantly chided herself. *What are you talking about? Whoever heard of friendly hands?*

Paolo returned with their plates, and they attacked their pasta with enthusiasm. After a few moments, Sylvain lifted his head to look at Maya.

"What you said about my parents, I know it is probably true."

She looked back at him, shrugged her shoulders, and continued eating. An awkward hush ensued. Finally, knowing she needed to lighten up, Maya said, "Don't worry, Sylvain, you are obviously not your parents. You don't need to take on that responsibility."

His look pleaded with her to make it so.

"So, what do you major in when you want to become a hot-shot environmental lawyer?" she asked him, a saucy smile on her face.

"Environmental law," he smiled back.

By the end of the evening their conversation had covered rain forests, the state of Haiti's vegetation, the depletion of the ozone layer, vegetarianism, activism, Haitian politics, Miami politics, national politics, movies, books, their friends (he couldn't wait to meet Colin), which Haitian band would soon be coming to the area, their tastes in music, and how it was time for the rain to stop. The rapport between them was easygoing and fun, serious but light.

As he walked her to her door, with umbrella in tow, he reminded her, "So, how about that ticket for Sunday's performance. Can you really get me one?"

"I can get you two. Don't you want to bring anyone?"

"If I come alone, can we grab a bite to eat afterward? Are you usually hungry after you perform?"

"Ravenous. Someone has to stop me from munching on my tights."

"Great," he chuckled.

"I'll leave the ticket for you at "will call," she promised.

"Thanks. I had a great time tonight," he said as she fumbled with her key at the door.

"I did, too. It's nice to know you're in town," she said, turning around to look at him with a smile.

She stepped into the building lobby.

"Good night, Sylvain."

"Bye. See you Sunday," he added, waving as he walked away.

She watched him get into his car and drive away, then she walked toward the staircase on suddenly wobbly legs and sat down hard on the next to last step.

Seems like such a nice guy, her heart thought delicately. *Too bad*, another voice, the louder one, chimed in.

6

For a solid twenty minutes Maya sat at the bottom of the staircase of her building's lobby, oblivious to all but the jumble of thoughts and sensations that flooded her mind as she reflected on the evening she had spent with the son of the man of her nightmares. The night was still young, and as various tenants brushed past her on their way up or down the stairs, Maya ignored the curious looks she was attracting. One middle-aged woman with a pink raincoat and silly, black knee-high galoshes nearly stopped to ask the lost-looking creature if she was all right, but *Maybe I won't,* she thought, suddenly anxious to reach her lonely apartment.

Maya was sitting in the same spot when Simon, the building manager, walked in, all a-flurry with "Oh my Gods" and "This horrible weather!" and "I'm just soaking," completely unaware of Maya's presence. She looked up at him, knowing there was no ignoring this human beast. It wasn't only that he was physically revolting—his pockmarked face reminded her of quicksand, his dead, opaque eyes, those of a soulless shark; his black greasy hair evoked a filthy oil slick—it was his contempt for anything dealing with tenants' concerns; as if he deserved a life of ease, much like a lizard, baking in the hot sun of a deserted beach. To top it off, the man was an obvious pervert. The way the 60-something greaseball leched after Colin was hard to watch. It was as if his mind played a tug-of-war with his hands, which crept toward his groin whenever he looked at her friend.

"What do you want?" he spat, as if he'd been avoiding her all day. "Were you waiting for me? I hope you're not going to tell me that there's a leak in your apartment. One more call like that and I'm handing in my keys!"

"In that case, there's a leak in my apartment," Maya said without smiling.

A chill scurried up his spine and he shuddered. Maya decided he looked like an iguana.

Just then, the front door opened once more and Colin walked in, his rain slicker dripping. He took one look at the scenario, muttered "Good evening" to Simon, and held his hand out to Maya, who took it and walked off with him down the hallway to his apartment. Behind them Simon half-wailed a need to ask Colin his opinion about something or other, and would he stop in for tea, anytime, really!

"Of course, Simon," Colin responded, never turning around.

"Oh, that's lovely, thank you, I'll get the water on right away, and won't that be nice..."

"Why don't we kill him?" Maya suggested to Colin once they were safely inside his apartment.

"How would you like to do it?" he said, flicking off his rainwear, revealing his usual black and white wear. "Should we inject him with a deadly virus that will eat him alive from the inside out? Or should we just open up my jar of scorpions and let them loose in his kitchen cupboard—especially where he keeps his teabags?"

"Maybe the scorpions; that deadly virus might choke on the likes of Simon."

"No razzing about having to decide between my theoreticals tonight? Just what did Simon say to you tonight?"

"Nothing. It's just that he exists."

"Yes, I see what you mean. Were you planning to spend the entire night on the steps, or just the evening? How long were you sitting there?"

"Just a few minutes. I felt a little dizzy."

"Dizzy? Why is that?"

"Maybe I had a little too much wine," she said, not knowing how to answer.

"Ah, yes. The big date," Colin said.

He sat down on the couch next to her and reached for the round black wooden box on the coffee table. Pulling out the makings of a joint, he started rolling. Soon enough, the air turned light gray and fragranced with the scent of marijuana. Maya leaned forward, picked up Colin's lighter and lit the black candle that sat in the mouth of the giant dragon-shaped candelabrum. Getting up, she walked to the door, clicked off the overhead light, and returned to sit next to her friend.

"Mmm, smells nice," she said, taking a breath.

"I know it's futile to ask, but do you want some?" he asked.

"I don't think so," she laughed.

"Really. First wine, then pot. We'd have to call out the marines. So, are you going to tell me about the big date or not?"

"Not the big date. Just a date."

"Not the big date. Just a date," he mimicked. "Just the first date you ever had. Just the first date you ever had and never mentioned to me."

"Relax, Colin. I just met him two days ago. I was busy hiding from the world of *Dance* Magazine, remember?

"Yes, I do. Have you made peace with that charming Penelope of the Valley of Death yet?"

"I wouldn't say 'peace,' and I hope never to run into her in public *or* in a dark alley, but yeah, I'm over it."

"That's pretty good. I'd still be sitting here trying to figure out whether she should die from a thousand vicious vampire bites, or be mauled to pieces by a pack of ravenous werewolves under the light of a full moon."

"Oh my," Maya shuddered, laughing.

"But then again, you have been busy, haven't you? What with starting up with strange men who end up being your old childhood friend turned new neighborhood boyfriend, who might have a fit of jealousy even now if he knew you were down here chewing the fat with yet another childhood friend."

Maya laughed softly.

"In any case, how is the new boyfriend? Are you seeing him again?"

"He seems to be a lovely guy, Colin. His name is Sylvain Chenet, and I did enjoy myself with him. He's smart, good-looking, and not full of himself, like most Haitians from his part of town."

"You mean he's one of *them*?"

"Yes."

"But if I understand the ridiculous politics of Haiti correctly, aren't you one of *them* now, just by virtue of being an educated person with a career and a life outside of the system?"

"I could never be one of them. They would never accept me, no matter how much money I made, no matter what recognition I attained. They might come to the theater and applaud my performance; they might even feel pride in my accomplishments, but I would never, ever be welcomed into their lives as a family member. That just wouldn't happen."

"But you're saying he's different?"

"He wants to be, but I don't know. It's hard to say." *It's hard to say anything about him since I feel totally blindsided by this whole evening! And I'm supposed to be so good at reading people...*"In any case," she said, "we are not doing that. He is a pleasant memory from my past, as I think I am for him. The company is enjoyable. That's where it stands. To consider anything else would be foolishness."

"On whose part?"

"On my part, his part, your part, you name it."

That Sunday, Sylvain sat in the audience, open-mouthed. Transported to a primal place, he could not interpret the feelings Maya's dancing caused within him. She was wild and powerful, yet graceful. Her feet moved at high speed, while her body seemed to sway as if in a dream. She maneuvered her frame into positions that bedeviled the mind—high side kicks that ended in snake-like undulations; a lissome pirouette dovetailed into a forceful handstand that triumphed into leaping backbends across the stage. Soaring karate-esque front kicks propelled her bouncing body back down onto the floor in a spin that propelled her like a jet, back into the high kick once more—a motion repeated at least five times in a row in an incredible show of strength, speed, and elegance. She twirled like a ballerina born of a wild lioness and a tame wolf. Her body glistened with sweat, becoming a mirror that reflected the glow of the stage lights; and all the while, the drums beat a relentless rhythm that felt almost like physical blows.

"Other-worldly," "haunting," and "intense" were some of the words he heard whispered around him once Maya left the stage. Through the rest of the show, whenever he caught sight of her again—being partnered with a strong, hard-bodied male or gyrating in unison with other corps members—a surge of adrenaline shot through him, filling him with pride, heat, and a crazy urge to leap up and shout her name.

Afterward, he walked in a trance toward the will call box where they had agreed to meet after the performance. He hoped she would be a while so that he could work on his composure, but to his surprise she exited the theater almost immediately, bounding toward him in a hurry.

"Come on, let's go. I don't like to hang around after a show. I can't really talk to people now."

"Where do you want to go?" he said.

"It's the first beautiful day in ages and it's still light out. Let's go walk through Graceland Cemetery. It's a beautiful walk; it's green and peaceful there. I go there to ground myself. Is that okay?"

"A cemetery? Graceland Cemetery?" he said, perplexed and amused. "I guess that's perfect, isn't it?"

It was a short drive to Graceland, and they'd ridden in silence, both of them overwhelmed in their own way. When they arrived, the sun was just beginning to set, a slight breeze stirring in the palm trees that lined the entryway.

"Come this way," Maya said. "There's a great little path with pretty flowers and shrubs and other things. They've really done a nice job of landscaping this place."

He turned to look at her, wondering if she was making a joke about the other "things" planted in these grounds, but she didn't seem to notice. Still silent, they walked with slow steps past gravestones that had been systematically arranged in unusual patterns instead of straight rows, and through a clearing that seemed to go on endlessly. Finally, Maya spoke. "So, what did you think of the show?"

"Maya, I don't know what to say. I'm thunderstruck. I just sat there thinking, 'I know this person. I *know* her.'"

"Oh, don't worry," she chuckled, "you'll get over it. That often happens to people who have never seen their friends perform. *Capoeira*'s pretty different, huh?"

"*Capoeira*? Forget *Capoeira*, it's you that's different! I felt captivated, so caught up. Maybe the word is ensnared. I couldn't move. There was such a force coming from you that... You affected me beyond words, Maya, as you may have noticed. I'm barely able to speak. I still can't get over it. You were amazing—ah, forget it, I'm sputtering."

"*Capoeira* is very strong stuff, not for the meek."

"Not *Capoeira*, Maya. *You*. Don't be so modest. You are a genius talent; own up to it."

"Thank you, Sylvain. That's very kind. Hey, want to go this way? I've never been to this part."

"How long do you want to stay here? It's beginning to get dark."

"Are you scared?" she chided him.

"Maybe," he said. "Will you know how to get back?"

"Oh, sure."

He followed her down another path that veered away from the graves to a deserted area full of brush, alongside majestic magnolia trees. She stopped and looked around for a moment, as if lost, then walked toward one of the trees. When she reached it, her breath caught in her throat as she noticed something: carved into the trunk was a crudely scratched penis and balls, emblem of the *Baron Samedi*.

I did not imagine it! That morning, as she had prayed to the Baron for guidance, she thought she'd seen a graveyard in her mind's eye and then a dagger. The ornately carved dagger she'd purchased months ago in Little Haiti and placed on the Baron's altar called to her sometimes. She did not know when she would use it it, but it was there, waiting.

She turned around swiftly, not wanting him to see the carving in the tree. "Come sit here under this tree for a minute. Look, there's a nice soft patch of grass here."

Obediently, he walked toward her, filled with some unnamed sentiment. They both sat down, shoulder to shoulder, leaning on the tree for support. Maya's sigh filled the air as the last vestiges of light disappeared from the sky.

"What are you sighing about?" he asked, looking straight ahead.

"Oh, nothing. It always takes a little time for me to wind down after a performance." And almost as an afterthought, "How's your family?"

"Oh, they're fine, I guess."

"How's your mother? Has she recovered a little better now from the death of your sister?"

"Of course, you knew about that. Yes, it took some time but she finally became her old self again, except for this sadness that creeps into her face when she's unaware. I don't think that will ever go away."

"And your father? His boats? Is he still doing that?"

"Oh yeah, till the day he dies," Sylvain said, laughing.

"I remember how crazy he was about you. He probably comes to Miami a lot between you and his boating business."

"Yeah, it almost feels like I see him more now than I did when I lived there! In fact, he should be here in another couple of weeks."

"Oh, you'll have to let me know so we're sure not to run into each other."

After a short silence, he said her name so softly that she wasn't sure she'd heard him speak. When she turned to face him, the look in his eyes stopped her cold, and her heart was beating so loudly she thought he must surely hear it.

"Maya," he almost whispered, "I don't know what's come over me, but I feel like I want to touch you. Can I just touch your arm, your face? You are so extraordinary to me."

Not knowing what to say, she nodded in response. Slowly, he reached over and stroked her long, thin arm with the back of his hand. She tried not to shudder as she felt a gush of warmth fill the spot between her legs. After a moment, he lifted his hand to her face and caressed her cheek.

"Your skin feels like a petal." He followed the curve of her nose. "You are so opposite of what I was taught to find attractive in a woman, but I am so attracted to you. Can I please kiss you?"

Though she didn't answer, he leaned over and brushed her lips with his, moving hesitantly over her mouth until her lips parted just a little, and he licked her lower lip shyly, respectfully. Feeling the impact of emotion that pumped through her, Maya lifted her arm and placed her hand around his neck. Their mouths opened, and as their tongues explored each other, she experienced the fulfillment of a longing now ten years old, while he gave in to the passion she'd stirred in him that afternoon. Caught in the moment, he recognized the same feeling he'd been fighting since the day they'd met in the rain. Moments later, when they pulled apart, she looked into his face. Seeing the man she'd conjured hatred for—and she had to admit it now—*also loved* for so long, panic seized her.

No, don't do it.

"Come on," she said, getting up. "We should go now."

"Now? Are you sure?"

"I mean right now. Let's go," she repeated, extending her arm to help him up.

"Okay, if you say so."

They walked silently for a while, her quickening steps becoming almost comical.

"Hey, hold up," he laughed. "What's the hurry? Are you trying to get away from what just happened back there?"

"No, I just want to get out of here, that's all. I'm starved," she said, thankful for an excuse.

"In the mood for seafood?"

"Sure!"

Finally out of the woods and into his car, Maya relaxed.

"You were really agitated there," he remarked.

"Mmm, well, that was agitating stuff back there."

"You mean us smooching?" he laughed, showing off his beautiful white teeth and Adam's apple.

"Ye-es."

"Life is a funny thing, *n'est-ce pas?*"

"It sure is. What should we do now?"

"Nothing. We don't jump the gun. We don't try to second-guess anything. We just keep moving slowly and carefully until, well, maybe until we don't feel like moving slowly and carefully anymore. All I know is that I want to keep seeing you. Is that all right with you?"

Maya stared out the front windshield.

"Please don't say no," he said.

"All right then, I won't," she said.

A few minutes later, Sylvain pulled into The Fish House, a popular seafood joint that drew a casual crowd and the younger piña colada set. Painted on the bright, chalk blue door was a big fish standing on its tail. It welcomed patrons with words written in a bubble that read: "We taste so good, it's a crying shame!"

They were laughing at the silliness of it when Maya suddenly froze. Sitting at one of the tables, engrossed in conversation, an unlit cigarette punctuating the salient points of her conversation, was Penelope Long.

"Table for two?" a friendly blond waitress asked. "Follow me." And away she strode, hips swaying, toward the table where the writer was sitting. She looked up and noticed Maya approaching. Sauntering past the table, the waitress didn't notice that her patrons had stopped, and turning, she walked back to see about the holdup. Maya was standing at the columnist's table, staring into her as Sylvain looked on.

"You have a problem, or what?" the nervous reviewer demanded in her best no-nonsense voice.

"Thanks for the piece," Maya said, enunciating each word so that they sounded like hail bouncing off hard plastic. "Sorry you didn't think much of the subject."

"I don't like or dislike anybody. I just call 'em like I see 'em," she said, lifting her spoon and shoveling Manhattan clam chowder into her mouth.

Maya stared at her another full thirty seconds. The people sitting at neighboring tables stared; the waitress, wanting to intervene with a cheery *would you like to be seated now?*" found herself tongue-tied. The dance critic's dinner companion sat frozen in place like a cartoon figure. Sylvain leaned over, about to ask Maya if she was okay, when she broke her stare, smiling slightly before moving on. The waitress and Sylvain breathed a sigh of relief.

As they sat down, and before Sylvain could ask, they heard the voice of Penelope Long rising.

"Gosh, I feel like I have ants crawling all over my skin. I'm burning up, oh my God! What's wrong with me? Get me out of here!" she screeched loud enough for the entire restaurant to hear. "Get me a doctor! I feel like they're crawling inside me! Oh...oh...oh noooooo..." And then she fainted.

The next few minutes were choreographed madness as Penelope Long's companion ran around the table to see if her friend was all right, while waiters and waitresses dropped plates and trays in an effort to provide assistance. A man in a white leisure suit jumped up, announcing, "I'm a doctor! Give her some air!" as he rushed over to the table. He bent to take her pulse and listen for a heartbeat, while the restaurant manager directed his wait staff to lift the sagging body out of the chair and move her to a private room in the rear. Minutes later, the manager returned to announce that everything was taken care of, that the young woman would be all right—an ambulance was on its way—and to please enjoy a glass of Chardonnay on the house.

A roar of approval joined boisterous clapping, while some still looked around, nervous, whispering to each other and trying to recuperate from the frightening disturbance. Over in her corner, Maya just stared at the table so recently occupied by ***her***.

"Maya, what was that whole thing about back there?"

"That was the woman who mutilated me in her review."

"Oh my God. What do you think just happened to her? It was creepy how she went into those convulsions right after you stood there giving her the evil eye."

"Pretty cool coincidence. I hope she does think I did it. I don't know what happened to her, but I can't say I feel much sympathy. "

"What if it's something serious?"

"I'm pretty sure it was a panic attack. I've seen it happen before. She probably forgot to take her drugs today or something."

"Hmm. I think you spooked her. Man, I've never seen anybody get so intense! You were like some mafia boss back there. The many faces of Maya; I've seen quite a few of them today."

"Want to take some time to re-think your fine opinion of me?" she asked, her expression cold.

"Take it easy. Strong women turn me on," he said with a wink. And as he said it, he reached across the table to cover her hand with his.

She felt herself relax.

Later, as he walked her to the front door of her apartment building, he suggested, "Can I walk you upstairs? Would you like to offer me a cup of tea? Coffee? Something? Anything?"

"I'd love to," she smiled, "but not tonight. My place is a mess; and besides, I have to get up early in the morning, and uh...I'm doing a terrible job at coming up with an excuse, aren't I?"

"What's the matter?" he asked gently.

"I'm just not ready," she confessed, her mind a blur, her heart pounding.

"Don't worry; you can offer me a beverage some other time. But I warn you, if I get completely dehydrated waiting..."

"Don't be silly," she laughed.

"I'll try, but I am feeling kind of silly," and turning serious, he added, "I like you Maya. I like you."

"I like you, too," she said, leaning over and hugging him to her.

"I've got exams next week, so I'll be hitting the books mostly, but I'll call you to see how you're doing, and we'll make a plan to get together soon, okay?"

"As soon as possible?" she said shyly.

"Sooner, if possible." He leaned in and kissed her softly at first, then more forcefully. Her body folded into his, and she felt the tension in her shoulders dissolve into his strong chest. She was the first to pull away.

"Bye, Sylvain."

"Bye, Maya, I'll call you."

During the next 48 hours, Maya St. Fleur became a haunted thing. Lying face down on her bed, she cried and prayed; then she cried and raged. Refusing to answer any calls, she stormed through her apartment, kicking at walls, punching pillows, and slamming things on counters. Sitting down at the foot of her altar, she tried going into a trance but failed, provoking yet further frustration and fury. When Colin knocked at the door, insisting she let him in, she asked to be left alone in a tone that quickly sent him on his way. Caught somewhere between insomnia and troubled sleep, her mind furiously debated with itself. *Did his father lie about letting Sylvain in on his plan? Or did Sylvain know but is now feeling smug because I didn't die on the boat? But, I don't think Sylvain does "smug." His bastard father probably did lie...But I can't be sure. And now, Sylvain is falling for me, and damned if I'm not feeling like my 12-year-old self back in that garden with him; like a silly, smitten fool. God, no! I can never be with him. It will never happen. Too many lies! That vile father of his would never let us be, anyway. And do I really want to be with his son? It's too close. Sylvain is probably a good man, but Henri Chenet hasn't paid yet. And, he needs to pay. He will pay with his son's life. There's nothing to be done for it. It has been in the works for too long now; there is nothing that can stop this train. Not even me. I'll do it and the misery will stop. I won't have these nightmares anymore. I will be free to stop plotting and worrying. I will stop hating that man because I won't have to anymore. It will all be over. I am sorry, Sylvain, but there is nothing I can do about it.*

On the third day of her self-enforced seclusion, the phone rang, and knowing who it would be, she picked up the receiver.

"Hi, Maya."

"Hello, Sylvain. How are you?"

"I'm okay."

"You sound funny, what's up?" she said.

"Boy, you must be psychic if you can pick it up from me saying just two words."

"Uh-huh."

"Well, the thing is my father just called, and he's coming into town earlier than expected. He's arriving tomorrow for a few days."

"Yes?" The mention of Henri Chenet filled her with angst, and something much darker.

"I was planning to call you tomorrow to see about getting together, but I'm calling now because I think it will be kind of difficult while he's here, especially since he's staying with me. I'm not ready for him to know about us yet."

"What's to know?"

"Maya..."

"Sorry, I'm being obtuse; I know what you're saying. I can't say I'm ready for that scene, either." She changed the subject. "Where will he sleep?"

"Probably on the couch."

"How long will he be staying?"

"Just a couple of days. This was an unexpected trip."

"Well, call me when he leaves, if you like."

"Maya, I do like! I will definitely call you the minute he's gone.

"Okay. Oh, can you give me your address? I want to send you a card."

"Are you going to write me something I don't want to hear?" he said.

"No, just things I find hard to say."

"Does this mean I won't be seeing you soon?"

"No. It just means you will be receiving a card from me in the mail," she laughed.

"Okay then." He recited his address and then asked, "Will that be all, oh Mysterious One?"

"I am not mysterious and yes, that's all. Talk to you soon?"

"Absolutely."

Twenty-four hours later, as nighttime surrounded the city, Maya prepared to do what she must. Dressed in navy blue sweatpants, sweatshirt, and black sneakers, she slipped out of her apartment, unnoticed. In her hand was the tied-off top of a black stocking, her driver's license, and car keys. Tucked inside her waistband, the sharp point of the dagger she'd retrieved from her altar scraped her leg as she quietly ran down the stairs and out onto the empty street. It was two o'clock in the morning. With hardly a car on the road, within fifteen minutes she was a couple of blocks away from Sylvain's apartment building, and she pulled into a parking spot. Reaching into the glove compartment, she pulled out the address she'd hastily written on a piece of paper. Sitting there in her car, she realized she hadn't thought this thing through at all. All she knew was his address, that he lived on the ground floor, and that he slept with his window open. And here she was with a knife in her pants!

I am totally out of my mind.

Stop!

Don't think.

Reaching under her car seat, she pulled out a pair of latex dishwashing gloves, pulling them on tightly over her slim fingers. Leaving the car door unlocked, she stayed close to bushes and trees as she sprinted toward his building. There was no moon in sight, but the streets were well lit, and soon she could see the number indicating she'd reached the right place. The open courtyard was just as he had described it. No security gate, no doorman. *Just walk on in and take care of business. How convenient. Is this how easy it is to commit crimes against the rich?*

Don't think, just move.

She'd become an automaton, ice water running through her veins now as, eager to complete her mission, she sought out Sylvain's apartment number.

No more nightmares.

Unit #101 was part of a cluster of three apartments nestled center left of the courtyard. Just two steps up and his door stood to the right. Walking back out to the courtyard, she could see an open window under a flowering jasmine bush. Crouching low beneath his window, she lifted her sweatshirt and pulled out the stocking cap, pulling it on over her head.

No more hate.

It took only one small heave for her to seat herself on the window ledge. Looking into the room, she could see the outline of Sylvain's body, lying face down in his bed, snoring gently.

Fuck you, Henri Chenet.

He had pushed the covers off, wearing only pajama bottoms and no top. After removing the screen, she pushed against the window glass in an upward motion. It was unlocked. Once inside the room, she wasted no time. Tiptoeing over to his bed and pulling out the dagger, she lifted it high up into the air and prepared to strike, but then Sylvain suddenly moved, turning his head over to the other side. On his face was a look of sadness, as if he was dreaming about something unhappy. Her heart reacted violently and she froze. *What am I doing?* Indecision suddenly engulfed her. *Am I completely insane?* And then fear attacked with a full frontal assault. *Can't do this. I have to get out of here.* She stood there, the effigy of a masked criminal, hand still poised in mid-air, tight grip on the dagger, when she heard something. Breaking out of her stupor, she turned to find someone stumbling through Sylvain's bedroom door. The man was uttering some half-formed question when he realized there was an intruder in the room escaping through the open window.

Running to the window, he saw a tall, thin figure, dressed in black, making a dash for it through the night. Throwing caution to the wind, he decided to follow. Tripping on the way out the window, he fell headlong into the bushes. It took a few seconds for him to recover, but he was quickly back on his feet, running after the person who had sped ahead of him and was already turning the corner. Cursing himself for having drunk too much, the man tried to catch up, but, upon turning the corner all he saw was the empty street with palm trees swaying gently in the nighttime breeze.

Lying quietly in a nearby flowerbed, Maya held her breath, hoping he would turn back. *Who the hell was that? Sylvain's roommate? He never mentioned anything about a roommate.*

"Where are you, shithead?" she heard him scream as a light went on in the building across the street. She could see him approaching, and she closed her eyes, awaiting her inevitable discovery and capture.

"Don't move motherfucker. The cops are on their way!" he bluffed. "I know you're around here somewhere! You just stay right where you are."

He was getting very, very close when he stopped, standing just on the other side of where she lay hidden. Then she heard him mutter, "Damn, I didn't even check on Sylvain!" And with that, he turned, jogging back toward the apartment.

As soon as he was out of sight, Maya leapt from her hiding place, ran to her car, and gunned the engine. As she drove, periodically peering into the rearview mirror to see if anyone followed, she realized that somewhere along the way, she had lost the dagger.

Oh my God! What have I done?

Coming out of her robot-like state, Maya pulled over and stumbled out of the car. Heaving violently, she retched pain, history, nightmares, and guilt for what seemed like hours. Having to stop twice more before finally making it back, Maya continued to vomit for two more days, unable to stop expelling the vileness that had made itself at home for so long within her.

The Baron

My, my, my, my, my. She hears my twisted suggestion about offing her boyfriend to get back at his father—*Exxxxcellent*. Now she's killing herself with guilt over *almost* carrying out my instructions. Drama, drama, drama. *Yesss*...I do love a good shot of drama. Keeps things spicy, red hot and sizzling. Exactly what needs to happen before things cool down to ice cold.

7

"In all probability, it was a burglar hoping to get in and out quick. Happens all the time when they stumble onto someone inside. They panic."

Sylvain stared into the eyes of Valentina Ruiz, the pretty, dark-haired police officer sent to take his report. Her partner was outside dusting for prints. His roommate, Carl Regis, a beefy, light-skinned mulatto with chestnut-brown hair falling into his eyes, was in the kitchen rustling up a glass of milk. Henri Chenet was pacing the length of the living room, one dying cigarette lighting a new one. Sylvain and the attractive woman with the severe face sat across from each other in what was, without a doubt, a male living room.

"Wow. I was almost the victim of a violent crime," he said after a while. "That makes me a statistic."

"Well, that's one way to look at it," she said. But you don't have to be an open-ended one. Maybe you can help us catch the guy. Sure you've never seen this before?" she asked, holding up the clear plastic bag containing Maya's dagger. They had found it at the foot of his bed.

"Looks mean, doesn't it?"

"Yes?" she said, all business, shaking the bag a little to remind him.

"Sorry, I have never seen it before. Hoping it might belong to an acquaintance of mine?"

"That would be helpful."

"And pretty sad, too."

"True. But do me a favor and take a real close look. Any of these markings mean anything to you? I know where a person can buy one of these, and I believe you are Haitian, right?"

"Yes, but what does that have to do with anything?"

"Can you please carefully inspect this knife and the markings on it?"

"Sure," Sylvain said, taking the bag from her, surprised that his hand trembled just a bit. It was four in the morning now, and although he was wired, he suddenly felt exhausted. He was barefoot and wearing a T-shirt over his pajama bottoms; his hair and face completed the picture of someone just rousted out of bed. His white T-shirt read "HAITI" in big blue letters.

"All I see are these two crosses etched into the knife," he said after inspecting the knife closely. "These markings mean something to you?"

"Well, I know they can be purchased at the open-air market down in Little Haiti. I believe these are *Vodou* symbols, but I don't know for which spirit."

"I know the fundamentals of *Vodou* but not the particulars."

"Let me see that thing," Sylvain's father interrupted, grabbing the bag from the officer's hand.

"The crosses I've seen tend to have curlicues on all sides, not like these straightforward ones," Sylvain said.

"And how would you know anything about *Vodou* fundamentals?" Mr. Chenet said to his son.

"It's part of our culture, Papa. How can you not know the basics?"

His father ignored him and resumed pacing.

"How do *you* know about *Vodou* spirits?" Sylvain asked the officer.

"I'm half Cuban, and our form of *Vodou* is called *Santeria.* My grandmother knows quite a bit about this stuff. Maybe I'll ask her."

"So you think this person could be Haitian?"

"Maybe. Nothing else you can tell me? Any enemies? Anyone who might want to hurt you? Rob you? Any snippets of conversation that come back to you as potentially meaningful right now? Anyone you've met recently who may have a motive of some sort?"

As she mentioned someone recent, she noticed a flicker in his eye and waited.

"I can't think of anything like that."

"Are you sure?"

"Yes, ma'am."

"Officer will do," she said cracking a smile. "Do you remember hearing anything at all after waking up? Did the person speak, make any kind of sound?"

"I don't think so. It was all pretty fast. One minute I'm sound asleep, the next thing I know, Carl is trying to get out of the apartment through my window. And Carl is a pretty big guy. From my perspective it looked kind of funny. Maybe surreal is more like it."

They had gone over his and Carl's story several times already.

"All right," she said, giving up. "I am going to give you my card." She reached into her pocket and handed him one. "Please call me if you or Carl remember anything else. If the lab results yield anything interesting, I will let you know. Tomorrow we will be back in your area to talk with your neighbors, check the grounds in the light of day. Try to get some rest, Mr. Chenet, both of you. Good night, Mr. Regis!" she called to Carl, who lumbered into the living room, crunching a piece of toast.

"Thanks officer," Sylvain said, smiling as she walked out the door.

For a moment, the two roommates looked at each other, heads shaking.

"Thanks, man," Sylvain said.

"No problem," the hero of the moment replied.

"Maya? It's Sylvain again. Where are you? I don't know why you haven't called me back. I would really like to talk to you."

It was his third message in two days. About to hang up, concern etched into his brow, Sylvain sighed with relief when he heard her pick up the receiver.

"Maya?"

"Yes," he heard her answer softly.

"Where have you been? I've left so many messages."

"I've been sick. Must have been something I ate. I've been throwing up a lot."

"I'm so sorry to hear that. You should have called me back. I would have come over to take care of you."

He heard a muffled sound. *Is she crying?*

"Are you all right?"

"Yes," she said. "I'm better now."

"You want to hear something funny? Well, not funny exactly. Someone broke into my apartment two nights ago and tried to stab me while I was sleeping."

"Oh my God," she whispered. "Are you all right?"

"Yes. My roommate, Carl, came in just in the nick of time and scared him off."

"Oh Lord," he heard her say, and then she started to cry.

"Maya, it's okay. Nothing happened. It was probably just a burglar who panicked when he realized the apartment wasn't empty. That's what the police think anyway. They think the guy probably saw my father leave for the evening and figured he was home free.

"That is so frightening, Sylvain! You were almost killed?" She sounded frantic and sad now.

"Maybe, but that didn't happen."

"And I didn't even call you back," she said, swallowing tears. "I am so sorry, Sylvain. I am so sorry."

"It's okay, don't worry about it," he comforted. You were sick."

"Are you home?" she said. "Can I come see you right now?"

"That would be great," he said. "You know how to get here?

"Yes. I mean, I have your address."

"Yeah, weren't you going to send me a card or something?"

"I decided against it. Where are you exactly?"

After giving her directions and hanging up the phone, Sylvain shook his head, smiling in anticipation of the attention about to be showered on him. *I would not have pegged her as the hysterical type.*

After hanging up the phone, Maya prostrated herself on the floor to the unseen God who had prevented Sylvain's death, thanking him, thanking the spirits, thanking all of the powers responsible for giving her another chance. She had committed a grave error for which she could never forgive herself. That she had almost gone through with it frightened her beyond reason, and she had been unable to leave her apartment, look at herself in the mirror, or dare to lay eyes on another human being. She did not deserve another chance, this she knew. But she would make it up to him.

A few minutes later, her face ravaged with tears, Maya ran to her car, sped all the way to his apartment, flung herself into his arms, and unable to restrain the impulse, wept with relief that the one she loved still lived.

They were inseparable over the next few days and weeks, the bond between them growing deeper, along with the dread of having to face his family one day. She resisted his attempts at making love, knowing somehow that it would set in motion an unstoppable train. She realized now that the love between Sylvain and her was the ultimate punishment for Henri Chenet, but the virgin in her still feared the intimacy and the angst that would follow should he abandon her after conquest. She relished the day that her nemesis would come to know about their relationship, and she worried that it would accelerate the inevitable meeting between them. She worried about the hate coming back full force; and she fretted about being a part of that family, foreseeing the social repercussions to come.

The Baron

———

She worries about everything instead of simply coming to me for help. Ooo, that just burns my ass.

———

It was early afternoon on a crisp and beautiful Miami Saturday when *Madame* Mirta opened the door, wondering who it might be.

"Bam nouvel ou chéri!" she screeched in pleasure upon seeing Colin clutching a trio of sweet-smelling gardenias.

"I had lunch with my parents today, and thought I'd stop by to see you before heading home. Are you busy?"

"Never too busy to see you, baby." Her pudgy arm waved him into her huge bosom for a bone-crushing hug.

"You're not wearing red today. What happened; did somebody die?" Colin asked as he followed her into the house.

"You so crazy. Nobody die. I love red but I no always wear red, you know that. What you want to eat, darling?"

"I just had lunch, remember? You're not going to make me eat again, are you?"

"Of course I do. How about some nice *pain pouding*, then? I sure you no have dessert."

"I may as well give in now. Who can resist your bread pudding anyway?"

"Good boy!" the boisterous queen clapped her hands. "Sit down. I have a little bit, too."

A few moments later they were both munching on dessert and drinking tea, and *Madame* Mirta was extracting as much news as she could from Colin.

"You ever hear anything more about that magazine writer?"

"You mean Penelope Long?"

"Yes."

"Why?"

"Nothing, I just wonder if Maya ever go see her or anything?"

"Worried about something?" Colin asked, knowing full well what she was after.

"Worry? No! I just think—"

"You just want to know if she ended up in the hospital or something wonderful like that, right? I know what you're thinking. Remember when that kid in our class stole her Nestlé's Crunch chocolate bar that time, and she kept asking everyone, one by one, if it was them?" Colin giggled fiendishly at the thought.

"Hmpphhh," *Madame* Mirta grunted.

"And then she comes around to Jason Tipton, and he says no, and she says 'No?' It was amazing how she just knew! And then next thing you know, he starts looking at his hand, and bam! He's hopping around, shaking it like crazy, claiming it was burning up. That was great! I wish I could do that. But no, I haven't heard anything like that, sweetie. I haven't heard much of anything from Maya these days. She's very busy with her new boyfriend."

"Boyfriend? Maya has boyfriend and she no tell me?"

"She certainly didn't tell me. Not that she's the kind that runs around talking up her business anyway, but I usually know what's going on to some degree."

Honing in on a tone she'd never heard before from him, *Madame* Mirta's head jolted up in surprise. "You jealous, Colin?"

"Jealous about what?"

"You know."

"About Maya's boyfriend?"

"Who this boyfriend is, anyway?" she said, distracted for a moment by the bigger news she'd just heard.

"A guy she used to know in Haiti, she says, and you can just forget that silly idea about me being jealous of him."

"Why you no could be jealous?" she teased, amused by the intensity of his denial. "Maya is beautiful girl."

"We've been friends for ten years, for God's sake," Colin said, reverting back to his usual unaffected and cynical self. "Beauty has nothing to do with anything."

"But, she beautiful, no?"

"Yeah, she is," he admitted, looking a little flustered by the directness of the question.

Noticing, *Madame* Mirta thought it best not to pursue this tack. Still curious, though, she asked again. "So, who this boyfriend is? Who she know from Haiti?"

"A guy named Sylvain Chenet. Apparently a rich Haitian with fabulously disgusting parents."

"A mulatto?"

"I believe so."

"Oh boy. That big trouble."

"Although I still can't figure what's so great about all this light skin crap," Colin continued. "Black skin is so much more daring and absorbing."

"What mean daring and absorbing? You always talk with words I no understand so good, Colin. Is that good thing in your eyes?"

"Yes, of course."

"That because you white. Maybe if you dark-skinned, you not think so. Anyway, that whole other conversation. I am worry about Maya. This not so good thing, I think so."

"Yes, I think so not, too,"Colin said, his eyes in a far away place. "Maybe I'll have to do something about it."

"What you mean?" she asked.

"I've got some ideas," was all he would say.

"Hey, this is kind of like being in a carnival."

Maya turned around to see who spoke, both surprised and pleased to find Sylvain. It was just a little before three in the afternoon, and The Mysterious Light Bookstore was packed with regulars—a healer looking for herbs and oils, a witch looking for the latest version of the *Book of Shadows*, a magician, two Zen monks, and assorted regular people, too. Writers were there, researching the supernatural; artists were browsing as well, leafing through books of patterns for "the perfect wave," "the perfect mandala," the perfect puffy, cloudy sky." Everywhere, people sat in chairs and on the floor, or they stood in corners, reading. Marla, the resident psychic, a sixty-three-year-old overweight mamma who dumbfounded advice seekers with a double-barrel shot of body odor and blistering personal truths, sat in her customary corner fast asleep, as usual. The lighting made for a cozy and intimate place to spend some time; the music, a whisper of flute, tinkling bells, or harp, set a low-key mood. One of Maya's duties was to make sure the scent of incense always filled the air with that sweet, pungent reminder of things mystical.

Outside, Mrs. Sky, the bag lady who had long ago substituted shopping bags for suitcases, could be found on The Mysterious Light Bookstore steps, greeting patrons, amusing them with astounding tales of her various travels, and assuring them that she had "been places" and "was going places." Her shopping cart was piled almost as high as the sky with small and medium-sized cases of all shapes and colors. One hand pulled a luggage carrier on rollers that held at least four masterfully arranged Samsonites; the other hand gripped four soft canvas valises that ranged from duffel bag to garment bag. Both shoulders drooped with smaller totes, makeup and toiletry bags; and around her belly were several belts that further weighed her down with leather and canvas fanny packs and pouches. Her creased face tried in vain to conceal the load she'd chosen to bear over the years, but her joyful spirit belied every hardship. She talked non-stop, but no one knew her real story. Maya usually tried to avoid her. Something about the woman unnerved her.

There was the time Mrs. Sky had patted her on the shoulder as Maya passed. When she turned, Mrs. Sky spoke confidentially, with a bright smile on her face, "All that traveling you did? You have a lot more traveling to do." And then there was the time she was heading to the theater after a long, difficult day in the store filled with rude returns and customer complaints. Mrs. Sky had greeted her as she pushed open the door to leave and announced, "You can only go so far, you know, before that trip catches up with you." Each time, Maya had looked at her, waiting for an explanation, but Mrs. Sky had looked at her in a serious, unsettling manner, as if to say, "Well, you know it's true." Everyone thought she was loveable and fun, but the woman gave her the creeps.

"Did you meet Mrs. Sky?" Maya asked Sylvain.

"Is that the suitcase lady?"

"Uh-huh."

"How could I miss her? What's her story?"

"Hey, what's your story? What are you doing here? I thought you were going to be up to your ears in law books."

"I was in the neighborhood?"

She laughed, tickled, "Yes, that works."

"I feel like a silly kid, but I haven't been able to get you off my mind."

"As a kid, you were never silly. You were very serious."

"I still am! Usually. But this thing with you is—it's so unusual, so unexpected, so kind of delicious that I want to keep after it."

Her heart did a back flip as she heard the words that a woman in love longs to hear, and she took a deep breath to dispel it.

"Am I bothering you?" he asked, anxious and embarrassed at the possibility.

"*No!* Not at all." She smiled, enjoying the feeling of being wanted by this man who had occupied so much of her thinking for such a long time.

"Here's what I'd like to do," Sylvain said. "I would like to go back to my apartment, study for the next four hours, and then open my door to find you there, waiting for me to feed you. How does that sound?"

"How about you go back to your apartment and study for the next four hours and then come over to my place where dinner will be waiting? How does that sound?"

"Even better! Can you cook?

"Of course I can! How's 7:30 sound?"

"Perfect."

He took her hand and held it for a moment, his eyes dancing with mischief. Her eyes danced back.

Later that night, at 7:30 sharp, Maya's telephone and doorbell rang at once. Colin reached for the phone and talked to Elly for a minute, informing her that Maya was catastrophically engaged at the moment, what with cooking up an entire meal for her "date" and trying to get him, Colin, out of her apartment. Having given up on the idea of shooing him out before an introduction, Maya buzzed Sylvain in, explaining over the intercom that her apartment was right at the top of the stairs.

"Come in," Colin intoned dramatically, opening the door before Sylvain's ring.

"Hello," Sylvain answered, surprised to find this ghostly creature instead of Maya.

"That's Colin," Maya explained, coming out of the kitchen with a bashful smile on her face. "He's the best friend I have in this city and he insisted on meeting my mysterious date."

"Am I mysterious?"

"No, it just seems that everyone thinks if I have a friend he has to be mysterious."

Colin zeroed in on Sylvain, fixing him with a "get ready" look. "If you had to choose between being a poor, desperate, illiterate Haitian who risks his life on one of those rickety boats so he could make it to Miami, and a lowlife Cuban criminal whom Castro let loose in one of those Mariel boatlifts heading for Miami, which one would you be?"

Sylvain looked stunned.

"He does this to everyone," Maya jumped in to explain. "If you know Colin, you know you'll eventually end up having to choose between two of his impossible scenarios."

"And if you decide not to choose?" Sylvain asked.

"You have to!" Colin said, "If you don't, your mother will have each of her fingernails and toenails pulled out slowly by cannibals who will then use those nails to scratch her eyes out before devouring her."

"Oh my God!" Sylvain laughed out loud, a look of horror on his face.

"So?" Colin pushed, antsy with anticipation.

"I would choose to be the Haitian," Sylvain said with certainty. "Even though our fates would be the same, at least I would have character."

"Appalling answer," Colin announced dryly as he walked out the door.

"Wow. Was that a test? And did I pass it?"

"If Colin says it's appalling, that means it's great. But no, it's not a test. He just uses these make-believe do-or-die situations as fodder for the creepy stories he writes."

"Science fiction?"

"Comic book creepy stuff."

"I see. And he's your best friend. Very interesting. Where on earth did you find him?"

"Long story. Did you get any studying done?"

"Some. All I can think about now is food, and it sure smells good in here. What's that you've got there?"

"Want to taste this rice?" she asked, spooning some from the steaming pot and walking toward him, a crooked smile on her face. "Yeah! Let's see...mmmm, delicious," he said, feigning ecstasy as he reached around her waist. She did not resist, and he lifted his arm to the back of her head, inviting her into his embrace. It started as a sweet, simple kiss, but minutes later, after she'd dropped the spoon to the floor, it had turned much more serious. His hands caressed her back, then the sides of her body, lightly touching her breasts as they did so. She shivered as a searing sensation filled her already-wet sex with a desire for closer contact.

"I want you, Maya, I want you," he murmured as his hands explored further, now rubbing her ass with hungrier hands. "You're all I think about. It's crazy."

She responded with her body, molding herself into the curve of his chest and his groin, touching him between the legs hesitantly at first, then with more intent as the urge mounted to feel the bulge that pushed against his jeans. *Can't fight this forever.* When her fingers found cold metal, she fiddled with his zipper for a while. Momentarily delayed by this obstacle, she looked up at him, suddenly self-conscious.

"I need to tell you something," she whispered.

"Tell me," he said, running his index and middle finger down her cheek.

"I've never done this before with a man, and—"

"Yes?"

"The food is burning."

She detached herself from him, giggling while he bounced after her to look at the damage. "You said all you could think about was food but you lied, and now look!" she laughed, trying to hide the embarrassment of her earlier confession.

Sylvain reached over and took the two pots off the burners and placed them in the sink. He found the light switch in the kitchen and turned it off, and then extended an arm to Maya; she followed him to her bed, which now lay adorned in moonlight streaming in from the windows.

He sat down on the bed and motioned for her to sit by him. When she did, he gently pushed her down, then joined her, their faces nearly touching, their bodies aching for closer contact.

"It is absolutely, completely, and thoroughly okay with me that this is all new for you. I promise to take care of you, to give you pleasure, and to make sure you enjoy every minute of it. Trust me?"

"So far, so good," she smiled, hiding her face in his chest.

For two hours, as the moon spilled like a silver river onto soft dry shores, the two lovers drank from the cup of forbidden love and passion, willingly fulfilling destiny's desire.

8

Strolling home from a popular bar where Elly and Colin had tried unsuccessfully to pry details from Maya on her flowering love affair, the threesome walked slowly, even though the rain had returned to the Southland in full force. As they approached the building, Maya was the first to notice a tall, black figure huddled against the door, his face turned away from the rain and toward the lobby interior.

"Talk about wonderfully shady characters," Colin said.

He'd been in a really bad mood of late. Either in a bad mood or unavailable to the point where Maya wondered if there might be someone in his life; but she didn't dare ask. Feeling lighter than she had in years and missing their closeness, Maya grew more exasperated with him with every passing day. She had initiated tonight's outing, but Colin had become irritable at her refusal to talk about Sylvain.

"Quick, either one of you," he said now, suddenly brightening at the thought that flooded him. "If you were walking toward this building right now, but *alone,* and you noticed this scary-looking guy crouching by the door, looking like he was just waiting for a victim to pounce on, what would you do?"

"I'd start praying like crazy," Elly answered first.

Maya said nothing and kept walking, but hurrying now a bit more than the others to get to the doorway. Left behind, Colin turned to Elly, whose face registered surprise and concern.

"Don't ask," he responded to her unasked question.

As her heels clacked noisily on the sidewalk, the silhouetted figure turned around, and then Maya broke into a run.

"Jacquy!"

Jacquy rushed from his shelter toward his oldest friend.

"Maya!"

Colin and Elly stopped to watch, struck by the intensity of emotion between the two.

They broke into fast and furious Kreyol.

"It sounds like African," Elly said to Colin, her eyes still focused on Maya and her mysterious friend, whose smile lit up the night around them. "Can you understand any of it?"

"It's Haitian Kreyol. Maya says it has elements of French, English, Spanish, and African, so you're not far off."

"Do you know who he is?"

"It's her best friend from Haiti. Whenever a letter from Jacquy arrives, she gets in a better mood. She never tells me what he says, but it's like the news is something she waits for as if her life depended on it."

After a moment, Colin and Elly approached the friends, who turned as if surprised by their presence. Colin held out his hand. "Jacquy, I presume?"

"Colin se yon bon zami mwen," Maya said. Colin's a good friend of mine. *"Et Elly, se yon danseu kankou mwen."* And Elly's a dancer like me.

"Enchanté," Jacquy grinned, shaking both their hands with vigor.

"Listen guys, we're going in now. I'll catch up with you tomorrow, huh?" Maya said, reaching for her keys, then giving Colin a hug and a wink. "Bye Elly." With that she disappeared inside, mounting the steps to her apartment with Jacquy close behind. When they reached the top of the stairs, Maya stepped toward the door to slip the key in the lock, but the funny expression on Jacquy's face stopped her.

"What?" she smiled.

"Look at your hair," he said to her. "You have long hair just like white people."

"Except white people don't have hair like this," she laughed, holding up one of her locks. "Guys wear their hair like this, too, you know."

"Really?"

Once inside the apartment, the two friends stood for a moment looking at each other, emotion bubbling up around them. Laughing like two giddy children, they threw their arms around each other. After all those years, here he was, her sweetest reminder of home—those hot and hazy afternoons spent chasing each other, swimming together, the secret reading lessons. When the reverie reached its inevitable conclusion, she stopped laughing, chilling him with her dead-serious eyes. Her voice took on a harsh, icy coating, and in the lilting, yet guttural language of Haiti, Maya spoke:

"I told you a little bit about it in my letters, Jacquy, but you will never know how awful that trip was. How terrifying. How degrading." She motioned him over to the bathroom, where she pulled out two towels and handed him one. She stood opposite him, wiping her hair dry, her mood changing to lightness and ease again. "But do you realize that because of you, learning English was so much easier because I knew the alphabet? Hey, you're so wet. All I can give you is a sweatshirt and sweatpants that will be ridiculously short on you, but they should work, since I like my clothes big."

"Anything dry would be great," he said, relieved to see the other Maya vanish.

"How long have you been waiting out there?"

"Two hours."

"Damn! You must have arrived just as we left. But when did you get in? Aren't you staying with that guy you're working for? Why did you stay out there so long?"

"I wanted to surprise you!"

"You're too silly! I hope you won't get sick. Can you spend the night? We have a lot of catching up to do."

"Yes, we do," he said in a way that made her uneasy. "I am sure Mr. Porter won't mind one night.

"You mean you have to ask permission? This isn't Haiti, Jacquy. You can do as you please, here."

"He's all right, Maya. He worked very hard to get me here, you know.

"Are you hungry?" she said.

"No, I'm okay."

"How about some tea?"

"I brought you some *te ti bom* from home, but it's back at Mr. Porter's house with my things. I will get it tomorrow."

"No problem," she said, placing two mugs, spoons, and sugar on a tray. As she carried them out to the main room, she motioned Jacquy over to the floor pillows. Placing the tray down on her makeshift table, she proceeded to light candles, unable to keep the edge from her voice.

"So, how all right is he? How much is he paying you as a butler? Have you discussed that yet?"

"Sure," Jacquy said, wishing he didn't have to tell her, sensing it was not enough. "He's starting me at $6.50 an hour, and if he likes my work, in six months, I will get a raise of .50 cents."

Maya turned to look at her friend with incredulity. His blue-black face, now illuminated by candles, made her melt inside, and she stopped to study him for a moment—his square jaw, full wide lips over even white teeth, his hair cropped close to his scalp, his wide forehead and intelligent eyes that seemed somehow both amused and sad. He was very thin with long legs but a rather short torso, and kindness hung about him like a halo. The words of rage on her lips screeched to a halt, bumping into each other so as not to tumble out. She fought back the urge to curse this Mr. Porter for exploiting her friend. That $6.50 an hour over a forty-hour workweek would yield him $260—enough to make anyone from their old neighborhood earning $500 in a *year* envy the likes of Jacquy with passion untold. Never mind that the average butler in Miami earned $20 to $25 an hour. Jacquy was in nirvana, and in spite of the unfortunate circumstances that had led her to this place, she'd been damned lucky, too. Lucky that Colin found her, that *Manman* Mirta embraced her, offering her what any bourgeois child in Haiti took for granted—a home, an education, new clothes from real department stores.

"Never mind me, Jacquy. I am a selfish, cold-hearted bitch. Pay no attention to me."

"You? Why do you say that? That's not the Maya I remember!"

"I am not the Maya you remember. I have been through hell and back, and it's only recently that I have decided to tackle the wall of ice around my heart. I grew comfortable with it, though, so it is hard work."

"Why do you want to get comfortable with that? What happened to you, Maya? Was it the trip in that boat?"

"No, you'll never know," she cut him off, looking away from his face to stare out the window at the rain. Quietly so that he could barely hear her, she said, "Something's had a hold of me all these years. It's something very much like...murder. I have had murder in my heart, Jacquy, and it's difficult to let it go."

"Murder? What you talking about, Maya? Murder? You mean you want to kill people? What has this white man's country done to you?"

Hearing the fear and consternation in his voice, Maya shook off the feeling of wanting to spill her heart and soul to her friend. *He could never understand. No one can ever understand.*

"Of course not," she smiled, assuaging him. "I don't mean it literally. I mean the hate and pain and darkness of that word. I can't shake it. My parents abandoned me to that icy black ocean. They made me go, knowing I would probably die. They said they had no choice, but didn't they? Don't we always have choice? I would like to say, 'It all turned out all right in the end, so what the hell?' I would like to forgive them and never think about it again, never have those nightmares again. But I can't do it."

"Do what?"

"Lose those night terrors. Allow myself to feel love without holding back."

"That's not true, *ma che*! I know it's not. Don't say that! I don't believe it!"

"Well, like I said, I am working on it."

"So, is *lwa* here, too?" he asked, changing the subject.

"*Lwa* is everywhere! What do you think?"

"I wasn't sure how it would be on the white man's land."

"*Lwa* is here, all right, and I am on very friendly terms with them. The woman I call my mother here is a big-time *mambo,* and she is the best! Every Saturday she has ceremonies, although it's been a while since I went to one. I've sort of gotten my own system down for communicating with the *lwa*. But it would be fun to go, and you'll get to meet her. She is the most wonderful, most generous woman alive, and I'm so grateful to her."

"Could it be love?"

"It's gratitude as big as the sky."

"The *lwa* don't help you with this pain you have in your heart, Maya? You ask them for help with that?"

"No, I haven't asked them for that," she said, feeling the weight and burden of her statement. "I haven't asked for that. But enough about me and all this wretchedness. Don't worry I'm doing just fine, Jacquy. It's you we need to worry about now. You're here in this big new country, and you don't know anything about it. I have to teach you how things work around here. We have to teach you English! I'll have to find out about evening classes for you."

"Everyone says if you watch lot of television, you can learn very fast," Jacquy said, looking around the apartment. "Where's your television? Doesn't everyone in America have one?"

"Yes, everyone but me. Sorry. I hate television, never watch it. So silly, most of it. I spend most of my time dancing; when I'm not dancing, I'm rehearsing or taking class, and when I'm not doing that, I'm working. I have a part-time job at this great little bookstore on Lincoln Road. It's called The Mysterious Light Bookstore, and all kinds of freaks come in there because there are loads of books on magic and witchcraft and herbs and Eastern religions, and tons of information on gods and goddesses from different cultures. They even have books on *Vodou*! You'll have to come. There's always incense burning and some mellow zigzagged music playing."

"Zigzag?"

"That's my word for things that are weird and wavy," she laughed.

"It sounds great, but I don't read English, and my French is just okay. I never had anyone to talk to in French, you know."

"Don't worry. You always wanted to learn. That hasn't changed, am I right? You'll pick it up fast."

"I hope so because, you know, a simple Haitian is what I am, and being here is already blowing my mind. Did you see the size of that airport?? Oh my God! I almost ran back on the plane! And those moving stairs! What the hell! And then no one was grabbing my suitcase, trying to take me to their nearest cabbie friend. It took me a lot of time to find the taxi stand. And the price! That thief charged me $30.00 to get to the house of Mr. Porter. THIRTY DOLLARS! I nearly fainted right then and there and got into a fight with him. I was sure he was trying to gyp me because he can see I don't know my way around."

By then, Maya was shaking with laughter at her friend's tirade.

"And nobody say hello or good morning or good evening here. Isn't that strange to you?"

"Americans are definitely not Haitian, Jacquy. You find that out real fast. They think differently from us. Of course, by now I probably think more like them."

"Hmphh," Jacquy said as he stretched his legs, which nearly crossed the entire apartment's length. A bear of a yawn escaped his lips.

"I'm getting kind of tired, too," Maya said looking at the time and standing up. "Where are you going to sleep? I have another bedspread—it's very thick—we can use it as a mattress for you, and I think I have another blanket to cover you with."

"Maya."

"Yes?" she said looking at him, wondering at the sound in his voice.

"There's something I have to tell you, but I do not know how. I am afraid to tell you."

"What is it?"

"Your mother—she is dead."

She felt as if a wall of bricks had fallen down from the sky on her head. "When?" she said in a small voice.

"Two weeks ago."

Unexpected tears flooded her eyes and dripped down her face. A sudden pain in her stomach felt probing and sharp like a killer's switchblade.

"How?"

"She had a heart attack."

"Was she sick?" she asked dully. "Had she developed a condition?"

"No, it was sudden. I don't know all the details, but your father says it had something to do with that family she worked for. You know the one you always ask me about in your letters?"

Maya felt her back stiffen and a slow rise of the feeling she'd become all too familiar with over the years.

"What do you mean?" she asked, her voice ominous and low. Now a pain was forming in her head, making her lift her hands up to hold it as if it might burst.

"Like I say, I don't know everything, but it seems she wanted to quit the job because he was so mean and nasty to her all the time, and it kept getting worse since the son went away; when she told him, he said he would call the police. He said he would tell them she stole from them. Your papa said that was not the first time he said this to your *manman*. But this time she didn't take it so well, and she got sick right then and there and fell down on the floor. At least he took her to the hospital, then went to get your papa. But when Raoul got there, she only stayed alive a little more—only long enough to tell him what happened. Nobody understands why he didn't want to let her go so bad that he had to threaten her."

Maya made her way over to the floor cushion, lowering herself before responding in a lifeless voice, which made Jacquy cringe. "Because the sick bastard has been molesting her since before I left, and I guess he did not want to lose his sex slave."

"Oh my God, Maya. I didn't know that."

Maya did not answer. She could not.

Two hours later, Jacquy awoke to whimpering sounds coming from Maya's bed. Sitting up, his eyes heavy with sleep, he watched her toss and turn like a woman possessed.

Two nights later, the two friends walked arm in arm along the beach, enjoying the fine Saturday mist that drizzled down from the sky, impregnating skin and sand with what felt like morning dew. An atmospheric shroud made it hard to see more than ten feet in front of them; but because of the heat, what should have felt like cool moistness seemed more like a light steam bath. As they drove up Collins Avenue toward *Ma-*

dame Mirta's house, Jacquy had jabbered non-stop about Maya's earlier performance. Having to shout now above the crashing waves, he carried on still in the lightning-fast Kreyol they both naturally spoke to each other.

"Maya, I can't stop thinking about you up there on that stage. I was shocked. How did you learn to move your feet like that? They were moving so fast, but your body looked like it was in slow motion. It was as if you were in trance. Was the *lwa* there inside you?"

"Yes and no. It's like feeling their presence, but I am still conscious. After the performance is over, I know exactly what mistakes I made," she said smiling.

"What mistakes?"

"If you didn't notice, then don't worry about it."

"That was a beautiful thing to see. I am glad you invited me to come. Your mother..." he said, hesitating, "and your father—they would have been so proud."

Maya stiffened and let go of his arm.

"Give me that damn arm back," he said, snaking it back through his own. "It's true and that's all there is to it. They were so sad every time they got your letters addressed to me. Your *manman*, she would stand there while I read, waiting to see if there was even one small word for her or your *papa.* Can you forgive them now for whatever it is they did to you?"

"You mean now that she's dead?" she said, her body coiled tight as a spring.

"Yes, I guess so. I never knew why you were so mad at them. They always refused to say why they sent you to Miami so fast like that."

"They had their reasons."

"Did they sell you to this woman we are visiting tonight?"

"No! No, it wasn't like that at all," she said, reliving the conversation with her mother, while her father stood silently in the shadows, crying. "I don't think they had much choice.

It wasn't really their fault. It's just me. I'm a hard person. I understand why, but it has still been hard for me to forgive them. They abandoned me, hoping desperately that I would survive the trip, but knowing I probably wouldn't. And why? In the end, it was the money. They had a better life after I left, didn't they?"

"Well, it's not like they became millionaires overnight or anything like that, but they did buy a few new things in the last few years. They fixed up the house and *lacou* real good, and they got a newer truck, and they've been very generous with many, many folks in the neighborhood. Including me."

"Good for them. Good for you. I knew God must have had a reason to make me get on that boat."

"Maya..."

"I'm sorry. I didn't mean that. Don't listen to me. This is a bad subject for me. I don't see clearly on it. Look, we're here. It's been way too long since I've seen my big ol' *Manman* Mirta. Come on, I'll race you. Follow the drums!"

When they reached the front door, it was ajar, left that way so everyone could walk right in.

"Koté ou yé?" Maya shouted. Where are you?

"Koté pitit mwen an?" a booming voice could be heard from the kitchen. Where's my baby?

The unexpected sound of a motor approaching caught Jacquy off guard, and he looked from right to left trying to locate its origin. Just as he turned toward the kitchen, *Madame* Mirta appeared in her red-satinned glory, looking for all the world like the belle of the ball at Haitian *carnaval*. Maya ran to her and threw her arms around the queen's neck.

"Bam nouvel ou, pitit mwen! Ki jan ou ye? Gad jan ou bel. Dépi konbyen tan ou pa vin we manman ou?" How are you, my baby? What's been going on? Look at you, how beautiful you are! How long has it been since you come to see your old *manman*?

"Trop tan, cé vrai oui." Too long, it's true.

"Et ki es jeunom sa?" And who this young man?

"This is Jacquy, *Manman*! He just arrived from Haiti last week," Maya said, smiling.

Jacquy stepped over to the chair and extended his arm. The queen refused his hand, insisting he greet her properly by kissing her on the cheek.

"Ki lontan map tande pale de Jacquy, Jacquy, Jacquy! Min ou finalmen!" she said, laughing. How long have I been hearing about Jacquy, Jacquy, Jacquy! Finally, here you are!

She steered them into the kitchen, wanting to be private with them while a stream of regulars filed through, shouting their hellos as they headed toward the living room. The lights were low throughout the house, and the sound of drumming could be heard over the talk and laughter of those who regularly came together to celebrate. *Cérémoni!*

Maya, Jacquy, and *Madame* Mirta huddled in the kitchen for a while, talking—with much hugging in between—before finally moving into the other room. They could feel the pull of impatient *Vodouists* waiting for the ceremony to begin. By then, *Madame* Mirta felt adequately caught up—*No, Jacquy was not Maya's boyfriend, and the show was going well; no, she did not have a boyfriend; yes, she was sure; and wasn't her daughter great on that stage usually reserved for white peoples? And what about Colin? Mr. DeVilla? Was Maya still working at the bookstore? Did she need anything?* Maya barely had time to answer before the queen's next question, fired at lightning speed. Not wanting to spoil the jovial mood, Maya did not mention the news about her mother, and Jacquy followed her lead. *Madame* Mirta had other burning questions, but knew she would have to wait until she could get Maya alone. The drums were beating faster now and mundane cares receding, as the realm of possession took over, promising to turn ordinary human beings into gods and goddesses to be served, fed, admired, and worshipped.

This night's ceremony was dedicated to Erzulie, governess of love. To welcome her, the *ounfo*'s ever-changing altar honored the Virgin Mary's alter ego with pale blue, pink, and white swatches of lace on which were lovingly placed some of the coquette's favorite things: sweet wine, cakes and other pastries, perfume, and flowers. Behind the altar, the transformed living room wall shimmered seductively with a half a dozen *Vodou* flags powerfully colored in blazing reds, deep blues, burnished yellows, and glistening greens. They all bore the goddess's symbol of love, a filigreed heart embellished with ornate and graceful curlicues. About twenty-five people, all of them Haitian and excited, swayed to the beat of the drums, whose tempo edged faster and faster toward a delirious pitch meant to entice the spirit and loosen up the congregation for potential possession. *Madame* Mirta, having already beseeched Papa Legba to open the door for the spirits to slide down the *poto mitan*, now whirred around in her wheelchair, rocking her head back and forth to the drums, inviting the spirit of Erzulie to take over her form.

Several minutes later, she lifted her head, her eyes flirty as she looked around, a coy smile on her face. A *hounsi*, *Madame* Mirta's current assistant and *mambo* in training—one of many since Maya—stepped in to help. The young girl, outfitted in traditional white dress and head kerchief, her eyes gleaming the joy of servitude to the gods, walked forward bearing a light blue lace cloak, which she placed around Erzulie's shoulders. She returned to the altar and grabbed a bottle of *Anaïs Anaï*s perfume, daubing the goddess's temples and wrists with the sweet golden scent. Erzulie smiled her approval at the care being given to her.

Sandwiched between Jacquy and a mother who clung to her seven-year-old daughter, Maya smiled wistfully to see the young *hounsi* attend to her duties. Not so long ago, it had been she who dressed the spirits.

Next, the *hounsi* placed several gold chains around the seated virgin's neck and handed her a fan, for which she was thanked by a bow of the head. Erzulie then asked for a mirror so she could inspect herself. She demanded rouge and lipstick. Once done, she looked up smiling, waiting for adoration. Everyone shouted compliments to her, which she loved.

"You are the most beautiful woman in the universe!" a young man screamed above the drums.

"And you smell so nice!" chimed in another voice.

"Come to me! Marry me, please!" an older man joined in.

"Look how pretty she is," women remarked to each other.

And in fact, *Madame* Mirta had become a different woman, exuding charm, poise, and sensuality. The desirable but unattainable virgin slowly rose from her iron prison and pranced around the room, joking with and taunting the men, speaking softly with the women. Years earlier she had been struck by a car while crossing US1, shattering her pelvis and putting her in a wheelchair; yet now, no one showed surprise to see the time-ravaged body of *Madame* Mirta practically waltzing around the room without showing any sign of pain. Fanning herself and tossing her head back as she laughed, Erzulie headed toward the two friends and stood squarely in front of Jacquy.

"And what can I do for you?" she asked in a throaty, sexy voice.

Jacquy had hoped he might get a chance to ask a favor. Whispering low in order to be private, he said, "My friend here," he said taking Maya's hand, "she needs help getting love back in her heart. You are the Goddess of Love. Can you help her?"

Maya stopped breathing as the goddess turned, looking her up and down with great interest.

"This is something you cannot understand," she said to Jacquy, "and you would be well advised to stay out of it. There is another among us who is already helping your friend. He will come later tonight to talk to her himself." And with that, she walked away, hips swaying.

Erzulie moved on, speaking briefly to the next woman and circling around the room for several minutes before returning to her chair to depart. But before she had a chance to leave, a crotchety old man on the other side of the room belted out a howl, then wild laughter. Outside, thunder bellowed from heaven to earth. Everyone in the room knew the Baron had arrived.

He stood waiting for the items he needed, and a couple of people rushed over to him with a pair of sunglasses, a black jacket and hat. The *hounsi* quickly walked over to him and handed him a cigar, then lit it for him; another young man furnished him with his cane. The ritual completed, the Baron wasted no time. He ambled over to where Maya stood and looked her straight in the eye.

"So, young woman, what do you want to do now?"

Nervous because of the crowd but uncaring, Maya responded, "I've been waiting for you to tell me."

"Is that right?"

She said nothing.

He pounded his cane on the floor, frightening her, "You have to choose for yourself!" Then he lowered his voice, now smooth as silk, "Or you can have me take care of it...In whichever way I see fit. When you decide, you know how to summon me. But remember *thisss*," he said, "There is no turning back when you call on *Baron Samedi*!"

Maya relived the scene over and over in her mind that evening, too engrossed to speak, much to Jacquy's frustration.

"What was he talking about, Maya? What is going on?"

"Nothing. It's private, Jacquy. It's nothing you might imagine. You know how he always speaks in mysteries. I am trying to decipher it myself." And she would say no more.

She was giving him a ride home, but first they had to stop at her apartment to retrieve the wallet Jacquy had inadvertently left behind. They rode in silence. Once upstairs, she said, "I'll just be a minute." She stepped into the bathroom; and catching her reflection in the mirror, she looked into her own eyes, wondering what she should do. She loved Sylvain and did not want to hurt him, but the urge to avenge herself and her mother had taken on a life of its own once more. It felt like a living, breathing presence that dwelt within her, an animal ravenous for blood, tormenting her with its need for vengeance. She sat down on the toilet to relieve herself, but real relief felt so far away. She closed her eyes tight, pulling on her hair and scratching at her thighs in anger. *Dear God, tell me what to do.*

When she walked out of the bathroom, she found Jacquy standing between the screen and her altar, holding Henri Chenet's picture in his hands.

"What are you doing?" she asked, stunned, landing back on earth with a thud.

"Who's this?" he asked.

"My altar is my *private business.*"

"Nobody in Haiti hides their altars, Maya. What's the big deal anyway?"

"The big deal is that I decide what's private and what's not, regardless of what all the Haitians in Haiti do! This Haitian is in Miami, sent here by the Haitians in Haiti, so I do things my way. Got that? Now give me that." She wrenched the framed sketch from his hands, suddenly empty and hanging in the air like two lost souls.

"Who is that man?" he said, deciding not to be offended by her rudeness. "You doing something to him?"

"Jacquy," she said, her back to him, her tone ominous.

"Never mind," he said. "Ready to go?"

"Yes."

"You going to be mad all night? I'm sorry I touched your things, all right?"

"It's okay, Jacquy, I'm sorry, just forget it." She tried to say it casually, but her words fell to the ground like a sack of wet sand.

"You sure are a different person than what I remember, Maya. I miss her."

"Sorry." Looking at the expression of concern on his face, she melted. "I'm sorry for being such a bitch, Jacquy. I'm very confused right now. I've got a lot to sort out. It's very complicated up here," she tried to explain, pointing to her head and walking to the door to open it.

As they walked down the stairs, he tried again. "Why don't you talk to me? Why don't you let me help you? We used to talk about everything!"

"That was a long time ago. You're the same wonderful guy I used to know, but me, I'm damaged."

"You keep saying things like that, but—"

"I know," she cut him off, "I don't know how else to clarify it."

"They say everybody in this country sees psychiatrists. Maybe that's what you need, somebody who will help you with all these crazy feelings you have."

She snickered at the thought, visualizing herself telling a shrink, "I'm thinking about murdering my boyfriend because I hate his father." The barely formed chuckle died as the thought of killing Sylvain jolted her back to reality, flinging her into inner torment once more.

I do love him. What am I supposed to do now? I can't kill him anymore.

And then another voice intruded, whispering, *"Revenge is the only way to get rid of the hatred."*

But shouldn't love be able to overcome hatred?

She turned to the sound of Jacquy's voice coming at her from a distance.

"Hello? Hello? Maya? Where are you?"

"Oh, I was just..." *I'll think about this later. Things are turning out so different than I thought.*

"Oh, man. I have a bad feeling about all this, Maya. I'm worried about you."

Later that night, as her mind blazed with questions, fears and doubts, she thought she heard a voice inside her whisper: *Leave it alone. What you need to do is let go.*

"All right!" she said aloud, sitting straight up in her bed the next morning. The dreams had been particularly intense that night, when she was able to sleep at all. In the dream, *Monsieur* Chenet was watching her perform, shaking his head at her all the while, as if she were the worst dancer he'd ever seen. Then he'd started laughing. Then he'd turned into Jacquy, then into Sylvain, who also laughed, sounding just like his father. And, all the while, that same voice had whispered, *Leave it alone. What you need to do is let go.*

Later that day, Maya hung up the phone and stared out of her apartment window. It was barely 6:30 in the evening, and the day's humidity was just beginning to hint at a night of rain.

Standing resolutely in the middle of her living room, she thought, *I'll have to hurry.* Then, walking rigidly toward her altar, she prepared to keep her rendezvous with fate. *Okay, Baron, it's up to you to decide, 'cause I can't.* As she lit candles, adjusted *Monsieur* Chenet's picture on the top shelf, and tried in vain to calm the black rooster in the cardboard box at her feet, the words she'd just said to Sylvain echoed in her ears.

Meet me at our spot in the cemetery in an hour and a half. There's something I need to tell you.

Sylvain Chenet felt good. Anxious to be reunited with Maya, he hurried down the path to the small clearing where they'd first kissed. He wished he'd brought an umbrella.

Why would she want to meet here and now? A real eccentric, my Maya. He caught himself and laughed. *My Maya.* For a guy who'd never rocked the boat back home, he could visualize the firestorm of ugliness that was sure to erupt once his relationship with Maya was revealed. And erupt it would, because this was no passing fancy.

In no time he found that funny little space, full of brush and skinny trees that really did feel like "their spot." He was walking toward the tree where they'd sat when something rustled in the leaves overhead, startling him. Looking up to locate the creature at play, he noticed large, breathtaking magnolias and sucked in his breath. The tree was filled to capacity with puffy white blooms, and he wondered how he could have missed them the first time. He stood for a moment, transfixed by the startling, awesome charm of nature. Minutes later, he turned his gaze earthward and noticed a strange marking etched in the trunk of "their" tree. Bending down to take a look, he shook his head, chuckling. Some young boy had gotten a great kick out of carving a gigantic penis with huge balls. Preoccupied, he failed to hear the light footfall behind him. A couple of large raindrops fell on his cheek and arm just as he turned to face the presence behind him. But it was too late. His face registered a look first of surprise and then shock as the hard, thick wooden cane came down, hitting him squarely against the side of the head. Dusky blood fountained from his ear as he fell to the ground, oblivious to the rain of blows that cracked his skull, granting his spirit the chance to merge with deathlessness once more.

Part Two

9

Valentina Ruiz woke up panicked. The dream, gone now for two years since her mother's death, was back. Lying still for a moment, feeling her sweat-soaked bed sheets, T-shirt, and hair, she inhaled and exhaled in slow rhythm. She could still feel the friction of thick, twisted, prickly rope rubbing her neck raw and red. A warm breeze blew her filmy pale green curtains open, sending clammy chills up her body. *Please don't start up every night again...* She needed to get up out of this bed. Turning to the clock on her bedside table, she jumped up. *Oh shit! The guys are gonna tapdance all over me.*

She ran down the hallway and into the bathroom while pulling the T-shirt over her head, tugging at her panties, and trying to avoid tripping over her feet as she pulled the shower curtain open. She pushed the faucet all the way to hot. As firehose-strength water pressure gushed from above, for just a few seconds she closed her eyes. Her tattoo of the *Santeria* goddess, *Oya*, glistened with the heat and moisture of the enclosed space. It covered her back completely. A strong mix of earth-brown, wine-red, silver-white, and burnished gold, the tattoo represented Cuba's compassionate warrior spirit in all her glory—a spear and red gourd at her side, and atop her head, a crown bearing nine charms: a hoe, a pick, a gourd, a lightning bolt, a scythe, a shovel, a rake, an ax, and a mattock. On her arm, nine copper bracelets shone beautifully, testament to the tattoo artist's special skill.

One of a dozen thoughts speeding through Valentina's mind blinked open her eyes. Peering out around the shower curtain, she took a look at herself in the mirror just above the sink. No, as usual, there were no burning red rings around her throat; just a reflection of the dark, wavy hair she inherited from her Cuban father, the hazel eyes her American mother gave her, and the smooth, golden-vanilla skin their union bequeathed to her.

Of course it's not there. It's never there when you wake up. "Thank God," she said out loud. Ten minutes and a flurry of soap, rinse, wipe, deodorant, and a shake of wet hair later, Valentina was navigating the morning traffic in Miami, trying very hard not to speed. *At least I don't have to worry about what to wear in the morning.*

Walking into the precinct at twenty minutes past seven, the one thing Valentina would have given another hour's sleep for was a strong cup of Cuban *espresso.* At least with coffee, she could better deal with the jive remarks, jabs, and jokes at her expense. *Oh, well.* Being treated like one of the guys was better than the taunts and sneers that so many female cops endured. She was lucky. She had realized from the start that parking her macho nature, and asking for guidance instead would improve her chances for survival on the force. Ten years later, and at a wise thirty-four, Valentina was still treated like a kid sister by most of the officers. It irked her sometimes, but *What the hell,* she also found it amusing. Less than amusing would be Sergeant Muñoz this morning. Lateness bugged him a lot, and here she was, a full twenty minutes into the hour. *Coño.* She was walking as fast as she could when the memory of the dream slammed her, leaving her foggy and fighting panic again. She brought her nail-bitten hand to her throat, closed her eyes, and tried to will away the flash of heat that overtook her body. *Aren't I too fucking young for menopause?* She didn't have time for this, she needed to go about the business of eating shit for breakfast.

The last thing she expected was the smiling face that greeted her when she entered her work station. With alarm, she noticed that everyone seemed to be smiling at her.

"What?" she asked looking around, the thoughts racing through her head crashing and banging against each other like bumper cars. *Relax*, she tried to tell herself, but couldn't. Sergeant Muñoz was standing by her desk with both hands on the sides of his ice cream cone body—thick, pudgy face, neck, arms, middle, and bottom, with legs like a bird's.

"Since you're so damn late, I shouldn't tell you till tomorrow," he said, failing at the intended snarl, "but I'll tell you anyway: You can take off that uniform. You're a detective, Ruiz."

"No way!"

"Believe it."

"Congratulations, Val!" her partner Jimmy called out.

Sergeant Muñoz extended his hand, suffocating hers in a chunky shake, and suddenly a dozen guys' worth of slaps on the shoulders, pats on the head, strangleholds from back of the neck, and high fives stunned Valentina into unusual silence. She stood statue-still, trying viciously not to cry—No, *Jesus, no*—and being insanely happy and, *Yessss!* satisfied.

"All right, all right," Muñoz shouted, "I'm sure you're all gonna miss Ruiz here 'cause she's a good cop, but there's plenty of scumbags out there waiting for you to get your pants on, so let's move it. Ruiz, if you weren't so damn late, I'd tell you to go ahead and change out of your uniform, but a call just came in about a dead body over at Graceland Cemetery, and your partner's already on his way, so—"

"My partner? Who's my partner?"

"Carlson."

"No. Don't say that. Not Kojak."

"He may be a little rough, but he can teach you plenty."

"Well, I guess there's got to be a cloud in every silver lining."

"There you go lookin' at things from the bright side again."

"Sarge, I got a pair of khaki pants and a shirt in my locker. Could I do that?"

"No time. Do it later. You better get over there now."

"Thanks for the recommendation, Sarge. I know I wouldn't have gotten this promotion without your good word."

"You're a good cop. You'll make a good detective. You've got the nose."

"Yeah, I do," she said, smiling. "What car do I use?"

"Ask Dora for a temporary blue and white for today. From now on you'll be riding in the unmarked with Carlson."

Kojak.

Steering out of the precinct parking lot, she headed down 8th Street toward the cemetery, trying not to think about the implications. Detective Harry Carlson had as many names as there are Hollywood cops and action heroes because he *so* loved playing the tough guy. He was like a cartoon, except that cartoons made you laugh, and Carlson didn't. A few minutes later, she turned into the cemetery gates. *Let it go...*This was her first case as a detective, and she'd be damned if she'd let *the Jackal* ruin it for her.

Perfect place to find a dead body, she thought. Following the scent of activity, she soon found herself in a strange, isolated little clearing thick with trees and swarming with officers. Down on the ground was a sight she'd seen too many times before. This time, whoever it was had gone at it with meaning. The back of the poor guy's head was gone, but his face was surprisingly intact. Staring at the remains, a numb feeling of recognition hit her between the eyes. *She knew this man.* A strange sadness overwhelmed her, then disappointment. *His* disappointment. *I can feel what he felt!* Her reaction surprised her. After all these years, she'd grown accustomed to the violence in Miami and in her line of work; hell, violence had certainly touched her own life directly, so she was no stranger to it. Even now she wondered about such people—the ones with all the excuses in the world for the brutal crimes they committed, and the unlimited supply of motives that drove them to desperate acts. She'd seen enough to know that they were often damaged people who couldn't see another way out; but all the same, she felt better when she busted them. She could always sniff out the guilty ones, too—at least ninety-nine percent of the time. She had *the nose*. The trouble was proving they were guilty, and that job had always gone to the detective on the case. But she was the detective now.

Looking away from the lifeless body, Valentina glanced upward for a moment and was struck by the profusion of magnolias in full, splendid bloom above—the dichotomy of the two sights laid bare the best and the worst that the world had to offer. For the thousandth time in her life, she wondered what the deal was with God. The *Orishas* of *Santeria* she understood. They had names, characteristics, functions, likes, dislikes, and specific powers; you served them, they served you. But this God thing, she was still trying to figure out.

A voice deep and low behind her interrupted her thoughts.

"So I hear I got a new partner. Decided to stick with the blue, huh?"

It was Carlson, looking her up and down.

"I fought real hard to keep wearing it, so Muñoz said one more day, but that's it. I'll have to give it back tomorrow; enjoy it while you can. Find anything else here besides the obvious?"

"Just handsome over here, and the weapon."

She cringed inwardly at his cruel choice of words but didn't blink.

"Can I take a look?"

"Sure. I think you'll find it very interesting," he said, trying to hide a sudden laughing fit that burst through his fingers.

The other officers on the scene looked over at Detective Carlson, joining in the yuckfest now spreading like a summer bug.

"Can't wait to see what's so funny," Valentina muttered.

Carlson motioned to one of the officers who were now turning into mirthful tomatoes before her very eyes. "Show Detective Ruiz what this poor sap got whacked with."

"Right away, sir," he gulped.

The officer walked a few steps to a gray canvas sack lying on the ground. With a gloved hand, he pulled out the bloody weapon—a thick, heavy wooden stick carved into the shape of a giant penis with two very large balls.

Valentina hissed in a sharp breath, brows furrowed, aware that her reaction would be fodder for every joke that week. But she didn't care. This wooden phallus she'd seen somewhere before. Maybe not this particular one, but something like it, and she couldn't quite remember where, when, or in what context. Somewhere in the background, like an annoying message announced over loudspeakers at the airport, she could hear Carlson carrying on, milking the moment. Like those times at the airport, she listened with one ear, wanting to make certain not to miss anything important, but her mind was somewhere else, digging, digging, digging for the information buried in her memory.

"The only guy I know whose grave is gonna read, 'Murdered by a random cock.'" The guys were killing themselves laughing, with Carlson as ringleader. In spite of herself, she chuckled inwardly at all these grown men turned grade school boys in the bat of an eye.

"Very, very funny, guys." Turning back to Carlson, she said, "I've met this guy before."

"Oh yeah?"

"Yeah. Jimmy and I answered a B & E call last week. It was at his place," she said, indicating the dead body with a nod of her head. "His roommate walked in just in time to surprise some guy standing over his bed with a knife. He ran after him, but the guy got away through the window and disappeared."

"So it was an attempted murder. What'd you find out?"

"He had no clue why someone would want to hurt him. Figured it was just a burglar who panicked, but I had other thoughts on it."

"Yeah? Like what?"

"Our victim here is Haitian, and—"

"Never would've known it. He's not half as dark-skinned as they usually are."

"They come in all colors, Carlson, just like Cubans, Columbians, Brazilians—"

"Really?"

"But I guess you wouldn't have noticed that."

"I noticed all them immigrants are usually scum, that's what I noticed."

"Muñoz said I could learn a lot from you, *Kojak*. I hope that's not part of the lesson plan."

"No kiddin'? He said that?"

While they talked, Valentina eyed the crew that would take the body back to forensics lab for further examination as they bagged the body of the once handsome young Haitian.

"So as I was saying, the victim here is Haitian, and the guy who took off dropped his knife. It had familiar markings on it, which made me think he might have been Haitian, too. But Mr.—oh, what was his name again?"

"Sylvan Tchanett," Carlson said, mispronouncing the name off a student I.D. card retrieved from the victim's pocket.

"Right! Sylvain Chenet. Seemed like a real nice guy. So, any witnesses? Anyone see anything funny? Got any ideas?"

"Not yet; we didn't find any prints on the murder weapon. But I've got Benson checking things out at the University. Once we know what his story is, we can start talking to his friends, maybe get a lead on why anyone would want the kid dead. Of course, could have been another fuckin' freak weirdo just waiting around to get his rocks off. When we go back, first thing you should do is check the files to see if there's been any recent bludgeonings like this one. Any open cases; maybe even a shut one."

"Carlson, I doubt we're talking some 'freak weirdo' here. I just told you—"

"I say we cover all the bases first, just to rule out anything obvious, got it?"

Inwardly, she rolled her eyes, but held her tongue. *Don't make waves your first day on the job as a detective.*

"What are *you* going to do?" she said in an even tone.

"I'm following a lead on that rich singer broad's husband that got whacked in his car a couple of days ago. Let's meet in my office once you've checked the files and talked to Benson to see what he found out. How's 11:00 sound?"

"Okay with me."

Files my ass, Valentina thought as she walked into her new cubbyhole located outside Carlson's office; it was decorated with a regulation metal gray desk, and a chair that looked to be about a hundred years old. Right now, the only thing on the desk was a phone, and she walked over to it, dialed a number from memory, and plopped herself down.

The place was buzzing with guys on the phone; guys walking around carrying file folders; guys getting coffee; guys staring into computer monitors or stabbing at keyboards; guys talking softly, talking loudly.

After a few rings, the delicate but strong voice of Valentina's grandmother answered the phone.

"*Abuela*, it's me."

"*Hola mi amor, como estas?*"

"English, *Abuela*, remember? You're still trying to learn, right? You can say, 'How are you,' can't you?"

"Of course, I can," she said in her heavy Cuban accent. I can also say, 'Gimme a break.'"

Valentina chuckled. "So, guess what? I made detective today!"

"Congratulations, *mi amor*! I'ng so proud of ju. You been waiteeng long time for dis, no?"

"You bet. I'm very excited. I'm already working on my first case, and I think you can help me."

"Me?"

"Listen, where have I seen a big long wooden stick carved like a man's dick and balls?"

"You trying to shock your *abuela*, Valentina? Or you trying to make me say sometheeng funny and dirty?"

"No, I'm serious."

"You always so serious, of course you serious."

"Never mind about that. Do you know what I'm talking about?"

"Jes."

A thrill shot up Valentina's spine and she started fidgeting in her chair.

"Go ahead, tell me. It's on the tip of my mind; I know it has something to do with the *orisha*, but I can't put my finger on it."

"Well, the Haitians call the *orisha* "*lwa*," but eet same theeng. You ever hear of the *Baron Samedi*? In Haitian *Voodoo* he Spirit of Death. Those Haitians love heem 'cause he so nasty and funny; anyway, that stick you talking about ees the cane he always use."

"That's it! I saw it on an altar over at that place in Little Haiti where you can buy the hens. What does he use the cane for?"

"For walking. For dancing. For poking fun. For make people laugh. He very funny that one."

"Have you been to a ceremony where he came?"

"Only one time. He was the star of the show."

"What's his story beside being nasty and funny with his penis-shaped cane?"

"I no know too much about heem. Let me see. Oh jes! That night when he come, they give him a black suit to wear with a black hat and sunglasses. Also, jes, a purple scarf. I theenk that what he like to wear."

"Anything else?"

"All I know is in Haiti, Spirit of Death ees not bad theeng. He very popular. He like to have party. But I hear you can make deel with heem to take care of bad people in ju life."

"Hmm. Thanks *abuela,* you're great. I knew you could tell me. Listen, I gotta go, but I'll come by and see you on Sunday, okay?"

"Okay, *mija*. You come see you old *abuela*. I make special cake for you."

"You? You mean you'll go buy a fancy cake and say you made it, right?"

She hung up laughing. Hers was the ultimate opposite of a typical Cuban grandmother. Her *abuela* hated to cook. She loved to dress up and go out to eat at fancy restaurants. She wore understated makeup and designer dresses, and she flirted with men of all ages. At the age of seventy-eight, she was still knocking them dead with her sophisticated charm. She hated it that her accent made her sound like a *wetback*, but she was working on it by taking English classes. She payed the tutor bullshit money while plying him with fancy pastries he was convinced she made just for him. Valentina could just imagine Mr. Hansen's face if he could see his student, the lovely Mrs. Ruiz, caught up in the throes of ceremonial trance. People had ideas about the kind of folk who practiced *Santeria* and *Vodou*, but they were so wrong. It wasn't lower class people looking for escapism; it was everyone—whether anyone believed it or not.

That was the part her mother never understood about the Cuban half of her family—that the *Orishas* were part of the landscape; hell, they *were* family. Although most Cubans were church-going, Virgin Mary-lovin' Catholics, their faith reminded her of the saying she'd once heard about Haitians—that they were ninety percent Catholic and one hundred percent *Vodou*. Most would never admit it, of course. And it was true that Cubans prayed fervently to God—the Father and the Son—got on their knees at church on Sundays, made confession, and received communion. But even though they shunned ceremonies and didn't believe in the *Orisha*s of *Santeria*, when the going got rough, they often found themselves turning to "home remedies" from "leaf doctors." So what if the "remedy" called for candle-burning and incense-lighting and an offering or two, and praying to so and so for this and that? That wasn't really *Santeria*. Not really.

Yeah, right.

Valentina thought back to her first days on the force, when she and Jimmy had answered a call at an apartment building in Little Havana. Someone had lodged a complaint about a lingering putrid odor coming from the apartment next door. What they'd found had not been pretty. After breaking the lock on the door, they'd entered the small studio and nearly stumbled on the decomposing body of a man lying amidst the remnants of a full-blown *Santeria* ceremony gone awry. Evidence of objects, altar items and other paraphernalia typically used in many of the religion's rituals were scattered all about, including the bloody remains of sacrificed hens. Jimmy had been nonplussed at the tableaux before him, but Valentina had known immediately whom to call for information about the dead man. Her contacts had eventually led to the resolution of the case, and Sergeant Muñoz had unofficially made her the go-to officer for all religious and ritual-related assignments.

She didn't practice *Santeria* anymore but she sure knew her way around it.

Half an hour later, Valentina knocked on the door of the Bal Harbour apartment where Sylvain Chenet used to live. His roommate Carl Regis opened the door, looking far less like a hero than he had on her previous visit. There was a wild look in his eye. She'd seen it before—that air of shock and disbelief common to relatives and friends of murder victims.

"I'm very sorry about your friend, Mr. Regis. Sylvain seemed like a nice young man."

"He was a better man than I. Come on in, officer," he said, waving her inside. His Haitian accent seemed heavier than when she'd answered the breaking and entering call a few weeks earlier. He pointed to the nondescript, tan-colored couch in the living room.

"Why do you say that?" she asked, sinking into soft cushions. He took the chair opposite her.

"Oh, he was so much more decent than most, you know? He wanted to do things for the environment, for starters! Hell, everyone I know just wants to figure out how they can get their parents to buy them a BMW or something. Sylvain was different; a real serious guy. Humble, you know? But he also had a great sense of humor. Damn, and he was going to need it, too."

"Why is that?"

Sylvain Chenet's heavy-set friend shook his head at something he couldn't quite comprehend. "Because he fell in love recently."

Valentina smiled. "Is that so bad?"

"No, you don't understand," he tried to explain. "He fell in love with a Haitian *peasant*!"

"What exactly do you mean by peasant?"

"Well, you've probably never been to Haiti, so you wouldn't understand," he said, shaking his head again.

"Are you talking about the disparity between the classes there? It's not so different from the way things are throughout Latin America, you know."

"I guess not," he said.

"Except it is more intense in Haiti," she said, surprising him. "The separation doesn't just come from variations in skin tones and economics, right? From what I understand, it's the education gap that really compounds the issue."

"Hey, you seem to know more than most about our country," he said, impressed. "But I'll tell you what, though, it isn't that simple. Those people are different."

"Different from you?"

"Yes."

"In what way?"

"In every way."

"What do you mean?" Valentina pressed, interested.

"They are primitive. It's like they are from the stone ages. They don't think like normal people. It's impossible to treat them like equals. It doesn't work."

"Was Mr. Chenet's girlfriend that way?"

He shifted a little in his chair. "Actually, I only met her once; he spent most of his time at her place, but—"

"What is her name?" Valentina asked, pulling out a pen and notepad.

"Maya," he said in a way that implied distaste.

"Last name?"

"Don't know it."

"So, you were going to tell me what she is like?"

"Well, she grew up here. So it was kind of interesting, really. She's a dancer, apparently—a very good one according to Sylvain. And she spoke fluent French, which was really weird."

"What was?"

"Hearing a peasant speaking in French. They don't know how to in Haiti. They only speak Kreyol."

"Most Haitians don't know how to read and write, I'm told."

"*Haitians* do, it's the *peasants* that don't."

"You're not saying *peasants* as in *farmers*, right?"

"No, it's the word we use in Haiti for people from the masses."

"All right, but in that case aren't the peasants Haitian?" she asked, trying to understand.

"Yes, but..." He looked frustrated. "Look, the thing is that there are two worlds in Haiti—why that is and why it's always been that way, I don't know. But the two worlds just don't mix. And no matter how educated a peasant becomes or what they accomplish, they're still peasants."

"And no matter what, there's nothing they can do to change their social status?"

"No," he said, daring her to judge him for it.

"Okay," she said, shrugging. Then she remembered. "Oh, about *Vodou*. Is it true that everyone practices it in Haiti?"

He shook his head again. "The peasants do."

"No one from your social class?" she said, trying not to sound disbelieving.

"It's obviously what keeps them where they are," he said, ignoring the question. "The whole thing is so ridiculous. If something bad happens, it's because some *lwa* must be upset, so they spend every last penny buying animals and sacrificing them to appease the *lwa*—meanwhile they're starving, you know? Something good happens, same thing. Only this time it's to thank the *lwa*."

"Do you think Mr. Chenet's girlfriend practiced *Vodou*?"

"Who's to say? Probably."

"Because no matter her upbringing, it's still who she is. Roots or something, right?"

"You think I'm one of those *bourgeois* assholes, don't you?"

"Not at all. Just trying to understand how it all works in your society."

"In any case," he said, visibly agitated by the conversation, "what does all this have to do with Sylvain's murder?"

"In light of the fact that there was a previous attempt on Mr. Chenet's life, everyone he knew is a suspect, Mr. Regis. And the knife we found here the other night has *Vodou* markings on it. And if there was a new girlfriend in the picture, then she is definitely of interest to me."

"Well you'd be wasting your time, there," he said, smirking. "Sylvain was the most amazing thing that ever could have happened to this girl. He was her proverbial ticket, if you understand what I mean. There's no way she was *ever* going to kill him."

Riding back to the precinct, Valentina ruminated on her enlightening conversation with Carl Regis. *Complicated people, these Haitians.* Unfortunately, he hadn't been able to give her much help on tracking down the girlfriend. Aside from her first name and vocation as a dancer, the only other thing he could remember was that, early on in the relationship, Sylvain had mentioned having a strange evening with his new flame at a restaurant called The Fish House. That some woman had fainted or something, but not much else. Sylvain's love affair with the dancer had been a sore point between them, Carl had explained. *I tried to stay away from that topic.*

Back at her desk, she found a report from Officer Benson. He had uncovered fairly basic information from the university. Sylvain Chenet was a Haitian on a student visa. Unlike many of his rich peers, whose families paid for American educations so their children could return to take over the family business, Chenet had been studying environmental law. Benson had already obtained telephone numbers from school records, placed calls to the family, and broken the news to them.

It had gone badly, as usual. Shock. Grief. She remembered the older Chenet, the victim's father, from the night she had responded to the B & E call. He had been more upset than his son over the attempt on his life and had almost refused to return to Haiti the following day, as scheduled, for fear of another incident. Valentina could empathize. Her own mother had been murdered two years earlier—a random victim of a violent crime. She pictured her own mother, and wondered at all the violence, the injustice of it. *Or was, in fact, justice? Or something like karma—Stop!* She berated herself for revisiting that mystery for the umpteenth time and getting off track so easily.

In any event, it would be hell on the family for the next few years, and then they would start to get over it. *But your own child? Did anyone really get over that?* The dead man's parents would be here tomorrow to I.D. the body. They would be catching the first available flight out of Haiti.

It was past six o'clock when, eyes blurry from the strain of poring over old crime files, Valentina pushed her chair back. "That's it! That's enough," she said out loud.

She'd felt from the beginning that his murder was connected with the earlier attempt on his life; and, as expected, the search for recent bludgeonings had proven fruitless. She had gone through the tedious process anyway, because it was her first day on the job, and it was best to go along to get along. But she knew that when she had a gut feeling, it was usually right on the money. Carlson had never turned up for their eleven o'clock get-together, and she was feeling pretty hungry now. A good seafood dinner was all she could think about. Seafood and a dinner date with a dead man.

Totally at ease at her table for one, Valentina devoured a bowl of New England clam chowder as she surveyed The Fish House scene. Young people in their early twenties filled the noisy restaurant, chugging back beers at the bar and cracking crab claws at tables covered in white paper. Loud rock 'n' roll music turned any attempt at normal conversation into a shouting match. Even though she was barely through with her soup, Valentina looked up to find her perky waitress delivering the broiled grouper dinner she'd ordered. As she set it down on the table, Valentina tried to make light chit-chat with her, even though she wasn't any good at it.

"This place always this crazy?" she asked, loud enough to be heard above the blaring music.

"Pretty much; this your first time?"

"Guess so."

"How do you like your food so far?"

"Excellent but a little fast. You must have six-armed cooks back there just churning the stuff out, huh?"

The waitress laughed a little too delightedly. "Oh, I wish they were always this fast!" Then, her face turned into a picture of concern, "But hey, I'm really sorry if this is out too soon for you. Would you like me to give you more time with your soup? I'll be happy to take this back and keep it warm for you."

"No, that's okay," Valentina said. Then, doing what she thought was a good facsimile of easing into the subject, she added, "A friend of mine told me it got pretty wild in here about a month ago."

"In what way?" the waitress started to say, but her expression changed from perplexed to one of total recall. "Oh, you probably mean that drama when we all thought that woman was gonna die on us."

"Yeah, that's what I heard."

"Not to freak you out or anything, but it happened right here?"

"You mean my table?"

"Yep, that's right. But I think it turned out okay. My boss was totally panicked, so he made sure to get her phone number to check up on her. You know, lawsuits and all."

"Is your boss here tonight?"

"That's him right over there behind the counter."

"Would you mind asking him to come over to talk with me for a minute?"

The waitress turned suspicious. "Are you that lady's lawyer or something?"

"No, nothing like that, I promise."

"Okay, I'll get him." As she walked away with Valentina's soup bowl, she glanced back nervously. Valentina winked good-naturedly at her while digging into her grouper.

Less than a moment later, a lanky guy in cheap gray slacks, sweat-stained shirt, and a very bad, electric-blond hairpiece barreled toward her, a phony smile plastered on his face.

"Hi, I'm Howard Walker. I understand you have a question about that woman getting sick here a while ago?"

"Would you mind sitting down with me for a minute?"

"Well, what's this about? I'm a busy man here," he said, his oily face glistening.

"My name is Detective Valentina Ruiz, and I am investigating a case. You might might be able to help me with some information."

Extremely nervous now, Howard Walker quickly slid into the seat opposite her.

"I spoke to the woman myself the next day, and she was fine!" he protested. "You mean she's dead now? If she's dead, it had nothing whatsoever to do with us, I can guarantee you that."

"You can stop wringing your hands, Mr. Walker," Valentina said. "The murder I'm investigating is of a man, this man." Reaching into the small, long-strapped leather bag she carried,

Valentina pulled out her victim's driver's license. "Any chance you might recognize him?"

He looked at the license for less than five seconds before replying with alarm, "Of course I recognize him! He was with that girl, the one my waitress swears made that woman get so sick. Said she acted so weird and creepy like she was putting a hex on her, and then boom! Next thing you know, that poor woman is screaming like crazy, like she was in pain or something. Thank God there was a doctor sitting nearby. He took care of getting her to a hospital."

"So there was some kind of exchange with my guy's date and the woman who got sick?"

"If exchange is what you want to call it."

"You say you have a phone number for this woman that got sick?"

"Yeah, like I said before. She sounded a little embarrassed about the whole thing when I talked to her, like she didn't know what got into her to make such a scene. In fact, I was thinking maybe I should call her one more time."

"Well, I'd be much obliged if you'd get me that number."

"Sure thing, detective..."

"Ruiz. And is the waitress from that night working this evening?"

"No, she's off tonight. Want to talk to her, too?"

"Please."

Later that evening, Valentina unlocked the door to her apartment, wrestling the phone numbers out of her bag at the same time. Everything's going too smoothly, she thought with suspicion. *For sure, I'm going to get their answering machines.*

Kicking off her shiny, black regulation shoes and dropping down into her couch, she reached for the phone and dialed the waitress's number with one hand while chewing on the other hand's index fingernail. As she waited for someone to pick up, she glanced around her modest one-bedroom apartment and thought for the twentieth time that it needed a paint job. She was thinking blue. *Replace this shitty green wall-to-wall with a nice blue area rug. Get one of the guys to install a dimmer on that switch so I can stop spending so much money on candles. And maybe I can make some kind of deal with Manolo for that great painting so I can get rid of this stupid poster.*

The welcome sound of a human voice on the other end of the line interrupted her rumination, and she slapped her knee with satisfaction. *No answering machine for once—I'm on a roll.*

"I'm looking for Erica Coten," she said with a firm voice.

"This is Erica," the youngish voice answered.

Bingo!

"Oh, yes," the waitress was happily recounting a few minutes later, "she just stood there looking at that woman for all the world like she wished she was dead. Made her real nervous. And then not more than thirty seconds later, there she was screaming that her insides were burning up. It was way creepy. So was that black lady."

"Thank you for taking the time to talk to me, Miss Coten," Valentina said when she was finally able to interrupt the girl's long-winded blow-by-blow account. "Can I call you again if I have any more questions?"

"Absolutely, detective. Any time."

"Thank you very much. Take it easy, now."

By the end of her second phone call, Valentina decided she had been born to do detective work.

After listening to Penelope Long's whining invective against her enemy for life, the new detective had learned the name of her victim's girlfriend. It was Maya St. Fleur, and Valentina knew exactly how to find her.

The Baron

Let me tell you exactly what went down that night. The cop's recurring nightmare said, *Hello, I'm baaaack!* And Maya? She started dreaming something new and peaceful for once. Get this: you know my distant cousin, the Cuban warrior goddess *Oya*? *Yesss*, the one tattooed on Valentina's back. My girl couldn't see *Oya*'s face, no, no, no. But the nine charms dangling from her crown? Those nine copper bracelets of hers? She could see those real good; and she could hear the tinkling sound they made, like a melody she might remember when she wakes up.

10

The scream that escaped Valentina's throat hurtled against the walls of her bedroom, jarring windowpanes and waking her neighbors. Within minutes they were ringing her doorbell, fearing the worst. Sitting up in bed, still panting from acrid fear mixed with strange relief, Valentina managed to make it to the front door, apologize, thank them for their concern, and reassure them that she was fine, just fine, and that it was just a horrible nightmare.

"That must have been some nightmare," she heard Martina, the schoolteacher with the grieving face, mutter to her husband.

"Yeah, too many more of those and they just put you away," foul-tempered Raoul with the eagle-beaked nose responded loud enough for Valentina to hear.

She feared he just might be right. With the dream or scream or both had come a voice—maybe not a voice, but a message telling her what she needed to do to banish the dream forever.

Tell someone.

Like confession or something? She didn't go to mass, and when she had talked to priests, they had never been the kind you confessed to. *Santeria and Catholicism may share similarities, but not that one, thank goodness.*

Tell someone.

But, who? She'd carried the secret around with her for so long, she couldn't imagine divulging it to anyone in the family. It would wreak too much havoc and precipitate a boatload of drama. And if she told the authorities—hell, she *was* "the authorities"—what would the consequences be for *her*? No, no cops. She didn't know who she would or could talk to about it, but she knew now that once she did, the telling would set her free.

"Carlos DeVilla Modern," Valentina said to the operator. It was 7:30 the next morning, and traces of her rough night hung about her like cobwebs on a lampshade. After a brief delay, a familiar recording came on. *The number you requested, 538-6901, can be automatically dialed for an extr—"*

"I think I still know how to dial a number," she muttered as she jabbed at the numbers on the phone pad, expecting an answering machine. To her surprise, a male voice with an accent she couldn't place answered the line.

Still on a roll, she thought with a smile.

"Hello? Hello?"

"Yes, hello. You caught me off guard. I didn't expect anyone to be in this early."

"Yes?"

"Sorry, this is Detective Valentina Ruiz with the Miami Police Department; may I ask who I'm speaking with?"

"Carlos DeVilla."

"*The* Carlos DeVilla?"

"You know me?"

"No, but the company name is yours, I figure you must be the big gun—in person, no less."

"Who else at this hour?"

"Good point." She liked this guy.

"What can I do for you?"

"I would like to get in touch with a member of your company. I understand she's one of your star dancers. Maya St. Fleur."

She heard an unsuccessfully stifled intake of breath, then nothing.

"Mr. DeVilla?"

"Did she do something wrong?"

"I have no idea. I'll probably just be breaking some bad news, but I do need to talk to her. Can you help me out with a phone number and address?"

"Why don't you just come here to the studio at noon today? We have rehearsals until then. She will be here. Can you tell me what this is about?"

"I'm sorry, I can't, not until I've talked to her."

"All right then, but I am here if you need me. She is like a daughter to me."

"Wouldn't you say that about all your dancers?"

"Perhaps. But Maya is special."

"Thank you, Mr. DeVilla."

At 11:45, Valentina drove up and parked outside of the Carlos DeVilla Dance Studio. She wore a pair of gray, lightweight rayon pleated pants, a black short-sleeved cotton crewneck top, and black platform shoes high enough to be noticed down at the precinct but unremarkable anywhere else. Stepping out of the unmarked, dull burgundy police vehicle, she leaned on the hood, hoping the skies would hold up a while longer before letting loose. The humidity in the air was thick, dank and worrisome for hair like hers, but today it was slicked back and held down with a headband. At age 34, a bad night's sleep shows up the next day a lot more than it used to, and Valentina was no exception to this unfortunate rule of maturation. Faint lines of strain around her eyes confirmed the previous night's episode, and reaching around to the tingle in her lower back, she suddenly remembered. *The message!* Now she wondered if *Oya* might have sent it. Smiling, Valentina gently stroked that part of her tattooed back where a brown and wine-red goddess danced, pleased that her communiqué had been received.

Valentina looked at her watch and decided it was close enough to noon. *I'll be standing here, giving myself a backrub while my girl walks out the back door.* Hastening now, her strides long, she reached for the door and opened it. Across the spacious sunlit studio, her eyes met Carlos DeVilla's and she smiled. He didn't smile back. Nodding seriously and beckoning to her, all in the same movement, he turned toward the rear left of the room and called out Maya's name.

Valentina turned in the direction he called and saw a striking, long-legged dark-skinned stunner with spaghetti dreadlocks. The dancer looked up and around at her teacher, who signaled to her. With senses on high alert now, Valentina noticed that the girl with the licorice body instinctively looked around the room, sensing something amiss. *Just a little nervous, are we?* Seconds later, their eyes met. As the two women walked from opposite sides of the studio toward the imperious Carlos DeVilla, Valentina experienced a strange sensation: familiarity, as if she knew this young woman, though she was sure they'd never met before. And wasn't that recognition she'd seen flicker in Maya St. Fleur's eyes, too? Valentina pushed the thought to the back of her head, intending to revisit it later, and held out her hand to the man she had spoken with earlier that day.

He cut quite a dashing figure, his moist, golden brown skin a perfect complement to wavy black hair, combed back and ending in soft curls at the base of his neck. He wore a black fitted T-shirt, black sweatpants, and a pair of sneakers. She could tell he had perfect, iron-hard thighs. She wished she could get a look at his butt.

"Detective Valentina Ruiz," she said, returning his strong grip, "but then I guess you already figured that out."

Upon hearing the introduction, the young dancer reacted with concern.

"Carlos, is everything okay?"

"And you must be Maya," Valentina said, turning to shake hands with her.

"Yes, I am," Maya said. "How would you know that?"

"Ms. Ruiz called this morning, wondering how she could find you," Carlos explained in his distinctively accented English, which Valentina finally recognized as Brazilian Portuguese. "She is apparently investigating a case and says she needs to talk with you. That's all I know." Turning to Valentina, he said, "Would you care to enlighten us further?"

"What kind of case?" Maya said, alarm (*Or just curiosity?*) alive on her unusual face—a finely boned face with traditional African features and dimples that softened an obviously hard edge.

"Actually, as I mentioned on the phone, I'd like to talk with you alone. Is there a place close by where we could have an iced tea, maybe?"

"Well, I have to be at work in an hour, but yes, we can go to The Korner Kafe. It's just around the block from here. We can walk."

"Perfect."

As they turned to leave, the girl's teacher stepped forward.

"Maya..."

She turned, and seeing the look on his face, the young woman smiled. "Don't worry, Carlos. I haven't done anything wrong. I'll let you know what's up the minute we're done."

As they walked away from him, Valentina asked, "Why should he think you've done something wrong?"

"Because he's always worried I'm up to something funny."

"Are you?"

"No, but those suspicions seem to follow me around. I'm Haitian, you know."

"What does that mean?"

"*Vodou*, of course." She said it lightly, but she wasn't smiling.

"Oh, that," Valentina answered. "Well, I'm half Cuban, so I get that too."

"You don't sound Cuban at all."

"Your accent isn't typically Haitian, either." It had the familiar lilting island cadence but without the odd mix of angular edges and brittle curves she associated with the heavy accent of the ever-growing immigrant population in Miami's Little Haiti.

"I came here young. I think I sound quite American."

"Well, not quite."

Outside now, they walked for a while in silence. When The Korner Kafe was just a few yards away, Maya asked quietly, "So, what's this all about, detective?"

Valentina stopped walking and turned to face the young woman, wishing she didn't have to tell her. Maya stopped, too, looking at Valentina with searching eyes.

"I'd rather tell you when we're sitting down."

All motion stopped, and the humidity felt like thick fog all around them. "Tell me now," she commanded.

"There's been a murder. Sylvain Chenet is dead. We found his body yesterday morning at Graceland Cemetery. He was hit over the head with a blunt instrument."

Intuitive senses on overdrive, Valentina observed Maya St. Fleur's hand shoot up to her mouth in horror. The dancer stumbled backward a couple of steps, her left arm flailing in the air, looking for support. A parked car provided assistance, and she leaned against it with a hard thud, staring down at the ground for a long time without saying anything.

"I'm very sorry," Valentina said.

"How...how can Sylvain be dead?" she heard Maya say softly to herself. "I've only just found him again. It's too soon."

"I'm sorry? What did you say?"

Maya was looking all around her now in a bewildered state, tears streaming slowly down her face.

"He was the sweetest, most wonderful man alive. Are you sure it's him? Are you sure he's dead? Why would anyone want to kill him? I am feeling terribly hot," Maya added.

'Hey, look, why don't we go in and have that iced tea? It's too hot out here. I think a little A/C couldn't hurt."

Valentina took her by the arm and walked her the few remaining steps to the coffee shop. Even though it was lunch-time, the place was practically deserted. Valentina took the first available table and sat down opposite Maya, trying not to stare too intently at the distraught woman. There was something about her that wasn't quite coming together for Valentina. Strangely, she felt drawn to her, could feel her genuine pain. But there was something else. *Later.*

"I do have to tell you that you are not obliged to talk with me if you don't want to. You may prefer to talk with a lawyer before answering any questions."

She seemed to snap out of her distress.

"Should I be worried?" she said harshly. "Am I under suspicion?"

"Right now we're talking to any and all friends and relations. I understand you were his girlfriend?"

"Well, not exactly," she said with a sad smile, staring into space once again.

"Yes?" Valentina prompted.

"I loved him very much. I guess I always have." Suddenly she looked up at Valentina, a lost look on her face. "We made love for the first time just two days ago. For me, it was the first time. I don't know why I should tell you this; it is very unlike me. I'm not known for talking very much about my private affairs. I don't know what it is, but I have this feeling about you. When I saw you at the studio, you seemed familiar somehow, although I'm sure we've never met."

"I had the same feeling."

For a moment, the two women forgot—Valentina about her investigation, and Maya about her lost lover—as they strained to understand the mysterious connection between them that was like a gauzy cocoon of budding camaraderie.

"I can't believe this," Maya said finally, breaking the strange but not uncomfortable silence.

"You said something outside about his death being too soon or something. That you had just found him again. What did you mean by that?"

"I knew Sylvain when we were both very young. When I left Haiti, I didn't get a chance to say goodbye, but I never forgot him. He was so kind and respectful and smart. I always hoped I'd see him again, and four or five weeks ago, we ran into each other at the school."

"You mean the university?"

"Yes. It was a chance meeting. He was equally happy to see me. It all developed very fast. You could say we both became infatuated." She stopped, a sob clogging her words, and dropped her head in her hands, lost in something close to despair.

"Did you speak to him on Monday?" Valentina asked softly, all the while sensing something amiss.

"Yes. We made a date to meet at the cemetery, but—"

"Why the cemetery?"

"I know it sounds funny, but I discovered this wonderful little area that is so peaceful and pretty that it comforted me to be there. I had shown it to him, and he liked it too."

"Okay," Valentina said, her eyes locked on Maya's face, her body, her gestures.

"So, we were supposed to meet there, but I had had a really long, exhausting day, and thinking I had some time, I lay down for a fifteen-minute nap. I woke up an hour and a half later. I knew it would be useless to go there; I didn't think he would wait that long, so I called his place and left a message, but I never heard back. I'd only been to his apartment once, and I did not feel comfortable with his roommate, so I didn't know who to call or what to do. I've been going crazy with worry since then, imagining the worst, of course. You know, I make love with him one day and he disappears the next. I guess I wasn't imagining the worst after all.

Valentina's head was buzzing, her mind filled with questions she could not ask. It seemed the woman sitting across from her was telling the truth. But there was something else. Something that nudged her and poked at her, trying to get her to recall something. *But what?*

Is there any chance I might be able to see him one last time?" Maya said after a pause.

"Um, I don't see why not," Valentina said.

"Today's the busiest day at the bookstore—that's where I work."

"Which one?"

"Mysterious Light."

"Okay."

"I'll have to go for at least a couple of hours, but I'll tell them I have to leave early. Where do I need to go?"

"The city morgue."

"Oh my God," she whispered, raising her hand up to massage her forehead as if she were developing a headache. "Where is it?"

Valentina wrote down the address on a napkin, and stood to leave.

"See you between 2:30 and 3:00?"

Maya nodded *yes*, eyes focused on her glass of iced tea.

"All right, then. I'm very sorry about your friend," Valentina said, starting to walk away. But the sound of a harsh laugh from Maya stopped her, and she turned around.

"Do you think I had something to do with Sylvain's death?"

Valentina knew she was reading her thoughts. She looked back at Maya's defiant stare, damned if she would let it unnerve her.

"Until we find the killer, everybody is a suspect."

"I suppose that's fair."

"Can anyone confirm that you were in your apartment asleep when the crime occurred?" Valentina asked.

"An alibi? Is that what you're looking for? Then no, I was alone."

Valentina shrugged her shoulders, turned and walked out of the coffee shop.

"And just where the fuck have you been all morning?"

Carlson was standing at Valentina's desk, wearing his usual tacky polyester pants and white shirt with the short sleeves that reached his elbows. Carlson struck her as a study in self-parody. The funny part was, he wasn't a bad looking guy. Fit because he lifted weights, his body could have turned a head or two—if only he didn't shop for clothes at Bargain Fair; and his thick, wavy dark brown hair was the envy of the balding, middle-aged guys on the force. But she wondered if it was motor oil he washed it with, since the repulsive sheen on his face made her want to look away.

"Following up on a lead," she answered. "And why the language?"

"Whatsamatter, can't handle tough talk, missy?"

"Only when it's appropriate, know what I mean? Like I could see asking, 'Where the fuck have *you* been?'" You asked me to meet you back here at 11:00 yesterday morning, and this is the first I'm laying eyes on your gorgeous mug since then."

"So *you're* giving me the third degree, now?" Carlson said, raising his voice to include other people in the room. "Her first day, and she wants daddy to punch a time clock." A couple of guys stopped what they were doing and looked up, always interested in a scene if it involved *Baretta*, ace police detective and caricature in the flesh.

"Daddy?"

"That's right. Why don't you tell daddy all about what you've been up to on your first day as a big, brave girl detective?"

Valentina looked around the room and addressed the growing crowd. "Why don't you all get back to work? Believe me, there's nothing interesting happening here unless you consider Rambo trying to figure his gun butt from his own butt 'interesting.'" She turned to Carlson, "I'll be happy to talk in your office. You let me know when you're ready."

As she walked toward her desk, he stood in her way. She silently dared him not to move. "Get your ass in here right now," he said, grinning; and turning, he walked into his office.

She followed him in, breathing deeply to keep her composure. "Now, was that really necessary, Carlson?"

"Lemme tell you something, Ruiz, all those pansies you been workin' with may think you're the cutest thing since their kid sisters, but you're working with me now."

"Bingo. The key word here is with you, not for you. Can you just give it a break? What is your problem, anyhow? What's with the act? Don't you get tired of playing the clown sometimes, Carlson? It's okay to drop the performance once in a while and just be a good cop, which is what they say you are."

Surprise registered on Carlson's face, and then his expression lost its edge. "Listen Ruiz," he said, dropping the edge along with the volume, "the thing is I like to work alone, and, straight up, I'm not in the mood to train a new rookie. My plate is full, this case I'm working on is a bitch and I got my own problems, all right?"

"Fine with me, Carlson. Just don't take it out on me, okay?"

"So you been following a lead," he said, moving on, "why don't you tell me what that means?"

"I tracked down the victim's girlfriend and talked with her just now."

"Did you read her her rights?"

"No."

"No?" he said. "You interviewed a murder suspect without reading her her rights? Excellent job, Ruiz. What else did you do, tell her what the murder weapon was? Jesus Christ. This is what I'm talking about."

"I did tell her that she might want to consult a lawyer before answering any questions, and she volunteered to talk after that; got any problem with that?"

"Smart-ass rookies," he spat at no one. "Hey, that's a great name for you!" he said laughing. "Rookie Ruiz. You don't mind, do you?" Seeing the look on her face, he added, "Hey, you can lighten up a little too, right? So what else did you get?"

Fighting to remain calm, Valentina recounted her visit to the restaurant, her conversations with the waitress and magazine writer, and her call on Maya St. Fleur. She did not tell him about the conversation with her grandmother.

"And what do *you* know about this case since we last saw each other?"

Carlson's eyes shifted away from Valentina's for a half second. She noticed it and filed it away.

"I've been busy on this other case..."

"Yeah, the rich singer broad—"

"Hey!"

"Hey, yourself. That's what you called her."

"Fuck that. In any case, she's all busted up. It took practically all day to get any sense out of her. Sent me on a wild goose chase...fuck me if I can make anything outta that mess, but I'm still working on one or two leads."

"Well, I'm happy to take the lead on this one since you're so busy."

"Fine. Just make sure I know what you're doing."

"There's a note on my desk that the victim's parents are going to be at the morgue for I.D. in an hour," Valentina said. "Maya, the girlfriend, is supposed to meet me there in two hours, so I'll just take care of it, unless you want to." She knew dealing with grieving parents and girlfriends was the last thing he would choose to do.

"That's rookie shit. Perfect for you, Rookie Ruiz." He smiled, waiting for her to agree that his little joke was funny as hell.

She blew him a kiss and left his office without saying another word.

Great. If I don't fall in line with the bullshit, I'm the one with no sense of humor. This is the shit that makes me wonder about you, God. Assholes like Carlson.

Walking down the long, dark corridor to greet Sylvain Chenet's parents, Valentina prepared mentally for the coming ordeal. The despondency of bereaved family members often hung about her like ghosts. Shaking it off meant a requisite run on the beach, then a cold shower, followed by an aggressive toweling to rub her body back to life. She doubted she'd have time for all that later so she'd sent a silent prayer to *Oya*, asking for an invisible armor to keep the family's blues at bay.

Here we go.

Pushing open the door to the anteroom, Valentina was met with a middle-aged, well-to-do Haitian couple. Prepared though she was, the detective was struck by their air of utter misery, which lay about them in a broken heap for all the world to see. The strong, handsome, vibrant man she remembered from their last encounter had morphed into the epitome of defeat, with stooped shoulders, chin hanging low, looking like a giant question mark with features masked by hopelessness. The fair-complexioned woman with him wore expensive black silk pants, a white tunic top and a white scarf over coiffed black hair. She sat in a chair, looking down at the floor, shaking like a junkie in need of a fix. Alarmed, Valentina advanced, wondering how this man, even in his sorry condition, could ignore his wife's distress.

"Ma'am, are you all right?" she asked, kneeling in front of Mrs. Chenet. "Should I call you a doctor?"

"Oh, I will be all right. It is just so cold in here," she stammered in a Frenchified Haitian accent.

"The air conditioner's been broken for a week, ma'am. It's 80 degrees in this room." Turning to Mr. Chenet, Valentina said, "I'm no doctor, but your wife seems to be in serious trouble here. Maybe I should call an ambulance?"

"No, she gets like this when she is nervous. I don't think she should come in to see the body. I'm sure I won't be too long, right? I'll take her right back to the hotel. Don't you have your pills with you?" he said, turning to his wife.

"Y-yes."

"Well then take them for God's sake! What are you waiting for? Can you get her a glass of water?" he asked Valentina.

"Yes, of course."

As Valentina turned to leave, she heard the tears in Mrs. Chenet's words as she pleaded with her husband in French. She heard him utter what was probably an apology in a rough whisper.

Boy oh boy.

Valentina was back in a flash with water, and soon she and Mr. Chenet were walking down the long, gray hallway, turning left to the cold room where the recently deceased lay in narrow cylindrical drawers, waiting for loved ones to take their last look at the person they would never speak with, laugh with, fight with, or touch again. Entering the room, Valentina motioned to the attendant—a slight young man with skin as gray and sallow as this place, his home away from home.

"Sylvain Chenet," she said, trying not to hear the tortured sound that escaped Mr. Chenet's lips.

Turning, she touched him on the arm, motioning for him to follow the attendant. She steeled herself for the inevitable. Right about this time was when any last remaining hope got dashed to hell on the morgue's cold tile floors—the possibility that there might be some mistake, that the corpse waiting to be identified could be some thief carrying the deceased's wallet. That rarely happened, though, and this time would be no different, no matter how much Henri Chenet prayed for it to be so.

Standing side by side with the victim's father, Valentina deplored the grating, obnoxious sound of the drawer as it opened to reveal the pale, marble-still body of the man he once called "son."

The father sounded like he was being strangled. "Half his head is gone!"

"Yes, that's why you need to look carefully for any identifying marks so that we can be sure," Valentina explained in a voice that tried to be authoritative and comforting at the same time.

Mr. Chenet had turned his face away from the body, and with closed eyes, forced it back. After taking a moment, he opened his eyes, and bringing a tight fist to his mouth, bit down on his thumb until he drew blood.

"Mr. Chenet," Valentina spoke softly, motioning for the attendant to get a tissue, "it is best if you try to stay strong right now."

"*Oh, really?*" he screamed at her, "*And why should I?*"

Mr. Chenet turned his attention back to the body, and after a careful, minutes-long examination, he spoke in a frozen voice, "Sylvain was born with that birthmark right there just under his neck. He cut himself with a knife on his left thumb when he was six. That cut required stitches—you can see them here. Over here on his thigh are the stitches he had to get when flying glass from a car window cut him very deeply. That was the accident that killed his sister. He was only eleven then."

Valentina sucked in her breath. "I'm very sorry, sir."

"Are we done here?"

"Yes, but we will need to discuss arrangements for the body. If you'll come with me, we can use this office," she said as she led him out of the room and motioned to an open door. The morgue attendant followed, then stood by waiting to take notes. Valentina offered the victim's father a chair and sat across from him at the bare desk. Before she could speak, Mr. Chenet interrupted.

"What have you done to catch the person who did this to my son?"

"I am the investigating detective on the case, Mr. Chenet, and the killing took place just a day or so ago. Right now we're following every possible lead. Your son had few friends, so it is slow going. There were no fingerprints on the weapon we found, but we've only just started."

"I want to offer a reward," he said, his eyes hard. "I want this person caught."

"Yes, sir. And how much would you like to offer?"

"Twenty thousand dollars."

"That's a lot of money. Are you sure you wouldn't prefer to wait a week or so to see if we turn up anything first?"

"My son was the kindest, gentlest boy that ever lived, I am sure he had no enemies. I would guess this was a random killing by some crazy person. I can't let him get away with this. Maybe someone saw something, who knows?"

"That's fine, sir. I'll call the local TV stations right away so that, hopefully, it will make tonight's news."

"Thank you."

After making arrangements to have the body sent back to Haiti, Mr. Chenet stood up, more stooped over than when he arrived, and walked slowly down the hall, refusing her offer to accompany him out. She followed him with her eyes; then, on a whim, quietly walked down the hall anyway to look into the anteroom through the window of the swinging doors. Standing there, she could see him slumped into one of the chairs, bent over at the waist, sobbing uncontrollably. His wife, whose shaking was as bad as ever, tried to comfort him while asking questions in a low voice that only annoyed him as he tried to shake her hand off his shoulder. Just at that moment, the outer door opened and Maya walked in. For no earthly reason, Valentina's heart jumped. From her unseen vantage point, she watched the girl's reaction. Standing stock still, a long, black silhouette in gray surroundings, she stared intently at the couple who, drowning in the drama of the moment, ignored her presence altogether. For what seemed like ages, Maya stood transfixed, eyes locked on Mr. Chenet, as if his wife did not exist. Glancing back and forth between the broken man and dancer, Valentina at last saw Maya's face relax, a slight but unmistakable smile on her lips.

II

Startling Maya out of her trance-like state, Valentina pushed open the swinging doors and beckoned her in. Although Mr. Chenet looked up momentarily, his wife never even noticed the lithe young woman who glided past them, disappearing into the dark hallway beyond.

The Baron

Now, look at that. Neither one of the two grieving mulattos has the slightest idea that their roadtrip and my girl's head trip just collided with one another. Ouch! That's the way it is, baby. You go along minding your own business, and somewhere else, another human's business is getting ready to mess with your groove. All the while, the world keeps spinning 'round like a crazy ball, with folks meeting up with me at the cemetery, and others starting the adjustment to the light of day. That's the way it is, darlin'. Nothing you can do about it. No, no, no.

"How is it that you know them but they don't know you?" Valentina queried as she guided Maya down the hall.

"How long were you standing there?" Maya countered, somewhat taken aback.

"I usually prefer answers to my questions. Let's just say it was long enough."

By then they'd reached the office, and Valentina pointed to the chair occupied by Henri Chenet just minutes before. She closed the door before taking a seat opposite this strange young woman, who fascinated her for some unfathomable reason.

"Want to tell me all about it?" Valentina asked. As the girl started to speak, Carlson's face rose up before her, and Detective Ruiz held her hand up to stop her. "Wait one minute. I need to tell you that for lack of other plausible suspects, you *are* under suspicion, and I'll say it again, you don't have to answer any questions. You're not being charged with anything at this time, but you may want to consult a lawyer before talking to me."

"I don't know any lawyers," Maya said.

"Want to take some time to look around?"

Maya thought about that for a moment. Feeling like a lioness about to pounce on an unsuspecting gazelle, Valentina willed herself to uncoil, though her hands remained clenched in her lap as she waited. After a long, silent moment, Maya spoke, first with hesitation, then with conviction.

"I may be wrong, but for some reason it feels all right to talk to you—without lawyers. I can get one, you know. My mother has the means to pay for a very good lawyer, I'm sure. But I have nothing to hide. I'll tell you the truth, whatever you want to know, because I sense that with you, it's okay. Call me crazy, but I usually do pretty well on instinct. Besides, who needs that kind of expense?"

"You don't know me, but you're right. I'm not going to jerk you around and play the kind of cop games you see in movies. And there *is* some kind of strange *déja vu* thing going on here between us, but I can't figure out what it is—it's something just within reach, but I keep losing it. Like I met you in a dream I might have had but can't remember." Then she added wryly, "And with the kind of dreams I have, we probably didn't meet under pleasant circumstances."

"You have bad dreams, too?"

"You say that like you own the rights."

"I wouldn't call mine dreams, and 'nightmare' seems too tame."

"Maybe I'm a character in one of your nightmares come to life. Here I am investigating a murder you could have committed, right?"

Maya chuckled, then turned serious again.

"Oh, I'd recognize you if you were in one of mine. Unfortunately, they are too vivid for me to forget. In fact, most of my nightmares include Mr. Chenet. No, they don't just include him; he's always the star of the show."

"Go on," Valentina prompted.

"I find it very odd that I should actually *want to* tell you about this because I've never talked about it with anyone. It's always been my own private hell."

With those words, which so described her own personal experience, Valentina shifted in her seat, anxious to hear what Maya had to say.

"I have hated Mr. Chenet all my life. Outside, just now, was the first time I've laid eyes on him since I was twelve years old. But seeing him in that miserable state—and this is going to sound very cold—actually gave me pleasure, even though his pain is the same as mine. I'd like to apologize for feeling that way, but I can't." At this, her face turned hazy and distracted, and she spoke as if to herself. "Back when I was a child and living in Haiti, my mother was the Chenet family's maid; and that asshole's sex slave," she motioned with her head toward the outer door.

Valentina nodded understanding, and waited.

"I was the tag-along help because I made a good audience for him while he molested my mother. He made me watch, to cheer him on, otherwise I would get slapped around. He had other plans for me, too, some kind of three-way scene he hadn't put into motion quite yet, but something happened."

Valentina inhaled deeply, focusing even harder on the dancer's every move and every expression.

"I'm also good with plants and flowers," Maya continued. "Sylvain was interested in the environment, and growing things, so we used to have long conversations together. After a time, something began to develop between him and me. I could feel that he liked me. I liked him too; he respected me, and that's a rare thing coming from someone in his class. When his father noticed our *tête-à-têtes*, the thought that his son might consider me an equal disturbed him. He was so afraid it might lead to something more that he blackmailed my mother into sending me away. It was just as well, since his sexual interest in me was growing with each Thursday afternoon episode."

"What do you mean by Thursday afternoon episodes?"

"He raped my mother every Thursday. It was a standing 'date' he never missed."

"How long did this go on before you left?"

"Over a year."

Valentina's jaw tensed. "I'm very sorry. So, your mother was the Chenet's housekeeper? By Haitian standards, was your family very poor?" Valentina asked, trying to get the story straight.

"Extremely poor. Even by Haitian standards."

"Then how could your mother afford to get you an expensive lawyer?" she questioned.

"Oh, not that mother. My other mother, here in Miami."

"You have two mothers?"

"The one who gave birth to me died in Haiti recently—her name was Jizzeline St. Fleur. The one who took care of me when I first arrived here is called *Madame* Mirta. I've always considered her my real mother.

"Okay, I get it. Let's get back to Mr. Chenet."

"He told my mother that if she didn't send me away, he would tell the police that she had stolen things from his house, which meant hard time in jail for who knows how long—there's no real justice in Haiti. It's more a system of whims. And he also offered her money, a lot of money. So it was decided that I should go. I had no say in the matter." She stopped for a minute, her eyes hardening as she looked directly into Valentina's eyes. "I came here by boat."

"Whoa! If he offered her so much money, why didn't they put you on a plane?"

"Because he chose the mode of transport. I guess he was too chicken to have me killed so he was hoping I wouldn't make it...most people don't. No one else on that boat did."

"Jesus Christ."

"No, there was no Christ involved here, just fear and greed. His fear and my parents' greed," she said, spitting out a bitter laugh. To Valentina's ear it sounded like a brittle stick of wood snapped in half.

"But your parents had no choice."

"Didn't they? I'm sorry, although I understand it logically, my heart still resents them for it. That's just how it is."

Valentina waited.

"My mother—*Madame* Mirta that is—she is a very good person and she's also very wise. She saw the damage in me early on, but smart as she is, kind as she is, and powerful as she is—she's a high priestess of *Vodou,*" Maya added, stopping to see the effect of her words. When Valentina failed to react, she continued. "Even she couldn't rid me of the hate I've carried around for so long. She once set up a cleansing ceremony for me when I was fourteen-years-old. Everything was arranged—herbal preparations, several attendants paid for and ready to assist, the works. I decided not to show up. I've grown used to this feeling—bitterness toward my parents and anger and hatred toward that bastard. It's part of me. I guess it's true what they say about familiarity and contempt; I became accustomed to it. But there was nothing I could do about it. There he was across the ocean, in Haiti. All I could do was continue to despise him. I paid for it with recurring nightmares, I think, but it felt good to hate him. Then I walk in here today and find him grief-stricken, beside himself with despair. What can I tell you? I liked seeing him that way. I hope he never gets over it."

Maya's eyes flashed an icy fury that filled the room, suddenly making it hard for Valentina to sit still. Standing up, she shook her head to ward off the sudden coldness in the air.

"That's an intense story," she said, rubbing her neck and looking at Maya.

"That's what people say about me. Intense. Can I see Sylvain now?"

Seizing the opportunity to observe Maya under this most telling situation, Valentina walked over to the door and, opening it, she motioned for the girl to follow. Preoccupied with the story she'd just heard, Valentina led Maya to Sylvain's still body in silence. *It's possible the poor kid got killed by some random fuckhead. I can see a motive for killing Henri Chenet, but not the boy. Still, something's missing in this picture; I don't know what it could be, but there's something else. Maybe it has nothing to do with the murder at all. Maybe I'm just interested in her as a character study. The similarity to my own fucked-up history is so weird.*

The same gray-skinned attendant, who now seemed another shade grayer to Valentina, pulled open the drawer, which held Sylvain Chenet's body. This time, the sound of the drawer opening reminded her of steel on broken rocks, and it annoyed her acutely. But the small cry that escaped Maya's lips pierced right through her. In the time it took to turn sideways, her suspect's body had crumpled to the floor in a dead faint, a look of utter sadness rearranging her features, a teardrop huddled at the corner of her left eye.

Later, when Maya had recovered, Valentina walked her down the hallway, past the now empty anteroom and outside into the harsh brightness of the day's sun. Maya's blue, eight-year-old Honda civic was parked in the building's lot, the dull finish matching its owner's countenance. Maya stepped into the car and strapped herself in.

"I have to ask you not to leave town."

"I wasn't planning on going anywhere," Maya said in a numbed voice, and turning the key in the ignition, she started her motor, "Hey, maybe you can tell me about *your* dreams sometime," she said.

Tell someone.

Feeling an itch, Valentina reached around with her right hand to scratch at a spot on her back. "Maybe I will," she said.

The Baron

Maya goes home and spends hours looking into the mirror. No shit, she is devastated, baby. Somebody, please, please, please explain this to me! The thing she's been wanting for years has *fiiiiiinally* happened. The boy is dead but she's feeling dead inside—which is fine where I live, but not so fine if you're still alive, ow, ow, ow! She's stopped having nightmares about Henri Chenet and his son and her grimy boat trip—yet, she is devastated. Humans.

A couple of days later, Anthony Partridge turned up at Valentina's desk and sat down opposite her before she had a chance to notice him arrive. He had a way of doing that. That's why he was so good at his job. Just like a phantom. One minute, there he'd be, hanging out, talking with the guys, joking, making bets about some nonsense; next thing you knew, he was gone. Vanished. Real smooth. His face could jump from open book to steel vault faster than the time it takes to plunge a bright room into darkness with the flick of a switch. He liked to joke that he was the only gringo on the force—*I got blond hair don't I?* That wasn't true, but plainly, Cubans represented the majority.

"Want to hear what I got?" he asked her without saying hello. "It's not much, but who knows?"

Valentina had asked Anthony to tail Maya St. Fleur for two days and to report back to her. In the meantime, she'd thought it through fifty times. *She was Sylvain Chenet's girl, and passion is definitely a potent force in her life. But crime of passion? Somehow I feel she's telling the truth. Still, she's odd. And there's that* Vodou *connection with the murder weapon. So why do I feel badly about having her followed? She's just a stranger to me. And I'm a cop!*

But Valentina couldn't ignore the other train of thought. *Why do I feel like I want to spill my guts to this girl when I don't even know her? I bet this is exactly what an amnesiac feels like after running into an old friend. She feels like someone I know that I can't quite remember. And she's just as baffled as I over the pull that's drawing us toward each other. Weird. But I can't let it affect my work on this case. I have to follow this through.*

"Tell me," she said now to Anthony Partridge.

"It's like she told you, she works in that bookstore. And we might have gotten lucky, because in the last two days she had a visitor. Black guy. Could be her brother for all I know, but he came by, talked to her for a few minutes, and left. Looked like he was pissed off about something. I followed him. Here's his address. Maybe you want to ask him some questions."

Without taking her eyes off him, Valentina reached over and took the piece of paper he handed her.

"She went home after work. Nothing much there except that she stopped at some guy's apartment before going up to hers. Looked like some freak—you know, like those kids who wear white makeup on their faces and dress like vampires?"

"Yeah, I've seen them. She has a friend like that?"

"Seems that way. I checked his name on the mailbox. Colin Gardner, apartment 1A."

Valentina jotted down the information while Partridge talked.

"Next day, she went to that dance school and came out of there sweating. She went back home—to take a shower I guess, then she went to the bookstore again. So I went back to her place and took a look around."

"What do you mean, Anthony?"

"I mean that I knew she'd be gone a while..."

"So you broke in?"

He smiled sideways. "Well, I wouldn't put it that way if I was you. Doesn't sound so nice, you know?"

Valentina started to sweat.

"Do you do this often? Does the top brass know? You could get in a shitload of trouble over something like this."

"Relax. Nobody saw me. Hey, they don't call me *the shade* for nothin'." He sat back, pleased with himself.

"Oh, is that what they call you?" she said, playing ignorant.

"So you wanna know what I saw up there or not?" Now he looked positively mischievous.

"Uh, no, Anthony, I don't think so. I think I'd like you to walk away from this desk without telling me what you found up there. The way you look, it better be good!"

"You wanna know what I found?" He leaned over the desk to whisper. "Voodoo, lady, Voodoo." He sat back to see the effect of his words.

None too surprised, Valentina prompted him, annoyed. "Yeah, so?"

"She has this whole setup behind her front door, otherwise the place is like any chick's. It's almost like six or seven bookshelves, but I can't say I saw any books on them. All kinds of creepy, weird shit, like cigars and a black hat and hair and strange-looking plants and black feathers and little bottles with oils in 'em, and drawings. Yeah, that was it. It stood out from everything else; some kind of sketch of a guy. I don't know anything about this kind of crap, but I would say she was workin' some hex on the guy in that picture. You know, like some kind of curse."

Valentina shivered despite the 80-degree temperature in the room.

"What makes you think that?"

"I don't know. Like I said, I don't know anything about this stuff."

"Would you recognize the face in that sketch if you saw it again?"

"Absolutely. Not forgetting is what I do best."

His ego was starting to get on her nerves, but she decided to ignore it. She was too intent on retrieving the contents of Sylvain Chenet's pockets. Jamming her hand into the yellow legal size envelope, her fingers found the hard plastic of his driver's license and she fished it out. Holding her breath, she handed it to Partridge, who looked at it for half a second and returned it to her.

"Nope. Too young. This was the guy that got whacked, right?"

Valentina nodded.

"The guy in the sketch was old."

An audible sigh of relief escaped from Valentina before she had a chance to stifle it.

"Why does that make you happy?"

"Never mind," she snapped.

It was ten o'clock the next morning when Valentina knocked on Colin Gardner's door, wondering what she might find out. She felt ragged and worn out from her sleepless night of dissecting, analyzing, and assembling the bits and pieces of information at hand. Her brain hurt. And then this morning, just before waking, she'd dreamed again of her mother. Her hand shot up to her throat, and she listlessly rubbed the imaginary burn marks. She was stroking her neck, remembering, when the door opened and a tall, lean, frighteningly pale young man with straight black hair and red-rimmed eyes stood there, surveying her. Suddenly she felt conscious of the sloppy sweatshirt she'd thrown on over her navy linen pants. It was a bad-hair day worthy of a hat, but she'd chosen a bandanna instead. She regretted the choice, certain that it only accentuated the effects of her haggard night. She felt her jaw lock up tight, her teeth grinding away at each other.

"And who might you be?" the young man asked with an inflection that made her wonder if he was gay.

"Detective Ruiz. Remember I called you yesterday? You said ten was fine?"

"Oh, yeah. But that was yesterday. I totally forgot."

"Uh, do you think I could come in for a minute anyway?" Valentina said.

"I guess so. I'm too curious, anyway."

He ushered her into what felt like a black cave. Except for a series of strange drawings on white paper taped to every wall in the place, and this kid's face, everything was black. She thought she could smell marijuana in the air.

"Have a seat," he offered, pointing to the black couch, taking a black chair opposite her. "What can the likes of me tell you about the likes of Maya? And why do you want to know?"

"Maya is under suspicion of murder," Valentina said, coming right to the point.

"Murder," he responded, seemingly unaffected but obviously interested. "Murder of whom?"

"A man named Sylvain Chenet. You didn't know? It happened four days ago. Aren't you friends?"

"I thought so. And how would you know about us being friends, by the way?" he asked, switching subjects.

"I'm a detective, it's what I do. So you were saying about being friends?"

"Well, she hasn't been returning my calls lately. Been too busy with her new boyfriend, I suppose. But if he got killed four days ago, it makes even more sense that I haven't heard from her."

"Why? I would think she would need support just now."

"Then you don't know Maya very well. When bad things happen to her, she withdraws completely."

"Can you tell me anything you know about her relationship with him?"

He furrowed his brow for a moment. "She liked him, as far as I know. Actually, she probably loved him—I could tell." When he said this, Valentina thought she detected a brief flash of anger. *Jealousy?* "But it would be so unlike Maya to actually open up and show it. That's our girl, though. Comes packaged that way."

"Why do you think that is?"

"What do you know about her?"

"Only what she's told me. That she came over here on one of those leaky boats from Haiti, and that she blames Sylvain Chenet's father for her ordeal."

The young man stared at her without saying a word.

"Mr. Gardner?"

His eyes came back to life a bit more troubled.

"You know more than I do, detective. I never knew anything about this guy's father. And a few weeks ago, when we talked about her first date with him, she never mentioned anything other than having had a nice evening with this Sylvain person and how it would always be a platonic thing because of all that social class blather down there in Haiti. Afterward, when it was obvious that they were anything but platonic, she just clammed up, kind of like a snake digesting the giant rat."

"Whoa! That's a pretty grisly picture you just drew. Do I sense some resentment here?"

"You think it's grisly? I rather like it, too."

Alrighty, then.

"But as for resentment?" he continued. "None whatsoever." He stared through her, making her feel uncomfortable.

"Did you ever meet Sylvain?"

"Yes, the night he came to her place for dinner. He seemed horrid enough."

"Horrid? I've only heard good things about him until now."

"Oh yes, well, horrid is a compliment in my book."

"Really? Why is that?"

"I write and draw horror comics, so what's wonderful to most is horrid to me; and nice is well, so bland, so vanilla ice cream."

"Okay," Valentina laughed, rather relieved, "I gotcha. Can we get back to Maya and Sylvain for a minute?"

"Certainly."

"You seemed surprised about Sylvain's father's influence in Maya's life."

"She never told me about him. Maya's got her secrets, and she works hard at keeping them to herself."

Again she sensed anger.

"Is there any reason you can think of that she would want to kill Sylvain Chenet?"

Colin Gardner's face cracked a hideous smile, his eyes cutting through Valentina's, making her feel nervous again.

"It seems to me, Detective Ruiz, that figuring that out would be your job, but if you ask me, I would say first off that Maya might be mysterious and moody and keep to herself more than most, but she's too powerful to have to resort to murder. She can too easily bend people to her way of thinking."

"I think I know what you mean."

"Really? Then you must have spent some time together already."

"Yes," Valentina admitted, her eyes shifting away from Colin's steady stare and down to the floor.

"Uh-huh. And secondly, if I were trying to come up with a reason why Maya might murder this guy, I would say—and I do have to admit I have a warped mind—the number one motive would be to get back at his father. You know fathers and how they love their sons and all that drivel."

"You think?"

"I know, it's farfetched, but wouldn't it make a terrifically ghastly and ugly story for one of my comic books? Excuse me while I jot that down."

He bent over a stray piece of paper and scribbled some notes. "How did you and Maya come to be friends?" she asked him when he finished scribbling.

"Oh, I'm the one who found her on Miami Beach."

It was Valentina's turn to stare. Colin stared back, satisfied at the reaction.

As she looked at him, a thought occurred to her and she asked, "May I ask where you were on the night of Thursday the 18th?"

He raised his eyebrows at the implication. "Here in my apartment, drawing."

"Can anyone confirm that for me?"

"If you ask Simon, our building manager, I guarantee he'll be able to help you. He watches my every move."

"Oh?"

"He likes me," the creepy comic book artist deadpanned.

A few moments later, he walked her to the door. As she started thanking him for his time, he cut her off. "Hey, if you had to choose between having a root canal in every one of your teeth every day until they were all gutted and crowned, or having each and every one of your teeth pulled out and replaced with new fake ones, what would you choose?"

She looked at him, horrified.

"I'd rather die," Valentina said, before walking away.

"But that's not an option!" she heard him insist as she stepped through the lobby's front door.

12

At exactly noon that day, Valentina looked up to find a sixty-something, weathered, coffee-colored Cuban gentleman standing in front of her desk, an old-fashioned fedora-style hat in his hand, a long-sleeved, white cotton shirt tucked neatly into his black pants. She felt a surge of adrenaline shoot through her body. Not only was he the first person to sound even remotely plausible as a witness, he'd actually shown up!

"Mr. Cortez?"

"Jes," he answered with a smile that promised genuineness, and a heavy accent.

"Have a seat," Valentina offered. "Would you like something to drink? Water? Coffee?"

"No, thank you, Mees." Bigger smile.

"How are you doing today?"

"Oh, not so bad, mees. Not so bad."

"Well, thank you for coming in to talk to me. Why don't you tell me what you remember from that evening. We're talking about the night of September 18th, correct?"

"Jes, that is correct, mees.

"Go on."

"That night, I go to thee cemetery to visit my wife. She die two year ago, and I always come for her birthday to bring flowers, ju know?"

"Yes."

"After I ready to leave, I walking to thee gate and I see a tall, very *flaco,* old black man walking in direction opposite to me yust a few jards away."

"*Flaco*?" Valentina asked. "Tell me again what that means. I used to know that word."

Mr. Cortez held up the little finger of his right hand.

"Skinny! Right!"

"Jes, that is the word."

"Okay, go on. Wait. Were you able to see his face?"

"No, not so good. I maybe see heem from side, and then I turn around to look at heem because he a little beet strange, so I see him from thee back, too."

"What was strange about him?"

"Well, he maybe have mosquito that try to steeng him because he jell at sometheeng, so I turn around and he is waving hees arm up in the air like he shooing something away. And what is strange is hees voice. Ees very high, almost like woman, but maybe because it come from hees nose instead of hees throat."

"Ah, are you saying he had a nasal voice?"

"Jes, exactamente!"

"I see. Go on."

"That ees all, mees."

"Do you remember what he was wearing?"

"Oh, jes. He wearing all black. Even black hat and black sunglasses. That ees also reason I think he strange, because I see black sunglasses, but there ees no sun because eet look like eet weel rain and eet already getting dark."

"Did you notice if he was carrying anything?" Valentina asked.

"Oh, jes. I almost forget that. He using very beeg, theeck cane. I remember that because when he come out I notice he no have eet."

"When he came out? You were still there?"

"Jes. That night, I feel very tired, mees. Sometime, my legs not so good because I get arthritis, ju know?"

"I understand. So where were you when he came back out?"

"There ees leetle bench near to entrance of thee cemetery, just inside thee gate. I seet there for maybe twenty minute. Thee pain, ees very, very bad that day. So I yust wait for eet to get better before I leave. Just as I theenkeeng to go, I see him come out. Again, I no can see hees face, just from thee side. He walking very fast, and eet make me notice that now he has no cane, but he still walk very good."

"Do you remember what time it was when he came in?"

"Jes, eet sometheeng like 8:30 when he come een, and he leave about ten, fifteen minute later."

"Is there anything else you can remember about him or that evening?"

"I no theenk so, mees."

"Do you remember anything else about his cane at all?"

"I no theenk so, mees."

"All right then, thank you very much for coming in. We will follow up on everything you told me, and if we come up with something solid, I will definitely contact you about that reward. Here's my number," she said, jotting it down for him on a piece of paper. "Please call me if you remember anything else."

"Okay, mees." Big smile. "I hope you find thees person you looking for. Taking away life ees bad." He walked away from Valentina; but then he stopped and turned around. "But if you don't find thees killer, don't worry, God will." He winked at her and made to go. Just as he was about to turn the corner toward the elevator, she stopped him.

"Mr. Cortez!" she called. He turned. "Are you positive the person you saw was a man?"

He looked at her briefly, but replied without flinching, "Oh jes, mees."

Around four o'clock that afternoon, Valentina's thoughts were interrupted by the arrival of Detective Partridge and a tall, young man she assumed to be Jacquy Pierre. She was grateful for the break. While her morning visit with Colin Gardner had convinced her that something was up with Maya St. Fleur's bizarre friend, after her talk with Mr. Cortez, she was completely flummoxed. She'd spent the better part of the day ruminating and rearranging the pawns on the chessboard of her investigative mind. A perfect description of Haiti's *Baron Samedi* had come crashing in on the game, catching her unaware, rearranging all the players, and making everything crazy all of a sudden. But still, Colin Gardner seemed jealous. Strange—working hard at being strange—and jealous, resentful, and angry. *Of course, any friend would be after being shunned for a new love.* But theirs was an odd relationship to begin with. She needed to know more. Hopefully, whatever Jacquy Pierre had to say would help make some sense out of this jumble of innuendoes.

Just as she headed out of the office the night before, Partridge had called to say that Jacquy Pierre was the name of the young man who had visited Maya at the bookstore that day, but the problem was that he didn't speak a word of English. Valentina had asked him to invite Mr. Pierre down to speak with her; she would find a Haitian translator.

Having dealt before on occasion with Marius Valris, she knew he spoke Haitian Kreyol. She looked up his extension, praying he would be at his desk and not out in the field. His deep, friendly voice with the island lilt sounded like music; a brief conversation later, he had agreed to be there for the interview with Jacquy Pierre.

The tall, thin, dark-skinned man in well-pressed, pale yellow shirt and navy blue pants looked very nervous. Valentina looked up and flashed an automatic smile.

"Mr. Pierre?"

He nodded.

"Please have a seat," she said, pointing to the chair opposite her. "Excuse me for a moment."

Turning to the phone on her desk, she dialed her Haitian translator. Not long after hanging up, she heard the elevator doors open and Marius Valris turned the corner. A caramel-colored man in his early thirties, Officer Valris was all integrity, strength of character, and pride in his work. He was grateful for the job that kept his Miami family clothed and fed, as well as the one in Haiti, who depended on his monthly checks for survival. He had no patience for the whiners and victims of the world, given the dire circumstances that had landed him in this country. Approaching Valentina's desk, he smiled and, without waiting for introductions, turned to Jacquy Pierre, who sat there with a lump of clay in his throat. Extending his hand to Jacquy and gripping it firmly, Valris addressed him in the typical Haitian Kreyol greeting:

"Sak pase?" What's going on?

Jacquy just nodded.

"So, Ruiz, I'm gonna take off, all right with you?"

Valentina turned to Partridge. "No problem. Thanks for all your help. Oh," she remembered. "Where can I reach you in a half hour or so?"

"I should be around."

"I'll call you when I'm through here."

"I'll be waiting, detective." He winked at her before walking away.

"I suppose Mr. Pierre here can find his way home alone?" she said, turning to Valris.

Valris translated the question, to which Jacquy replied with a nod. Valentina pointed to the empty chair next to Jacquy and invited Valris to sit down.

Addressing Jacquy directly, she said, "So I understand that last week you visited Maya St. Fleur at the Mysterious

Light Bookstore, where she works on Lincoln Road Mall. Is that right?"

Valris translated while the expression on Jacquy Pierre's face turned from nervous to perplexed.

"Pou ki sa l'ap mandem kestyon sou Maya?" he asked Valris.

"He wants to know why you're asking questions about Maya."

"Tell him because she's under suspicion of murder," Valentina said, turning to look at Jacquy for a reaction even before Valris translated.

"Ki es ki mouri?"

"He wants to know who died?" Valris obliged, refraining from reminding Jacquy that he was the one being questioned.

"A Haitian man named Sylvain Chenet."

At the mention of Sylvain Chenet, the young Haitian practically leaped out of his chair. *"Koulanget!"*

"What did he say?"

"Holy shit!"

"Ask him why he's so surprised. Better yet, why he's so disturbed. Did he know him?"

Watching as Valris translated, Valentina observed Jacquy's body language go from one of initial shock to worried preoccupation to frightened guardedness. *He doesn't want to get her in trouble, so he's going to try to figure out how to give us as little information as possible.* Slowly, mindful of every word, Jacquy answered.

"He claims he's surprised," Valris said, "because he hasn't heard that name in a long time. Not since Maya worked for the Chenet family when she was very young and living in Haiti. He wants to know why you think Maya might have killed him."

"Because she was his girlfriend, and they were supposed to meet at the very place where Sylvain Chenet's body was found."

Hearing this statement as relayed by Valris, Jacquy found it very difficult to hide his reaction, and his hand shot up to his mouth, his brow wrinkled with apprehension.

"M'pa janm kon bagay kon sa. Li e kon mande'm pou fami Chenet a leu li te kon ekri mwen, e'm te kon bay li nouvel."

"He says he never knew anything about that. He says Maya used to ask him about the family in their correspondence, and he would fill her in. Kind of like updating her about news from back home."

"Ask him when was the last time he wrote her with any news about Sylvain."

After listening to Jacquy's response to this question, Valris said, "About two months ago, he wrote, saying that he had heard from Maya's mother that Sylvain was studying environmental law at the University of Miami."

"Does he have any idea why Maya would want to kill Sylvain or if she ever mentioned anything at all that might have sounded funny or strange to him."

Valentina could see Jacquy's eyes shift uncomfortably as Valris translated. She knew he would answer in the negative and that he would be hiding something. When, predictably, Jacquy shook his head no, Valentina struck.

"Ask him why he thought he was being brought in for questioning in the first place, since he didn't have a clue about this affair. Could it be he's anxious about his status as an immigrant here in the States?"

"Oui, mwen te panse ke se te pou sa men tout papye'm en od," he replied somewhat nervously, producing a sheaf of papers and laying them out on the desk.

"He says he wondered if that was it but that all of his papers are in order."

Valentina made a show of looking over the papers, which proved that Jacquy Pierre was, in fact, in the States legally. Shaking her head somberly, her mouth pursed, she spoke to him directly. "Do you know that withholding information on an investigation such as this one is as bad as aiding and abetting a criminal? And, if you are holding back, anything at all, even an innocent conversation that might give us some kind of clue, do you know that you could have your residency revoked and be sent back to Haiti quicker than that?" she concluded, snapping her fingers loudly, jolting him.

At this point in the conversation, Valris felt a momentary surge of sympathy for his compatriot, but the cop in him quickly took over. *Sometimes you have to bully a potential witness into spilling it.* He dutifully translated in his best reproachful tone as Jacquy visibly shrank in size in his seat.

Now begins the dance, Valentina thought. *How does he give us enough, and keep himself out of trouble without getting Maya into hot water?*

"Sel bagay mwen ka di nou se ke depi m'rive icit mwen we ke Maya change. M'wel vin tounen yon moun qui pa gen jwa nan keu li."

"The only thing I can tell you is that when I arrived here, I noticed that Maya had changed, that she's become someone with no joy in her heart," Valris translated.

Jacquy spoke again, and Valris continued, "And he feels that this could have something to do with some old history from when she was a little girl. He never got the whole picture, but he knows that she has a lot of anger at her mother and father, and that she once even told him that she had death in her heart."

"Death?" Valentina repeated. Then, going on a hunch, she repeated, "Death? Is that what she said? Or did she use the word murder?"

As Valris translated, Valentina got her answer, even though Jacquy fervently insisted *"lan mò, lan mò."* Death.

Noticing the beads of sweat forming on Jacquy's forehead, Valentina changed the subject. "Tell him just one or two more questions. An eyewitness saw someone around the murder site around the time of the killing. He described a tall, black, skinny man wearing black pants, a black jacket, and a black hat, and he was carrying a thick cane. Oh, and he was wearing dark glasses and he had a nasal voice. Does that ring any bells?"

Looking surprised, Valris volunteered, "That sounds like a perfect description of the *Baron Samedi*. Know who that is?"

Valentina nodded, then signaled toward Jacquy so that Valris would translate. As he did so, the beads of sweat on Jacquy's face turned into rivulets that slid down his now feverish face and neck. He looked completely taken aback, his entire body a picture of consternation and fear.

Speaking so low that Valris had to ask him to repeat his answer, Jacquy admitted, *"Kòm ou genle deja di li, moun li dekri a, se deskripsyon Baron Samedi. Men'm pa fouti explike ou sa sa vle di."*

"He says that, as I just told you, the person you described sounds like *Baron Samedi*, but he's at a loss to explain any of it to you."

"Ask him what he would think if I told him that the weapon found at the murder site was a cane carved into the shape of a penis and balls, and that that's what was used to bludgeon Sylvain Chenet over the head so many times that he was barely recognizable to his own father."

As Valris spoke, Jacquy became visibly agitated, all the while trying as hard as he could to remain unaffected by what he was hearing. When Valris was done, all Jacquy could say was that he didn't know what to say.

"Okay," Valentina said, ending the torture for him, "you can go now. But if you come up with anything you think I should know, here's my number."

Valris translated, and Jacquy stood up, grabbing his papers, in a hurry to disappear.

"Oh, and one last thing," Valentina said, standing too, and turning to Valris, "Could you ask him if he's ever seen a sketch of a middle-aged man in Maya's place?'

Jacquy listened, thinking back, trying to remember, and then answered.

"He did see a picture like that," Valris said, "and that when he asked her who it was, she got mad at him and said it was none of his business; and then, she took it away and put it somewhere else." *Where was she going with this?*

"Ask him if the man in the picture could have been Sylvain Chenet's father?"

Seemingly surprised at the question, Jacquy answered, *"M'pa jam kontre ak fami Chenet a. M'pa kon sa moun sa yo samble."*

"He says he's never seen anyone from the Chenet family before in his life."

As the two men walked away, Valentina reached for the phone and dialed Anthony Partridge's extension.

"Yeah," he answered.

"Valentina Ruiz. Got a few minutes for me, detective?"

"Hey, you don't gotta be so formal with me. You can call me Anthony if I can call you Valentina."

"Uh, sure," she replied. *Is he flirting with me?*

A few minutes later, Partridge swaggered over to her desk and perched himself on its corner.

"What can I do for you this time, *Valentina*?" he smiled mischievously.

"Remember Colin Gardner, the weird-looking guy who lives on the first floor of my suspect's building?"

"The freak? Sure."

"I need you to tail him for me."

"How long?"

"Next few days. That all right? Do you need to clear it with anyone first?"

"*The Shade* finds ways to do the things he wants to do. Would that make you happy?"

"It would make me even happier if you refrained from breaking into his place. That would make me very happy."

Before he could respond, a booming voice interrupted: "Happy? Who's got the nerve to be happy around here?"

"Kojak, my man!" Anthony stood up and hi-fived Carlson, who now waited for an explanation.

"I've been doin' a little surveillance work for Detective Ruiz here, and it looks like she's been real happy with me."

"Oh yeah? What work would that be?"

"I'll tell you all about it in a minute, Carlson," Valenina said, and turning to Anthony, added, "Let me know what you find out."

"Will do!" He slapped Carlson on the shoulder and started to walk away, but stopped in mid-stride and turned around. "Hey, I been thinking about it, and the guy in the picture could be the dead kid's father. I'd have to look at it again, but there just might be a resemblance. Make any sense to you?"

Valentina nodded dully as she watched Partridge's retreating back.

"Why don't you come into my office and tell Uncle Rambo all about it, rookie."

She didn't feel like dealing with this asshole and his head games right now, not with all the competing theories swimming around inside her head. "Give me a minute, Carlson," she said absent-mindedly, her mind racing.

"How 'bout *right now*? How does that sound? Does *right now* sound too soon for you?" He was smiling contentedly as heads jerked up to see what all the ruckus was about.

Don't lose your cool, girl. Deep breaths. She walked into his office and he followed her in, slamming the door behind him.

"I've hardly been around for the last few days. I want an update on the case a rookie's been working on, and she tells me to 'give her a minute.' I almost thought I heard you wrong."

"That's right, isn't it? You're supposed to be the guy I *learn* from, except you're never around. So I'm taking over this case, okay, Carlson? You can read the report just like Sergeant Muñoz and anyone else who's interested. I know what I'm doing, and frankly, I don't have the time to waste, telling you what's happening on a case you couldn't give a shit about. You're too busy holding your rich widow's hand and helping her wipe her tears away, isn't that right, Carlson? As a matter of fact, why don't we both go into Muñoz' office right now and you can tell him what it is that's got you so busy you can't even think about anything else."

He was standing fairly close to her already, and he stepped even closer now, eyes glaring.

"Don't fuckin' cross me, Ruiz," he said through gritted teeth, "or maybe I'll have to let Muñoz in on how you got *The Shade* to do a little B & E for you. The sergeant don't know it, but everyone else does; that's Anthony's specialty. Just try and tell me you didn't have him break into your suspect's place for you."

"What?" Valentina said.

"You heard me. And I just heard you talkin' about it with him."

"I gave Partridge a job to do. How am I supposed to—"

"Tell it to Muñoz, baby."

She felt a deadly familiar calm descend over her. She stepped into Carlson's face, hissing every word slowly and clearly so he'd get it.

"You don't want to fuck with me, Carlson. Just *don't*. Or you'll wish you hadn't. *Understand*?"

She stormed out of his office, slamming the door hard behind her. Inside, something fell to the floor with a loud thud.

13

"Hello?"

"Maya?"

"Yes, who is this?"

"It's Detective Ruiz."

"Valentina?"

"Do you know another Detective Ruiz?"

"I like that name. It sounds like a song about love."

"I've always liked my name, but I never thought about it that way."

"What can I do for you today, Detective?"

"I wondered if I could come by your place to talk?"

"About anything in particular?"

Maya's casual tone sounded forced to the detective. "About this case."

"Am I still under suspicion?"

"Well, I haven't caught the murderer yet."

"Why not? In the movies the good guys always get their man."

"Oh, we'll get him—or her—especially now with the reward offer being broadcast on TV the other night."

"Reward?"

"You don't watch the local news?"

"I don't own a television."

"Your friend's father, Henri Chenet, offered a $20,000 reward for any information resulting in the capture of his son's murderer." She waited for a reaction; hearing silence, she continued, "So, of course, every psycho, liar, prankster, and just about anyone desperately in need of cash has been calling with 'information.' It's a real interesting process, trying to weed out the bozos from potentially important witnesses."

"How do you do it?"

"I've got a nose for it. I just know when someone's bullshitting. It's part of the package. My mother made sure of that."

"What did she have to do with it?"

"That's a whole other story."

"So, any important witnesses turn up?"

Again, Valentina detected nervousness in the question. "A few. Any chance I could swing by your place?"

"Um, well...sure. How long will it take you to get here?"

"Fifteen minutes, max."

"Okay, see you then."

After storming out of Carlson's office, Valentina had fled the building, jumped into her car, and driven home feeling like a gorilla escaped from the zoo. She was afraid of herself when she got like this. She had paced her apartment, throwing a cushion, then another across the living room, banging kitchen cabinets, and kicking a dent in her oven door. Finally, deciding to act rather than react, she had located Maya St. Fleur's telephone number and dialed.

On the way over to Maya's place now, dodging in and out of rush hour traffic, she tried to convince herself that it was the altar she wanted to see, the picture of the old guy in the sketch; but she knew otherwise. She wanted to talk to Maya—about what, she wasn't sure yet. Stopped at a red light along Collins Avenue, she leaned her head out of the car window and looked up at the sky, searching for answers to unasked questions. The day's hazy sunshine was giving way to cloudy gray. Rain was predicted for that evening. Wanting to scream out the frustration stewing inside her, she hoped there would be thunder.

As she waited, a swift, rusted blue Chevy Impala slowly made a wide left turn in front of her. Its stringy-haired, dirty-fingernailed driver was blowing music on a shiny harmonica that Valentina couldn't hear. His right hand on the steering wheel, left arm and upper torso leaning perilously out the window as he played, the young man's eyes bulged with concentration and *menace.* Valentina craned her neck as she watched the car disappear, not wanting the surreal moment to end.

"What the fuck was that all about?" she said out loud, shaking her head. *Straight out of Kafka, and I'm on my way to a visit for God knows what reason with a potential murderer.*

She wondered if the harmonica player was some kind of sign, meditating on it all the way to Maya's, and unable to shake a sense of impending disaster. *What a day!* Her head was swarming with the disconnected data gathered from Mr. Cortez and Maya's friends, Colin and Jacquy. She needed time to put it all down on paper, study these puzzle pieces; see if and how they all fit together. Right now, with Carlson and his threats added to the mix, the puzzle seemed like a plate of scrambled eggs—exactly how her brain felt now. She couldn't think. All she could do was let disconnected bits of information materialize and then vanish from her head. Trying to suppress her issues with Carlson, she wondered what excuse she could give to Maya for wanting to see her.

Eventually, she found herself in front of the dancer's apartment building. The door buzzed open, and taking a deep breath, she walked up the steps to the second floor, praying to *Oya* for guidance. *Tell me what to do, PLEASE!*

Maya was dressed in gray sweatpants and a bright yellow T-shirt cropped at the waist, a hesitant smile on her face as she opened the door.

Wound up like a spring, Valentina blurted, "There's something I need to take care of, and I think you can help me."

"Really?" Maya said, showing her surprise. "Would you like to come in?"

"Yes, thanks."

Entering the apartment, Valentina looked around for the altar and noticed a screen just to the left on the other side of the front door. Something about it warned: "Private—No Trespassing." She could ask about that later. For now, she had more important things on her mind.

"The only place to sit is here on the floor. Care for a cushion?"

"Sure, no problem."

Valentina chose one of the pillows leaning on the wall just to the right of the front door, and Maya sat down opposite her.

"I'm curious. What is it you think I can help you with?"

"This may sound crazy to you, but hopefully it won't. There's a guy that I work with. His name is Harry Carlson. He's unbearable. I can't keep working with him, but the situation isn't likely to change unless I do something about it."

Valentina stopped, hoping for an encouraging comment or look of understanding, but none came.

After a brief silence, Maya simply said, "Yes?"

"Well, I'm half Cuban, as I think I mentioned once before. I used to accompany my grandmother to Santeria ceremonies all the time when I was younger, and became initiated. But, at some point—around the time I turned 18 or 19—it all started to feel ridiculous: the beliefs, the rituals, the heaviness of the religion and all its rules...Having a religion, period; so, I pulled back. Went in the other direction, where logic rules the day; but not before I witnessed some pretty incredible things. And they stayed with me. Basically, I know the spirits are real."

"Are you asking me to help you get rid of this guy with the help of the *lwas?*"

"I don't know. Maybe not get rid of him, exactly. Just resolve the situation."

"And—"

"I know the obvious questions is, 'Why not turn to *Santeria* since that's what I'm familiar with?'"

"Um, yes, that is a question..." Maya said. But after pausing for effect, she added, "And I'm supposed to know all about this stuff just because I'm Haitian?"

"No, not because you're Haitian. Because something made me call *you*, not the *Orixas*, not my grandmother nor any of the priests I could have contacted. I know it sounds crazy, since I don't even know you, and—"

"And you think I might have killed Sylvain," Maya completed the thought for her.

"Yes, that's still an open question," Valentina answered truthfully, "but...hell, I *am* totally crazy for being here and bringing you my problems like this. You know what?" she said getting up. "Forget I ever came here. I don't know what got into me. I can take care of this myself. You probably think I'm a lunatic, or a fool. I apologize for bothering you."

Valentina had her hand on the doorknob, ready to rush out, embarrassed, when Maya's quiet voice stopped her.

"Valentina."

"Yes?" she said, ashamed to look at her but turning around just the same.

"Don't go. It's okay. It's perfectly all right that you came here. In fact, I was expecting you."

"What?"

"Why don't you come back and sit down. I think we can take care of your problem very easily."

"Really?" Valentina said, coming back toward her and sitting down on the large cushion with a thud.

"This kind of thing is very simple. The only thing to be careful of is your rage. It's all around you like a whirlwind. We'll first have to do a short cleansing ceremony to rid you of it, and then we can work toward the other."

"What do we need? Don't we have to have something that belongs to him or a lock of his hair or something like that?"

"That's usually helpful. Do you have something like that with you?"

"No."

"That's okay. What's more important here is your intention. Although it is not my first inclination to think like this, I will tell you what *Madame* Mirta, my mother, counseled me and anyone else about to undertake this kind of work. It's a law of the spirits and a universal law. Everyone says it without realizing its truth, but there is no way around it. What you put out, you get back. So you need to be very clear about what you want for yourself—not what you want to have happen to...what's his name again?"

"Carlson."

"Mr. Carlson, then. If you want to have something terrible happen to him, then you must know and expect that something equally terrible will happen to you."

"I understand," Valentina said.

"Do you know what you want?" Maya asked.

"Okay," Valentina said, feeling some of the earlier tension ease away, and creasing her brow in thought, "what exactly do I want? I don't want to have to work with him anymore. I like working alone. And I would like him to be on the receiving end of the same garbage he puts out. He's vile and overbearing and without scruples."

"Hmm," Maya said looking up into space. After a few minutes of silence, she said, "The most effective rituals are the ones that come organically—not from some manual or from another priestess' tried and true method; and I just got an idea. I've never used this before, but it just came to me and I would be very surprised if it did not work."

"What do you have in mind?" Valentina asked, curious and suddenly excited. "I would have thought you'd want to summon the *Vodou* spirits for something like this."

"Don't forget, I'm an Americanized Haitian. I put my own spin on things. Besides, asking the spirits for help, or using the elements amounts to the same thing. I follow whatever suits the situation or my feeling at any given time. Make sense?"

"I'm not sure. *Santeria* and *Vodou* seem so specific in their ways and practices "

"They are," Maya said. "But just as you mentioned earlier, that's what bothers me too, sometimes, about the religion—the rules and all. It's all so limiting. That's why I do what feels right for me."

"Okay, I follow you."

"How much do you know about *Santeria*?" Maya asked her.

"Quite a bit. Although I no longer practice, I'm still fascinated by it and drawn to it—especially to *Oya*. See? She stood up, turned her back to Maya and lifted her shirt, displaying her tattoo.

Maya drew in her breath at the visual intensity of the image that would adorn the detective's skin for life. She raised her eyebrows, surprised. "Wow. And you need *my* help?"

"I'm familiar with the different spirits, what they like, and what they do; and when I feel the need, I call on them. But for the most part, it's *Oya* I turn to.

"And this time? Why didn't you ask her for help?"

"She's the one who led me here."

The two women looked at each other in silence, each with their own puzzled thoughts.

"Why don't you go into the bathroom," Maya said at last. Wash your face and your hands; and here—." She got up, went to the kitchen area, opened one of the cabinet doors and pulled out a clear plastic bag containing a mix of herbs, which she poured into a medium-sized plastic bowl. Walking back into the living room, she handed the bowl to Valentina. "Fill this bowl with water, dilute the herbs as best you can—they are specifically used for cleansing—and pour the mixture over your entire head. You need to shake your anger. You can use the towel in there to dry off. It's clean. In the meantime, I'll burn some van van oil to clear the room."

"Okay."

Struggling to fit her head into the tiny sink to soak her entire head of hair, as instructed, Valentina wondered if she was completely insane. *Does it get any stranger than this? She may have killed this kid—got dressed up in appropriate costume—tall, skinny black man with a woman's voice, Mr. Cortez said. Very sick. Morbid. And here I am about to trust her to help me with Kojak. She'll probably have me close my eyes for this ritual. She could easily kill me! Oh, Jesus. I'm not clear on whether or not she did it. I can't put my finger on what the real story is. Okay, one thing at a time.* The conflicted detective decided then and there to pursue Carlson right now and the rest later.

Emerging from the bathroom with wet, towel-dried hair, Valentina entered what felt like a completely different space. The curtains had been drawn, the coffee table moved aside. A plate containing a lighted black candle anointed with van van oil released a sweet, smoky haze into the air. Maya motioned for her to sit down in a designated spot in the middle of the room, and then she seated herself opposite Valentina. Placed around them in a circle on the floor were eight white candles, which provided the only other light in the room. Night had fallen by now and the rain, which had warned its arrival all day, was finally making good on its threat.

"Close your eyes and clear your mind completely of Harry Carlson," Maya instructed her. "Empty your mind and heart of the anger he brings out in you. Do you have a way to do this?"

"Yes," Valentina answered right away. "I just need to breathe deeply for a while. That usually works to calm me down."

"Good. With each inhale, breathe in whatever your vision is of a peaceful, hassle-free environment, and with each exhale, let go of the feelings you have for Harry Carlson."

After concentrating for a while, Valentina conjured up her vision of peace: clear blue skies, sweet, gentle breezes, and a warm turquoise ocean, waves lapping softly at a white, sandy beach. Her hostility, anger, and rage she envisioned as blackish-green toxic materials, spewing lava-like out into the universe and away from her forever. Breathing in invited paradise; relinquishing hell became her out-breath. She repeated this exercise for what seemed like an eternity, enjoying it more and more as it worked its magic on her spirit. When she next heard Maya's voice, it was harder, stronger, and commanding: "Now imagine a mirror, as big as you like." And after a few moments, "Is it there?"

The picture of a long mirror framed in Mexican white metal, and stamped with symbols popped into Valentina's mind. She held onto it, seeing it clearly and forcefully.

"Place that mirror in front of Harry Carlson now!"

As she heard the words, Valentina visualized Carlson in his office, the mirror coming down before him with a loud crack, halting him in his tracks, barring his way, forcing him to look at himself.

"Hold that image in your mind now, and call it up whenever you can. That will reinforce its potency. From this day forward, until you remove that mirror from the path of Harry Carlson, he will experience everything he puts out in the world three-fold. What you have done is to speed up the cycle of karma. It will hit him instantly. His karma will not wait. Now, keep this in mind: you are not doing anything other than helping Carlson to see who he is. You are not doing anything *to* him.

However, you have to remember that just as you placed a mirror before him, so have you placed a mirror before yourself. Are you comfortable with this?"

"Absolutely."

"Good. Our work is done."

The two women looked at each other silently for a moment, and Valentina smiled.

"Thank you," she said.

"Happy to help," said Maya, smiling back.

"Well, I guess I should get going now," Valentina said. And as she prepared to leave, she again noticed the screen and turned to look at her host.

"What's behind here?"

"My altar. Want to see it?"

"Sure," she answered, somewhat surprised.

She watched for hesitation in the girl's movements and found none as Maya got up, switched on the overhead light and walked to the screen, pulling it back easily with one swish. The altar was as Partridge had described it: three shelves filled with a variety of oils, herbs, sketches of symbols, and a fair amount of paraphernalia, all of which probably held a specific significance for Maya, but meant nothing to Valentina. There was no sketch in sight depicting an older man's face.

"Is each shelf reserved for a different spirit?" she asked Maya, who seemed to be holding her breath while watching Valentina's reaction.

"Yes. This one down here is to *Erzulie Dantor*. She is a warrior female spirit–kind of like *Oya*. The heart, the knife, and a black pig are her symbols. That's why that picture is there," she said, pointing to a newspaper clipping of a black pig taped to the shelf. "This middle one is dedicated to *Marassa*. They are twin spirits associated with children and procreation. They represent love, truth, and justice. And magic, too. I found these dolls at a flea market, and they reminded me of them.

The *Marassa* are usually represented by dolls. And this shelf up here is for the *Baron Samedi*. I love him. He takes care of me."

She didn't offer any other comment on the *Baron,* and Valentina did not ask. But she noticed that the shelf was covered with a black cloth and a purple velvet shawl. There was also a cigar, a black hat, black sunglasses, and a few other objects she couldn't quite identify. She did not notice the *Baron*'s cane anywhere.

"I'm familiar with *Baron Samedi*," she said, turning to look at Maya.

"Oh?"

"Yep. Remember I told you on the phone that there was a reward out for information leading to Sylvain's killer?"

"Yes?"

"Well, a witness came forward today and described someone near the scene of the crime who sounded pretty damned close to the *Baron*."

Valentina noticed something resembling fear infuse Maya's face.

"Is that so?" she said, turning her face away from Valentina's piercing eyes for a moment, "And what do you make of that?"

"I'm not sure. Either someone disguised as the Spirit of Death killed your boyfriend, or maybe the Spirit of Death decided it was time to take him. What do *you* make of it?"

"If this were happening in Haiti, it might make some kind of sense. But even then, *Baron Samedi* look-alikes usually come out at *Mardi Gras* or during ceremonies. Otherwise, it would be kind of strange." She shook her head. "I don't really know what to tell you."

"Did I tell you what the murder weapon was?" Valentina asked.

"No."

"The *Baron's* cane."

"Oh, my God!"

"Yeah. How come you don't have one for him on your altar?"

"I've never been able to find one that didn't look like a bad joke," she answered in what sounded like a natural tone of voice, except that Valentina instinctively picked up the lie.

"Really?"

"Yes. Really," Maya answered, her forceful tone seeming to bait Valentina.

"I think there's something you're not telling me," Valentina tried.

"It's irrelevant, " Maya answered.

"Try me."

"Well, the truth of the matter is that I used to have one, but I misplaced it a while ago."

"You *lost* a cane like that?"

"Yes," she said.

"When did you lose it?"

"It might have been when I moved, or it might have happened when someone broke into my car a while back. I can't really be sure."

"Do you think anyone you know could have taken it from here?" Valentina asked, suddenly flashing on Colin Gardner.

"Doubtful. I don't have too many friends, you know."

"I've met your friend Colin."

"Really? How did that happen? Oh," she said, remembering, "of course. You've been questioning people I know because I'm under suspicion." She looked sad.

Valentina shrugged her shoulders and nodded.

"I loved him so much." The disconsolate woman standing before Valentina whispered the words, a sob catching in her throat, and the detective accepted her declaration at face value. "This is why you really came here, isn't it?" Maya said.

"Well, it's true that this case is still very much open and that it is occupying many of my waking hours. But that's only part of the reason I'm here. Actually, I wasn't sure why I came; I only knew that I wanted to talk to you about Carlson; and I certainly did *that*. Again, I can't thank you enough." And, remembering something that had been niggling at her, she said, "By the way, what did you mean earlier when you said you were expecting me?"

"I have been thinking about you a lot since we last saw each other. And then there were at least seven messages from my friend Jacquy on my answering machine saying that he needed to talk to me—something about the police. I haven't called him back yet, but I wondered if he was talking about you. I couldn't imagine how you would even know about him, but I guess you have your ways."

Valentina nodded.

"And you know something else? I think your friend, *Oya*, has been trying to prepare me for you."

"What do you mean?"

"Remember the nightmares I told you about? The ones I've had my entire life? They're gone. But I've been dreaming of a woman with no face, and the number nine always makes its way in there somehow. Seeing your tattoo just now—I suppose there are exactly nine charms on her crown, right?"

"Yes."

"Thought so. When I saw it, I realized it was her."

"No shit."

"No kidding."

The two women looked into each other's eyes for a moment, at a loss for words, until Valentina raised her eyebrows, then turned and walked out the door.

The Baron

Two minutes after that lady detective leaves Maya's apartment, the telephone rings. Want to guess who it is? You got it: Jacquy, looking for some sense around all the crazy stuff he heard at the police station. Oh, no. Maya can't deal with him right now, darlin'. All that anger, and all those questions! She's worried about Colin too, since he's not picking up his phone. She thinks her head might burst wide open. She wishes it would. I could help her with that, if she likes.

Several days after the ceremony in Maya's apartment, Valentina stepped out of her car, anxious to get to her office. The forensics lab tests hadn't turned up anything of value, but Partridge had called her cell phone, saying he had some news on Colin Gardner, and she couldn't wait to hear what he had to say. But when she walked into the precinct, she could tell that something was going on. People were standing around in groups of twos and threes, whispering, shaking their heads, looking worried and disturbed. Furthermore, her entrance had the effect of a cannon ball. Seeing her, they scattered back to their posts like criminals attempting nonchalance. Before she could ask, Sergeant Muñoz bellowed her name from his office. She looked around at everyone, her face a living interrogatory as she walked toward his door. Most looked away or stared through her.

"What's going on here?" she asked, sitting opposite her beefy mentor, anxious thoughts now scurrying around inside her head like felons under siege. Muñoz seemed exhausted for such an early hour.

"I've got serious news about Carlson," he said in a low, angry voice.

Flashing for a split second on Maya and her sitting around a circle of candles, concentrating on Carlson, Valentina froze. Trying not to let the itch rising up her back excite her, she attempted unsuccessfully to seem casual.

"What?"

"We've had to suspend Carlson from the force while we investigate what looks a lot like his involvement in the murder of Edward Morrison—you know the case, don't you?"

"You mean the one he's been working on so hard he was never around anymore?"

"Yeah, the one with the singing, grieving widow who couldn't get enough hand-holding from Carlson, who lately was looking like her personal security guard."

"Holy shit," Valentina said, the breath knocked out of her. "Was he involved with her?"

"That's what it's looking like. Like he got together with the wife, and they decided to kill Morrison for his money."

"It's *Body Heat* all over again."

"Yeah, except this ain't no movie—this is real life Miami Heat, the kind of shit that stinks worse than dog crap for the force. Everybody hates crooked cops, and as soon as something like this goes down, every citizen and immigrant in Miami decides that all cops are bad. Makes me tired just thinkin' about it."

"How did you find out?"

"We got a tip from the old man's daughter. Months ago she spotted her father's wife in a bar with the same guy she thought she saw driving away from the house the night he was killed. She didn't figure Carlson in the picture until the son of a-bitch went out there to get her statement. She's spent the last three weeks telling herself she must be crazy to think the cop on the case could be the same guy she'd seen twice before. Both times were from a distance. Anyway, one thing led to another and she finally came in yesterday. Carlson can't account for his time the night of the murder. It's all fucking crazy—a good cop like him. Anyway, he's not guilty yet. We are investigating, as they say. In the meantime, you're on your own. All right with you?"

"You know there's no love lost between me and Kojak. I didn't figure him for something like this, but I'm not going to miss him, if that's what you're asking."

"Yeah, I counted on you saying that."

Valentina walked out of Muñoz's office in a daze. Thoughts of the ceremony, her intention and intensity in that moment crowded around her, nudging her. *Oh my God. Look what we did!* A smile playing on her lips, she floated to her desk, lost in a warm haze of personal satisfaction. She was grooving on the pleasant sensation when the phone rang.

"Ruiz," her old partner, Jimmy, laughed in her ear, "great partner you chose for yourself."

"That's what I was thinking."

"What do you know about this situation?"

"Same as you. Kojak didn't exactly confide in me, you know?" She didn't have time for gossip right now. She needed to think.

Hey, how's your first case going? I heard about that murder at the cemetery."

"Complicated as hell. Everything points to my main suspect, but I can't believe she did it."

"Why?"

"I like her."

"First rule, don't get personal."

"It's not personal, just complicated; plus, I've got no hard evidence against her. Listen, Jimmy, can I catch you later? I got somebody coming in right about now."

"Okay, babe. Later."

After hanging up the phone, Valentina turned to look at Carlson's office, her head reeling from the news. She walked into his now empty space and stood silently, feeling his energy, the menace he liked to exude, his greasiness—and she felt glad for his absence. She had decided to get him out of her life and, suddenly, the old man's daughter had come forth. Coincidence? Was there such a thing? She let the strength she felt wash over her. Somehow, somebody out there had heard her plea and helped her, bringing justice in its wake, too! It was perfect. Just perfect. Now if only she could solve this case without the murderer having to be Maya St. Fleur—except that every day, that outcome seemed less likely.

Back at her desk, Anthony Partridge was looking especially pleased with himself this morning. Valentina sighed inwardly.

"What do you know, Anthony?"

"And how you doin' today, Anthony? Oh, just fine, Valentina, and you?"

"Sorry, how are you today?"

"Great!"

"Glad to hear it. Now, can you tell me what's going on?"

"You don't wanna know how come I feel so great?"

"If it has something to do with this case, I'm all ears, otherwise, sorry, but no. I'm not trying to be rude or anything, it's just that—"

He held up his hand. "Okay, okay. Christ, just tryin' to be a little friendly."

"I understand, and I am sorry. I guess I'm just very preoccupied."

"Yeah, yeah, I get it." He stared at her for a while, regret mixed with anger on his face.

"So, you were saying?"

"Yeah, right. That freak kid? He's got some even freakier friends. You ever hear about that Cuban gang up in North Miami, callin' itself El Calle Ocho 'cause there's eight of them? Shake merchants down for protection money, operate like they think they're some kind of mafia outfit?"

"Yes?"

"There's been a few killings we're pretty sure they're responsible for, but we never been able to pin anything on them. They always come out clean."

"Yeah, so? How does this tie in with Colin Gardner?" she asked, trying not to sound impatient.

"Looks like he's friends with the head homeboy. Followed him to the dump he and his brother live in. Saw our boy go in there, and stayed a couple of hours. Two nights later, he goes back, picks up the brother, and they go to a local dive for some food. I could see 'em from the car. Looks like they had a lot to discuss."

"Hmm. What do these kids look like?"

"Head homey, his name is Jorge—big, greasy, slicked-back hair, tattoos all over his arms and chest. Wears those muscle T-shirts so's you could get a good look at them. Carries a knife big enough to see it real good from far away. Real motherfucker. The younger brother is skin and bones. Kinda tall, dark-skinned, shaved head—they call him Pat. Maybe short for Patricio or Patrick, I'm not sure. Doesn't look as mean. I hear he doesn't talk much, kinda keeps to himself. But they were talkin' up a storm that night!"

"Let me have that address," Valentina said, pushing a sheet of paper across the desk to him.

"What? You thinkin' of going over there? I wouldn't go by myself if I was you."

"Why don't you let me worry about myself?"

"Hey, it's your ass. They don't like cops. You might consider goin' in the daytime, then."

"Thanks for the info and the advice, Anthony." She smiled at him to make up for her earlier brusqueness. It seemed to work.

"Hey, no problem! *The Shade* at your service," he mock bowed, turned, and disappeared before she could say another word.

14

The next morning, Valentina stepped into her car, strapped on her seatbelt, and leaned over the steering wheel for a moment, rubbing her eyes, trying to sort out the torrent of thoughts in her febrile brain. She went over it in her mind once more. *Okay, we've got the suspect herself, the waitress who thinks she's spooky, the magazine writer who hates her, the witness who's confusing the shit out of me, and her friends who seem to know less about her than any stranger on the street. Next stop: the mother.*

The night before, Valentina Ruiz could have been mistaken for a sleepwalker. She'd spent a good part of it in her living room, staring into space, thinking about *Baron Samedi.* The man Mr. Cortez described *was* the Baron. But did he really exist? How could this be? Did spirits visit the earthly plane, take on human form, and run around town shopping and going to the beach? She'd never heard of such a thing. Usually, they came during a ceremony that explicitly summoned them and then departed before it was over. *Hello! Valentina, what are you even thinking?* She remembered the first ceremony she had ever attended. Dressed like the *orisha* and acting out, the *santero* had taken on the personality of *Oya.* Or was the *orisha* actually *in possession* of the *santero* for a certain length of time? She didn't know enough about *Santeria* to say for sure, but her own interaction with *Oya* had been so powerful that night, that after carefully considering the move, she'd decided to tattoo her entire back with the fighter spirit's image. She wanted her near—her essence, her warrior ways. She needed the strength to help her with her mother and the trauma that hounded her day-to-day existence. The few people who had seen her tattoo assumed she was a *santera*, but that was far from true. It was only that from the moment she'd met *Oya* so long ago, something about the goddess had gripped her and never let go. She also recalled the day, just a year ago, when she'd found her mother, dead on the living room floor of her childhood home. If not for *Oya*... No, she did not want to think about *that*. Willing herself back, she'd gone over the stray puzzle pieces of her latest murder case, arranging and rearranging them this way and that, until she'd remembered one forgotten link. *The mother.*

Finding her had been a breeze, but trying nonetheless.

Mr. DeVilla can tell me where she is!

When the thought occurred to her, Valentina had jumped to her feet and sprinted out the door, headed for the DeVilla Modern studio on the off chance he might be there. It was past eight and the odds were slim, but she felt too restless to sit still. Besides, she hoped a little night air and drive might relax her a bit. As she drove, the cool, musty breeze lightly whipping her face, a thought intruded on her thoughts, and a half smile broke out on her lips. *Taking a look at that butt won't be too difficult*. She'd never been much into older men, but this one was definitely hot! *Debonair, commanding, so mindful of his dancer's troubles. Swoon.*

Arriving at the DeVilla Modern studio, Valentina noticed the nearly empty parking lot and took it as a good sign. She was hoping to catch the dance master, but didn't relish the idea of running into Maya, or having to explain her presence. The door to the studio was unlocked, but the large, open room was empty. It felt a little spooky to her. *Door's open but looks like no one's here. Oh well, I'll call and make an appointment*. But as she turned to leave, a sound coming from the locker room stopped her. *Maybe he* is *here. One quick look, just in case.* Walking toward the open doorway, she called out, "Hello? Anybody here? Mr. DeVilla?"

What sounded like frantic rustling reached her ears, but before she could get to the door, Carlos DeVilla emerged, slightly disheveled, followed by an overweight Latin woman dressed in her Sunday best—tight black and white print skirt, white stockings with black high-heeled shoes, and a black silk blouse. The buttons were done up the wrong way, and her breasts were heaving. *Oh my God! She must be over fifty-five!* A wave of disappointment swept over Valentina as another part fought off the urge to laugh. *How fabulous, a handsome older man with a taste for older women! Right on, Mr. DeVilla! Too bad for me...*

She waited while he hustled his friend out of the studio. When he came back, he was all business, with no sign of embarrassment.

"Yes, officer?"

"It's detective," she corrected, "Detective Ruiz, and I'm sorry if I interrupted anything."

"Don't mention it," he said, cutting her off. *Cold eyes.* "What can I do for you?"

Oh, right. I'm a cop. Everybody hates cops on principle. She didn't really give a damn about that, though.

"I was hoping you might be able to help me. I would like to speak with Maya's mother, but I don't know her name or where she lives. And I would rather not ask Maya," she added almost defensively.

"May I ask why?' he said, his Portuguese accent ever so formal.

Valentina thought about this for a minute, wondering whether to go into hard-ass cop mode. She resisted the impulse.

"Well, as you probably know, I am investigating the death of Maya's lover. She was the last person to see him alive, and she can't provide us with an alibi. Unfortunately, Maya is on the list of suspects, and I have to follow every lead that I can."

"Maya's lover?" he said, almost to himself.

Unbelievable. Another intimate who knows next to nothing about her.

"You hadn't heard anything about him." A statement, not a question.

"No. But that's not unusual, if you know Maya."

"I'm beginning to get the picture.

"And why do you say she is 'unfortunately' a suspect?" he sidetracked, throwing her off, zeroing in on her soft spot.

"Unfortunately, because personally I like her," Valentina admitted.

"Is that so?" he asked with skepticism.

"Yes, that is so," she said briskly, the hard-ass cop in her pushing to the fore. "So, do you have an address for her mother or not?"

"Certainly. I will be happy to give it to you. Anything she might say could only help Maya. She is a lady of great character."

No, it hadn't been *easy*.

As she stood now before *Madame* Mirta, she understood exactly what he meant by "lady of great character." The woman had gone gray, and her once puffy cheeks sagged with the weight of years, but to Valentina she cut an awesome and majestic figure. Clearing her throat, she introduced herself.

"My name is Detective Valentina Ruiz, and I wonder if I could have a few minutes of your time? It's *Madame* Mirta, isn't it?"

The impressive woman dressed in a bright red mumu embroidered with navy blue dragonflies looked directly into her eyes with an expressionless face.

"You know my name and you ask politely. Of course you can come in."

She backed her wheelchair down the hallway, beckoning Valentina in. It was a humid day, cloudy and hot. Stepping forward as *Madame* Mirta floated backward, wheels whirring, eye contact unwavering, Valentina experienced a bizarre sensation, as if she were entering a *sanctum sanctorum* from which she might never emerge. She stopped for a minute to get her bearings. *Madame* Mirta stopped too, and the spell broke.

"You okay?"

"Uh, yes...yes. I'm sorry. I just felt a little dizzy for a minute."

"Come in and sit down," the large woman said, concern on her face.

Valentina followed her into the kitchen, vaguely noticing ceremonial accoutrements in the large living room, but she could not concentrate. The kitchen was a mustard yellow room gone dingy, with a kitchen table covered in a vinyl tablecloth of wild red roses against a green background. Four plastic garden chairs looked brand new. Still feeling a bit wobbly, she headed for one of the chairs but was arrested by the aroma steaming from a gigantic pot on the stove.

"Mmmm, that smells delicious! What are you cooking?"

"Is a beef stew like we make back home. From Haiti, you know?"

"Yes."

"Why don't you sit down and I serve you a bowl."

"God, that sounds great. It's hot as hell out there, but for some reason it sounds perfect."

"Well, is not so good yet because I just make it last night. Tonight it taste much better. But it should be okay."

As she talked, she ladled broth, meat chunks, and a multitude of vegetables into a bowl big enough to feed a king. Valentina laughed out loud, protesting, "Oh please, not so much!"

"It okay," *Madame* Mirta insisted, pointing to a chair at the kitchen table. "Sit down. I take care of everything."

Valentina did as she was told, and moments later was wolfing down the best-tasting soup she had ever eaten in her life, reenacting the enthusiasm of another little girl so many years before. Looking at her, the queen remembered and she shook her head, smiling.

"What are you thinking about?" Valentina said, noticing.

Madame Mirta moved her wheelchair back and around so that she could sit directly across from her guest.

"You remind me of someone, that all."

"Is her name Maya?" Valentina asked instinctively.

"How you know Maya?" How you know my name, anyway?" She asked, remembering that this was a detective.

Valentina also remembered that she was a detective, there on an unpleasant mission, and she stopped eating. Guiltily, she pushed the bowl away.

"You no want no more?"

"No, thank you. Your kindness made me forget why I came to see you, and I am afraid you probably won't like what I have to say." Valentina wondered why she was suddenly sweating. *Probably the soup.*

Looking instantly tired and even more regal at once, *Madame* Mirta ordered, "Tell me."

Valentina sucked in her breath, then exhaled quickly.

"There's been a murder. A young Haitian man," she added quickly, knowing what a mother might imagine. "His name was Sylvain Chenet. Did you ever hear that name before?"

"I have heard the name years ago, and also recently, but not from Maya."

What a surprise.

"Your daughter was very much in love with Sylvain Chenet, and they had just started seeing each other when he was murdered."

"Yes?" she said, waiting.

"I am following every lead I can in this investigation. And even though I wish it were not true, Maya is a suspect in the case."

"Why you wish it not true?"

"Because, for someone so young, she's been through so much hell already. I guess I feel like it would be a shame if she was involved in something as serious as murder." *There, I said it.*

"How you know Maya?"

"I only met her recently when I started on this case. It's hard to explain. It was a strange thing. There was mutual recognition the minute we met, like we knew each other long ago, or something like that. She told me some of her secrets."

"Did you tell her yours?"

"Not all of them," Valentina said, caught off guard.

"Hmph," she muttered under her breath; then, "What you want from me? Maya never tell me her secrets." Valentina could see she was hurt.

"That's just it! I've talked to the people closest to her, and most of them did not even know this boy existed in her life. I'm trying to understand, and I'm hoping you can help me get a better handle on her because she's so guarded. It's very hard to figure her out. I am pretty good at it with most people; it comes naturally to me. But Maya—she's different, to say the least. Anyway, I would like to find that she had nothing to do with this, and I figure anything you can tell me might help."

It was *Madame* Mirta's turn to take a deep breath. The navy blue dragonflies on her dress seemed to come to life as her huge chest swelled up and down with her labored breathing.

"Maya not like regular people. She special. She have a lot of pain inside her, ever since she little. That pain make itself at home inside her. She don't know how to be without pain."

Valentina remembered Jacquy Pierre's admission that Maya had death *or murder* in her heart.

"You say you heard Sylvain Chenet's name before."

She looked down at her hands, hesitating for a moment. "I hear her cry that name out in her sleep over the years. That name come only in her worst nightmares, but she always refuse to talk about him. Then, her friend, Colin—you know him?"

"Yes."

"He tell me two, three weeks ago that this *bourgeois* boy is Maya boyfriend. I think that big trouble."

"Why?"

"Because it never work. She only get hurt in the end. I try ask her about this bad business, but she clam up, tell me not to worry, they only friends. I want believe her so I not push. What else she tell you about him?"

"That she loved him very much. That he was lovely. Sweet and very kind."

"Hmph" again, now with ocean waves frothing under knitted brows. And after a few more moments, "There is a broken and confused little girl who live in Maya. But not a killer. She is a good girl. Did you ask her if she kill that boy?"

"Yes, I did."

"What did she say when you ask her?"

"She said she didn't do it."

"Then you should believe her."

That simple. Just believe her.

"All right," Valentina said after a while, "her friend, Colin Gardner? What can you tell me about him?"

"Colin is very strange boy, too. That why I think they such good friends all these years."

"When he came to see you, what did you talk about, if you don't mind my asking?"

"The usual. Maya."

"Did he say anything unusual to you about Maya and her boyfriend?"

"Everything Colin say is unusual."

"I know what you mean," Valentina chuckled.

"But did he say anything special about Sylvain and Maya or anything?" She was digging—for what, she did not know. But she thought she might have hit pay dirt when she saw a slow smile creep up from *Madame* Mirta's lips and spread up to the corners of her eyes.

"I never think about it before, but that day, I get feeling Colin might be in love with Maya," she said.

"I never got that far—him being in love with her—but I did think he might be jealous, which would make sense if he was in love with her." She thought about it, then asked, "Do you think Colin is capable of murder? He seemed quite angry when he talked about Maya and Sylvain. He seemed hurt that she didn't have time for him anymore."

"My dear, anything is possible," *Madame* Mirta said wisely, leveling her with a look, "but killing someone is very big thing. If you ask me, I think you barking up the wrong tree, as you Americans say. Colin may be strange, but he good boy."

Just what he said to me about Maya. Valentina sighed out loud.

"Do you think he could put somebody else up to it for him?" She was thinking about the tall, dark-skinned gang member named Pat that Partridge had told her about.

"I would not think so."

"Do you know how versed Colin is with Haitian *Vodou*?"

"Why you ask that?"

"Because an eyewitness described someone dressed like the *Baron Samedi* near the scene of the crime, and I'm thinking that someone with an exquisite sense of the macabre could get into dressing up as the Spirit of Death to kill someone. And I can't think of anyone more macabre than Colin Gardner."

Madame Mirta's face had transformed itself into a tableau of consternation and disbelief. "It true what you say about *Baron Samedi*?"

"I am inclined to believe this witness," Valentina replied.

"Then I say you better go find the *Baron* instead of wasting your time with Colin."

Reaching around to the back seat of her car, Valentina grabbed the black jacket she needed to hide the gun around her waist. She knew she would look out of place in this neighborhood, her soft, tan cotton slacks and expensive leather flats clashing dramatically with the low-riding jeans and tank tops that were the norm in this part of Miami. It could have been Any Ghetto, U.S.A.—bad graffiti mixed with good on grimy gray buildings shedding layers of paint and exuding neglect. Kids and grown-ups loitered on front steps, smoking joints and cigarettes, swigging beers, hanging out.

As she walked toward the address Partridge had given her, a voice behind her jeered, "Lookin' good, *mamacita*." Turning, she stared directly into the boy's eyes. His hair net made her want to laugh out loud, but she held back. He and his buddies needed to know they didn't scare her. She held his eyes as she kept walking, releasing her stare with indifference when they started laughing out of embarrassment. A few steps more and she stood in front of the building. The damp heat on concrete steps discharged a heavy odor of urine, and she quickly stepped inside for a welcome reprieve. The desolate, dark green lobby wasn't much better. Scanning the numbers on the doors, she figured the apartment she sought would be upstairs. As she assessed the filthy stairwell, Valentina heard the door open behind her and the boy with the hair net walked in. The look on his face told her he had arrived on a dare.

"I'm looking for Jorge and Pat," she said quickly in her best Spanish, catching him off guard. "Know if they're around?"

"What you want with them?" he said, trying to hide his surprise at this *gringa* who could speak his language.

"I'm sure they wouldn't want me to tell you. Private business."

"Yeah, Pat is up there," he grudgingly conceded.

"Thanks."

She turned and headed up the stairs, feeling his eyes on her back. Up on the second floor, concrete gave way to nasty green carpeting stamped with cigarette burns, chewing gum, and the grime of ages. As she stepped slowly down the squalid hallway, instinct told her that somehow, behind all these closed doors, people knew an intruder was in their midst. At apartment number 202, she knocked. The voice that answered was high pitched, young.

"Who is it?"

"I'm looking for Jorge or Pat. I'm a friend of Colin Gardner's."

The door opened swiftly, and to Valentina's surprise, the person who stood before her was a tall, shaved-to-the-scalp, dark-skinned, muscular girl. She could see how this lanky youngster could be mistaken for a guy. But the small, protruding breasts under her fairly transparent white muscle T-shirt took away any doubt.

"Pat? As in Patricia?"

"Patsy."

Valentina suppressed a chuckle. Her physical resemblance to Maya was striking. Flashing her badge, she said, "Detective Ruiz. Can I come in for a minute? I'd like to talk with you."

"Oh, fuck. I didn't do nothin'!"

"I never said you did. But maybe you can answer a couple of questions for me."

"You said you were a friend of Colin's." she said in a heavy Cuban accent.

"Well, sort of. Can I come in?"

She looked suspicious but stepped aside to let Valentina through. Once inside the apartment, Valentina took a quick look around. It was much cleaner than she expected, with not a thing out of place except for the big, black open coffin that stood in the middle of the room. Ignoring the young girl for a minute, Valentina walked over to it and looked in. A life-sized rubber doll lay face up, her red lips forming a wide "O."

"Mind telling me what this is doing here?" she asked half shocked, half amused, and totally curious.

"I don't have to tell you nothin'."

They were still standing, and Valentina gestured toward the spotless, overstuffed vanilla white couch just on the other side of the coffin. Pat walked over to it and Valentina followed, each sitting on opposite sides of the couch.

"Have you heard of a friend of Colin Gardner's named Maya?"

"Oh, her," she said miserably. "Yeah, I heard of her."

"Have you ever met her?"

"No, but I seen her."

"You sound like you don't like her much."

"Made me kinda mad when I saw her 'cause I pretty much figured out that Colin has feelings for her. And then I find out I look a lot like her. At first I thought maybe that was the only reason he liked me."

"Wait a minute. You mean you and Colin—"

She looked away shyly for a moment. She couldn't be more than nineteen. "Yeah."

"I see."

"What do you see?' she asked. "Why you askin' me these questions? What's it to you?"

She did see. He couldn't have Maya, so he'd found the nearest facsimile.

"Let me ask you something. Where were you on the night of September 18th? It was a Thursday."

"You're weird, lady. I know what day that was 'cause it's my birthday, and I spent it with Colin in his apartment."

"Can you prove it?"

"Why should I have to?"

"Humor me."

Rolling her eyes, the girl made an effort to remember.

"Well, we ordered pizza from Pizza Hut, and they delivered. They'd have some kind of record, wouldn't they?"

"When I asked Colin what he did that night, he said he was in his apartment drawing and that there was no one to corroborate his story except maybe his landlord, who might have been spying on him."

Valentina saw the girl's eyes harden.

"You know Maya?" Pat said.

"Yes."

"Well, he probably didn't want you to go tellin' her," she said, raising her voice. "He doesn't want her to know about us yet. Don't ask me why."

"Okay, I get it."

"Well, maybe you can explain it to *me*, then." She was getting herself worked up. Valentina tried to remember the boy/girl angst of her teenage years but couldn't at that moment. She shook her head.

"Maybe you should get Colin to talk to you about it." She got up to leave and remembered the coffin. "By the way, what in God's name is this doing here?"

"I'm studying to be an undertaker," the young girl deadpanned.

"Why am I not surprised?" she said before walking out the door.

Later that day, Valentina sat across from Colin at The Korner Kafe. His skin looked even paler than she remembered. It had begun to rain, and the wet, gray day provided the perfect backdrop for their morbid conversation.

"So where did you and Pat meet?"

"At my favorite funeral parlor."

"Your favorite? You frequent many of them?"

"I like hanging around them; I get ideas that way."

"Uh-huh."

"Anyway, Mr. Cordell, who owns Cordell Funeral Home, he's a perfectly twisted guy who loves to talk; all kinds of absolutely appalling stories. I could listen to him for hours, so I go see him every now and then. I think he makes up some of it, but I appreciate imagination."

"And Pat?"

"She was standing outside the shop, looking in the window when I arrived one day, so I encouraged her to come in and talk to old Cordell. He's teaching her the ropes." "Why would a young girl want to get into that kind of business?"

"You say that like it's bad."

"No, just creepy to most."

"Yes, quite," he said, looking pleased with himself. "She's fascinated by death—by that moment when the person that *is* leaves the body and becomes a person that *was*."

"I see. And you?"

"Oh, I am very interested in the supernatural, the unexplainable, the things most people are afraid to explore."

"And how familiar are you with the Haitian Spirit of Death? The *Baron Samedi*."

"Only what I've seen of him at the ceremonies I've attended with Maya."

"And where would those be?"

"At her mother's, of course, every Saturday."

"Can anyone go?"

"Probably."

"Why didn't you tell me that Pat was with you the night of Sylvain Chenet's murder?"

"I like mystery."

"And you're in love with Maya and didn't want her to know."

Sharp, cold eyes bored into Valentina's.

"Love. Strange word. I don't know about that." He seemed uncomfortable.

"You must admit your girlfriend looks very much like Maya, except for her lack of hair, which makes her look like a guy. I find that very interesting."

"Oh yeah? Is it? I hadn't noticed. And who said she was my girlfriend? What an utterly inane word."

"Can I give you some advice, Colin? If it's not going to happen with you and Maya, then embrace Pat completely. Don't deny what you feel for her, because she probably won't put up with it for too long."

He looked down into his coffee.

"Have you talked to Maya lately?" Valentina asked.

"Haven't had time," he said between tight lips.

"Piece of advice number two. Maya could be in a lot of trouble right now. She may have killed her boyfriend for reasons unknown to me. I don't think she did, but then again, anything is possible. So if you want to help her out, now is the time."

He looked at her and smiled cynically, honing in on the soft spot of her uncertainty.

"Anyway," Valentina said, snapping at his insight, "whether she did or didn't, she is in pain. No matter what happened, she loved him very much."

"Yes, I know," he said, resigned.

"And she could probably use your support right about now. If she is involved in this, she's going to need help. Get my drift?"

"And what do you propose to do to figure it out?" he asked, enjoying Valentina's obvious frustration.

"Saturday may be the only answer."

The Baron

Yeah, baby, that's probably true. Except that I only work with those who ***know*** me, get my drift? No? I'm talking about service, child. You serve me, I'll serve you; otherwise the only thing outsiders ever see is a giant black wall. That's how it works. She won't learn anything from me! Well, maybe just a little. I like to keep them guessing some.

Meanwhile, Maya is still staring into the mirror, searching, wondering, hoping to feel a little better each day. *Yesss.* She'll eventually come 'round, but it will take time. That's the way it works.

15

"Noooo! Stop! You're hurting me. I can't breathe!" Valentina sputtered and coughed as the rope tightened around her throat, rubbing, rubbing furiously as it choked off her breath.

Tell someone.

The beautiful face of Valentina's mother loomed large over her, watching, smiling wickedly at her daughter's fear and pain. "Please stop," Valentina cried, choking on the words.

Tell someone. Go ahead.

And then she was awake, gasping for air, eyes throbbing with the horror of the experience that always left her drained and weak, no matter how many times it happened.

"Oh my God, oh my God, oh my God," she cried to herself. "When will this ever stop?"

Tell someone.

As she wiped at the tears that soaked her cheeks, she wondered why it was so dark in the room. Turning to look at the clock, she let out another cry, "Oh no!" It was 9:30. She'd lain down at 7:30 for a short nap. "Fuck! I wonder if it's too late!" Within minutes, she was racing out of her apartment building and into her car, speeding to catch what might have already passed. It was Saturday night, and she didn't want to miss her dialogue with Dr. Demise, the Sire of Doom, King of the Dead. *Wait for me, Baron, I'm coming.*

"Ah, you are finally here. *Exxxcelent.* I wasn't going to... wait much longer."

Fifty pairs of eyes and humid bodies turned toward the only white woman in the room, and Valentina froze. The smell of liquor and cigar smoke was strong, suffocating. *Madame* Mirta was nowhere to be seen, but the man standing before her in full *Baron Samedi* regalia exuded power. She'd come flying through the front door and into *Madame* Mirta's living room, where frenzied bodies danced to the wild rhythms of three drums in full tilt. He'd stopped dancing the moment she entered the temple teeming with congregants, and was staring at her now, waiting. She was determined not to show any fear. Everyone said he was fun, a riot, hysterical. Why wasn't she feeling that right now? He was dead serious, and it made her nervous. She didn't know what to say. *What was it I wanted to ask?*

"You wanted to know who...killed that boy...wasn't that it?" he answered her thought, racking her nerves.

"Well?" she sputtered, "Will you tell me?"

"Death always comes at the perfect time. *Yesss* it does."

"I'm not so sure about that," she said, shakily. There was a chill around her, and his eyes seemed bottomless behind those black glasses.

"You know it's true, darlin'," he said laughing, a low sound that turned high-pitched, making her shiver.

"Did he have to die so brutally?"

"That was his destiny. *Yesss,* it was."

"Who decided that?"

"Who do you think?"

"You?"

"Who else, darlin'?"

"But, why?"

"Human beings are always hell bent on...trying to figure this stuff out, but they NEVER WILL." As he said this, he tapped his cane loudly three times.

"What about Maya?"

"What about her?"

"How did it happen?"

"Her will was done, as thine will be done, as all will be done—on earth, as it is in heaven. Hee hee hee hee!" he screeched, pleased with his clever quoting of the Catholic prayer. "Remember that," he continued in his slow, nasal voice. "Listen to what I'm saying...And while you're at it, why don't you also listen to...the one who's been trying to guide you all these years. Don't you...hear her voice? Don't you want release? Open your ears!" And then he was gone.

From the moment she left *Madame* Mirta's that night, right until the time she went to sleep the next evening, Valentina chewed and digested all the facts she'd gathered since the beginning of her investigation. She was daunted. While attending to paperwork during the day, returning calls, or checking her bag for keys, she pondered the mystery of Maya St. Fleur and her lover's murder. The evening air was breezy and without a hint of humidity. *At last!* Walking out of the precinct, Valentina stopped to feel it on her face. She closed her eyes, mutely praying to *Oya*, to God, to anyone who would listen to help her *get it*. As she walked toward her car, unlocked the door, slid behind the wheel, and started the engine, she continued to reflect. She wondered again if there had ever been a case of the *lwas* of *Vodou* or orixas of *Santeria* materializing in the physical realm to commit a physical act without using someone else's body? She didn't think so. She knew it was crazy, but she'd even checked with her grandmother.

"Where ju get thees *loco* idea? I never theenk of that. But who knows what is possible with the gods?"

Big help, Abuela.

And why Sylvain? It was his father Maya hated. What was this anger she admitted to having in her heart? Anger strong enough to kill the only man she ever loved? Of this, Valentina was quite sure—that Maya was undeniably and passionately in love with the dead man. Or had she made a deal with the *Baron*, only to have the deal go sour? Sylvain Chenet would not be the first man to be killed by mistake. But why?

Before she knew it, Valentina realized that she had pulled into the supermarket lot, parked her car, and shut off the ignition. *Holy shit, how did I get here? Wait. Is that how it could have happened?* She felt close. *So close.* She walked down the aisles of the overly lit and excessively refrigerated store, oblivious to the items she pulled off the shelves. *Tell Me.* Driving home was no different, performed in a hypnotic haze that erased the memory of carrying groceries up the stairs of her building, unlocking the apartment door, and unpacking her purchases.

Thinking out loud at times, she changed out of her clothes and into a large T-shirt. Lost in thought, she made a salad and poured herself a glass of red wine. Mulling over all the elements, she ate without tasting her meal; and all through the night, she thrashed in the arms of Morpheus, enmeshed in her meditations on murder.

When she opened her eyes the next morning, she knew.

She got out of bed and lumbered out into the living room to her briefcase, where she dug out Maya's number and dialed.

"Maya? It's Valentina. I have news about the wonderful Officer Carlson. And there's something else I need to tell you. Actually, two things. Can you meet me today at The Korner Kafé? One o'clock? Good."

They sat across from each other, two glasses of half-touched iced teas on the table, oblivious to the lunchtime bustle around them. The day was white-hot outside, but an ancient A/C breathed artificially cool air inside the cafe. Someone at the next table was smoking a cigarette, blowing fumes their way, but the two women didn't notice. Wearing a pair of jeans and a white T-shirt, Valentina was doing all the talking. She had just announced the news about Carlson to Maya, beaming at the efficacy of the work they'd done. Maya looked proud.

"See, magic, the spirits, God, whatever you want to call it, it's all at your beck and call if you approach it with good will. People don't know how powerful they can be."

"Yes, just like people don't realize how weakness can rule their lives," Valentina countered.

"Who could you be talking about? Not you. I would guess you're anything but weak."

"There's a part of me that's really strong; but there's another part that for years has been overwhelmed by the force that used to be my mother." Valentina stopped to take a breath and to take a long drink from her glass. Sensing her nervousness, Maya cocked her head to one side.

"Is this the thing you wanted to tell me?"

"One of them. I've never talked about this to anyone. Nobody. But for some reason, just after first meeting you, I got the message—and I'm sure it was from *Oya*—that if I told this story to someone, not just to anyone, but to you specifically, it would help free me of this weakness that lets these nightmares kick my ass. I've been having the same torturous dream since I was ten years old.

"I'm all ears."

Summoning strength, arms crossed on the table and leaning forward, Valentina began her tale. "I always walked to school by myself, because it was only three blocks from where we lived. It was no big deal, all the teachers at school knew it. One day, I forgot my lunch at home, so they allowed me to run back to get it. When I got there, my mother's car was in the driveway and so was my Aunt Cecelia's car, parked just behind hers. I thought that was strange, because my mother's sister worked during the day. My lunchbox was there on the kitchen table, right where I had left it. I was just going to grab it and get back to school, but then I heard voices upstairs. The voices sounded strange, like a fight, something I shouldn't interrupt. But I was curious, so I headed up the stairs quietly and paused at the top step, where I could easily see into my parents' bedroom. My mother was holding a gun to her sister and directing her to climb up on the bed. There was a wooden crate or box sitting in the middle of the bed, and my mother was telling her to climb on top of it. I couldn't understand it all, because my aunt was crying and screaming at her to stop, and my mother was saying things like, 'Don't you like this bed anymore? You liked it just fine when you were fucking my husband in it, didn't you?' I'm paraphrasing now, because it didn't make much sense to me then. Later, I realized that my mother had found out about an affair between my father and my aunt.

"'He's just going to love finding you here like this. Maybe it will help him to remember that this bed is mine, and he doesn't bring any whores into this house.'

"I didn't understand what my mother had in mind. Was she just going to stand there, pointing a gun at my aunt until my father got home? Well, just a little bit more stretching was all it took, and then I saw the rope. She had tied a rope from a beam in the ceiling, and at the end of it was a noose. She was ordering my aunt to step up on the box and to put the noose around her neck.

"I thought my mother must be trying to scare my Aunt Cecelia and that this must be a silly game. But one minute there was all this crying and screaming and pleading, and my mother shouting for her to shut up and to kick the box away; but suddenly there was a loud noise as the box hit the bedroom floor, and then silence. My aunt had hanged herself at gunpoint. I was too shocked to move or say anything, but it didn't matter because it took a long time for my mother to come out of that room. By the time she did, I had quietly gone back down the stairs and run back to school.

"That afternoon, when I got home, both cars were still in the driveway, and my mother was down in the kitchen, tending to business as usual. When I went upstairs, I noticed her bedroom door was closed. I didn't open it. I went back down and observed my mother carefully, trying desperately to find something different in her demeanor. There was nothing. She looked gorgeous, as usual: voluptuous, with long, black, wavy hair and big breasts that she showed off in clingy tops. She was wearing her favorite hot-orange lipstick and humming some tune as she started dinner, as if all was right with the world.

"When I got up the nerve to ask about her sister's car, she just said that Aunt Cecelia didn't feel well that day and had come over; that she was napping in her bedroom upstairs, and that I shouldn't make any noise that might disturb her. Later, when my father came home, he also asked about the car, and she told him the same thing. As the evening wore on and there was no sign of Aunt Cecelia, my mother suggested that Dad go up to check on her. When he found her, dead, hanging over their bed, my mother acted more shocked and bereaved than when her own mother died.

"I watched her call the police and answer their questions like a pro. No one ever guessed what had really happened, and I never told anyone. My father never cheated on her again."

"You've carried this around with you all this time?" Maya asked, aghast, "Why?"

"I didn't want my mother to go to jail. I was scared. I didn't want people to say she was a criminal. Seeing her anger that day almost made me understand what pushed her to do it. And over the years, watching her talk about it taught me everything I know today about dealing with the people I interact with on a daily basis—the ones who comit crimes and then come up with every story in the book so that they don't end up in jail. It's automatic. I can sniff out their lies in a minute."

They were both silent for a while, the weight of Valentina's revelation hanging awkwardly between them. Finally, Maya spoke.

"Where is your mother now?"

"She was murdered in her own living room. I was the one who found her."

"No!"

"Yes."

"Did you ever find the killer?"

"That was two years ago, and no. Nothing was stolen, no one ever figured out what happened. In the files, she is just another random victim of a violent crime. It must have had something to do with karmic justice."

"And your father?"

"I haven't seen him since it happened. Soon after, he got a job that took him out of state. It's better this way. For years, the child in me wanted to blame him for making my mother so angry—enough to turn her into a killer. I did not want to blame her. Of course, that's crazy; but sometimes, when you decide something in your heart, it's hard to let it go."

Again, silence filled the air between them for several moments.

"I still don't know why you were singled out as the one I should tell," Valentina said at last.

"Maybe it's because I won't judge you."

Another long moment of silence passed between them.

"How do you feel?" Maya asked, finally, curious.

"Kind of like I just threw up."

"Are you okay?"

"I'm not sure. I guess I'll know later. "

Maya turned her head to look out the window, lost in thought. Valentina studied her profile openly, sadness descending upon her, overpowering her own inner turbulence.

"You said there were two things?" Maya asked after a while.

"Yes. You know what I was just saying about being able to sniff out the good guys from the bad guys?"

"Yes?"

"It's about you and this unsolved case. This murder," Valentina said to Maya without malice, but rather with something approaching regret.

"Yes?" she said again, a little uneasy now.

Valentina took a deep, deep breath, taking in what felt like all the sorrows of the world.

"From our first conversation, I knew that you were telling the truth. And I also knew that you had killed Sylvain Chenet."

Maya's eyes showed both surprise and a hint of fear. She waited for more.

"That's why this whole thing has been such a puzzle for me. Plus, I didn't want to believe it, so my usual instincts got a bit muddled there for a while. I don't know why we have this connection—I feel like I've known you for thousands of years, lifetimes. Maybe that's why I know what happened."

"Tell me," Maya said simply.

"It has been confirmed to me by two different sources that you have or had a sketch of an older man on your altar. I believe that was a sketch of your enemy, Henri Chenet. I believe that picture was there because you contracted with *Baron Samedi* to get your revenge by killing his only son. You knew he loved him very much, didn't you?"

Maya just stared.

"You kept tabs on his comings and goings over the years through your friend Jacquy, and you found out when Sylvain moved here to study law. You didn't meet him by chance. You planned to meet him—so that you could kill him."

"And how did I do it?" Maya asked, her blank face a mask of neutrality.

"I realized that the only way you could be telling the truth about your innocence is because you're not sure yourself how you did it; and that's because you went into trance. You called the spirit of *Baron Samedi* to possess you and he, not you, committed the act you never could have accomplished yourself.

"Someone answering the description of *Baron Samedi* was seen entering the cemetery at the time Sylvain was supposed to meet you. He was carrying a cane. A phallic shaped cane. The same one that crushed Sylvain's head."

Maya's eyes closed briefly in pain at the thought.

"When he came out, he wasn't carrying it. It was left at the murder scene. I guess there was no way to wash the blood and brain matter off it, so there it stayed. What I don't know is how conscious you were during the act. How conscious you were afterward. How conscious you are now. Maybe you know exactly what you did and you're laughing at me even now. And maybe you tried to call it off but couldn't. But the bottom line is that you did it. Just like I've carried this hideous secret around with me all my life, so have you carried in your heart enough hatred to kill the man you adored. Why, Maya? Why? What has it brought you, finally?"

Maya stared at the agitated woman across her, but when she opened her mouth to speak, it was not to solve Valentina's mystery for her.

"This story you've dreamed up would make a great movie, or better yet, a great opera. Very dramatic. Why don't you arrest me?"

"I haven't able to find the proof. You did a good job of covering your tracks. But I know I'm right."

"I'm sorry you feel that way. If you think I'm capable of—"

"Of what? Killing him or hating so much?"

"Both, I guess. I've never heard of a *lwa* coming into this plane on his own and running around town. So what you're saying is that I was possessed by the *Baron*, who caused Sylvain's death."

"Right. Do you think that's what happened to you?"

"I think that's a fantastic premise. I did not kill Sylvain."

"My nose is telling me you're not really sure."

"Your nose may be a little off. You're under a big emotional strain right now."

"Yes, I am."

"I'm sorry."

"Thanks. However, I've done nothing but analyze this thing for a while now. I don't think I'm wrong."

"I loved him."

"I know you did."

"He's dead, and I have to live with that."

"Yes, you do."

"Believing what you think me capable of, where does that leave us?"

"Here in this coffee shop with an unresolved situation."

"I would have liked to see you again, Valentina."

There was nothing more to say. Maya stood and strode out into bright Miami sunshine, full skirt brushing against sandaled feet. Unable to breathe or move, Valentina watched through the glass door as she walked away. When she reached the corner, the young dancer turned to look at Valentina, a wistful look on her face.

In that moment, the detective froze in horror, gripped by the certainty of what she'd just seen: Maya, silhouetted in a tall, black top hat, wearing dark sunglasses and a knowing grin.

EPILOGUE

One year later

Valentina felt like jumping up and down and singing. This was her first Saturday off in months, and she didn't know what to do with herself. Crawl back into bed and sleep all day?

Tempting, but too wasteful.

She hadn't seen a movie in ages. *Maybe a marathon at the fourteen-plex.* She would watch movies till her eyes jumped out of their sockets. Maybe people would scream, thinking they were slimy frogs!

How grisly.

Maybe the beach? The weather was over-the-top *perfecto!*

Unoriginal for Miami, but so what?

She would pick up stacks of fashion magazines and have a silly fashion magazine marathon at the beach.

Great idea!

She was feeling giddy, punchy with the thought of all that free time. She'd have to go to the store, pick up some snacks, water, juice, and of course, the magazines.

She washed up quickly, leaped into her bathing suit and a pair of jeans, and headed down to her car. Twenty minutes later, the ocean loomed azure-green and sparkly on her left as she scanned Ocean Boulevard for a parking space. It was early enough that the crowds hadn't yet arrived, but the heat was rising, and Latin music already blared from passing cars. As she pulled into a convenient spot, she realized she had forgotten her morning coffee. *Boy, was I in a hurry to get here.* Finding good, strong espresso would not be a problem; the beach was lined shoulder-to-shoulder with oh-so-trendy bistrots. She walked a block or so before choosing a sidewalk table at News Café, whose starched white tablecloths contrasted with the typical hard white plastic furniture everywhere else on the beach. Feet up on the chair opposite her, she stretched her legs lazily. This was going to be her day.

Suddenly, the thought of scrambled eggs interrupted her espresso craving, and Valentina turned to look for her waiter. Spotting him taking an order, she started to raise her hand when something made her stop and turn to look behind her. Frantic drumming switched places with her formerly steady heartbeat, and she gripped her chair to stop from bouncing out of her seat. After all these months, here was Maya St. Fleur strolling down the bright morning sidewalk, totally absorbed in a seemingly amusing conversation with a pre-school boy. Maya, and the heaviness that hung about her like shadows, seemed totally incongruent in this *tableau*. She willed the young woman to look her way. As if responding to a call, Maya lifted her head, and their eyes met.

She halted in mid step, jolting her young companion backward in the process. Valentina stood up, feeling stilted and stiff. They stared into each other's eyes for a long moment, all activity around them a frozen blur until Valentina broke the ice. Walking quickly toward the pair, she greeted the enigmatic dancer—once the prime suspect in a still unsolved murder—with what felt like markedly inadequate words.

"Hello, Maya."

"Hello, Valentina," Maya said, softly. "I've thought about you a lot this past year."

Senses on overload, Valentina skipped right over the small talk.

"Who's your friend?" she asked. Maya looked down at the little boy with light brown skin and soft, curly hair, then back at Valentina, and hesitated. "This can't be Sylvain's son; he's too old," she said, feeling like an idiot the minute she said it.

"Right..." Turning again to the boy, she said, "Lionel, say hello. This is *mon amie*, Valentina."

Smiling shyly, Lionel extended his hand.

Valentina felt herself breathe for the first time as she reached out to shake the tiny hand. The kid was adorable.

"...He's my brother."

Valentina's head jerked up. "Who? Your brother! How?..." A headache was on its way. "Say, do you want to sit a minute? I haven't had any coffee yet, and I really feel like I could use some right now.

Maya nodded in agreement.

Valentina marched over to the waiter, ordered two coffees and an orange juice, and headed back to the table, where the two were settling in.

"So tell me. Please."

"Do you remember my mother? She died in Haiti last year."

"Yes."

"Lionel is her son."

"But he looks mixed."

"To be precise, he is my half-brother. His father is Henri Chenet."

"Oh my God." Valentina bit down on her knuckle. "Henri Chenet's son. That means he's also Sylvain's brother."

"Yes," Maya whispered.

"And how on earth did he end up here?"

Just then, the waiter arrived with a tray and set down two cups of coffee and a glass of juice. The strong scent of sweetened espresso wafted up in the air like a ghost. Lionel asked if he could have a straw, and the waiter obliged. As only a four-year-old can, the child occupied himself with his drink and straw, completely oblivious to the intensity of the conversation around him.

"You were right about me," Maya said, looking into Valentina's eyes.

"In what way?"

"You said that I allowed hate to run my life to the point of killing the only man I ever loved."

Valentina waited.

"And you were right."

"I get the feeling there's more to this."

Maya sighed before continuing.

"Our last conversation left me with a giant question mark. It was a question that haunted me every day, and every night for that matter; but I didn't dare explore it. I didn't want to know. It was easier to mourn Sylvain and to miss him. But after a while, I had to face myself...and the Baron. So I asked him to tell me what happened."

"You asked the Baron," Valentina said.

"Yes," Maya said.

"So, you're telling me you didn't know?"

"No, I didn't."

The two women stared at each other again, one searchingly, the other openly.

"How did you ask him? I mean, how do you communicate with him?" Valentina said.

"I just asked. And he came to me in a dream."

"Is that how you usually communicate with him?"

"It was, that time."

"How do you know it wasn't just a dream?"

"I know," she laughed.

"Go on."

"He told me what I already knew," Maya said. "Once you call on *Baron Samedi*, there's no going back. I was mad with grief over my mother. I was mad with hatred—for myself, for my life, for Henri Chenet most of all. Long ago I decided to kill his son because I wanted him to know pain. Real pain. But I was so in love with Sylvain that I couldn't bear the thought of it; so I left it up to the Baron. I hoped he would make the right decision."

"You asked the spirit of death to make a life-or-death decision?"

"It's not that black or white," Maya said. "There can be no death without life. The two are intertwined. And it's the same with the Baron. There are things we will never understand—about timing and fate and karmic forces, not to mention the power behind our thoughts and intentions. I was horrified when I realized what had happened. If I could have killed *Baron Samedi* for what he did to Sylvain, I would have." She stopped to shake her head with a sad smile. "But is he really to blame? He is the one who told me I would have to pay for what happened. He's the one who told me about Lionel. He's the one who suggested I take care of him. Jacquy had told me in a letter some time ago that my parents had another child, but that's all I knew. My father was more than happy to part with Lionel. He certainly didn't need the daily reminder of the rape and humiliation my mother had suffered for so long."

"Does Mr. Chenet know about him?"

"I don't think so."

"Are you planning on telling him?"

"I'm taking it one step at a time." And then surprising Valentina, she asked, "By the way, are you still having nightmares?"

"No. Not anymore."

"I'm glad," Maya said.

"So why didn't you tell me, if you thought you didn't commit the murder?" Valentina asked brusquely. "Or rather, if you thought you were not responsible for what happened?"

"You're a police detective, remember? He used my body. Technically, what does that make me? Insane?"

Considering the implications of this statement, Valentina found herself at a loss for words. Finally, she said, "This was my first case as a detective. It frustrated me to no end that I couldn't tie it up, nice and neat, with the bad guy in jail. But then again, I knew I was dealing with another kind of animal here. You have to understand, I let my mother get away with murder. Somewhere deep inside me, I never wanted to let that happen again. I still don't. But the sorry truth is, people get away with stuff all the time. It's in the news every day: corporations that foul up our rivers, crooked cops who abuse their power, kidnappers who never get caught, husbands who beat their wives..."

"You think I belong in that group?"

"I guess—and that's *if* this is all true or even possible—you're somewhere between them and an abused wife who snaps and kills her husband."

"In other words, nothing to write home about."

"Or list on your resume," Valentina added, snickering. "But more importantly," she added, "what I want you to tell me now is whether *you're* still having nightmares?" She looked over at Lionel, who was beginning to fidget.

Maya laughed quietly. "I haven't had them in a long time. You don't need to worry about Lionel, if that's what you mean. I have to work through it every day—who he is and what it all means. He's my daily reminder of that monster of a man, of what little satisfaction I got from his pain in the end, and of a precious life lost because of me. But the boy is well taken care of, and I love him very much." Maya stood up to leave, adding, "I have to go now, Valentina. But is there a chance we might see each other again sometime? I'd like that very much."

After a pause, Valentina said, "You have to know one thing about me. I won't stop working on this case. It's frustrating, but I'm still not sure about you. Maybe you're insane and maybe you're not. Perhaps a supernatural act really did take place—I don't discount that. Then again, maybe you were just really good. Very careful. No evidence to link you to the crime. Honestly, that eats at me. Here was a pre-meditated crime, resulting in the death of an innocent man; and this 'unsolved case' nonsense just doesn't work for me. But you know what? Today is Saturday, and on this day, I figure anything's possible."

The End

About the Author

Saturday Comes is the fifth book by Carine Fabius. She is a contemporary ethnic art dealer, museum curator, body art pioneer, and blogger on issues relating to the arts, culture, and lifestyle. You can read her blogs at HuffingtonPost.com, at FiftyIsTheNew.com, and at CarineFabius.com. She is currently at work on a collection of short stories. A Haitian native who grew up in New York, she currently lives in Hollywood, California.

Made in the USA
Charleston, SC
26 November 2011